THE
TUESDAY
Erotica
CLUB

Lisa Beth Kovetz

SOURCEBOOKS LANDMARK™
AN IMPRINT OF SOURCEBOOKS, INC.®
NAPERVILLE, ILLINOIS

Published by Sourcebooks Landmark, an imprint of Sourcebooks, Inc.
P.O. Box 4410, Naperville, Illinois 60567-4410
(630) 961-3900
Fax: (630) 961-2168
www.sourcebooks.com

Library of Congress Cataloging in Publication Data
Kovetz, L. B.
  Tuesday erotica club / Lisa Beth Kovetz.
       p. cm.
  ISBN-13: 978-1-4022-0664-1
  ISBN-10: 1-4022-0664-X
1. Erotic stories—Authorship—Fiction. 2. Women—Societies and clubs—Fiction. 3. Female friendship—Fiction. I. Title.

PS3611.O74945T84 2006
813'.6—dc22

                                                2005025115

Printed and bound in the United States of America.
DR 10 9 8 7 6 5 4 3 2 1

About the Author

photo © Michael Rosen

Lisa Beth Kovetz is an award-winning writer, producer, playwright and stand-up comic. Her company, Flying South Productions, produces children's media and short films. Kovetz's play *David's Balls* appeared at the Edinburgh Fringe Festival, has been translated into Romanian for the Pearl of the Carpathians Theater Festival and is now on a three-year run in Bucharest. She lives in Los Angeles, California.

For Jonah and Aubrey

And also for the girlfriends who have kept me going through the years: Beverly Crane, Jennifer Gunzburg, Tina K. Smith, Star-Shemah Bobatoon, Margot Avery, Lara Schwartz, Sandi Richter, Cookie Wells, Nataly Sagol, Margo Newman, Pascale Halm, Deborah Hunter-Karlsen, Antonella Ventura Hartel, and Michael Rosen.

And thanks to Adam Chromy who picked me out of the puppy pound of hopeful writers and sold the book to the perfect publisher. And a special thanks to Hillel Black of Sourcebooks who polished the story into a professional manuscript.

1. *Mahogany*

"...AND THEN AGAIN AND again against the fine mahogany china cabinet, and then he pressed the warm flesh of her buttocks, which is really just a fancy word for ass, against the cool glass, ok, and then that sent these ripples of like sensation through her back, ok, and, it was because of the cold you know, and then also her front, ok but that was his hot tongue because it like, it tickled her neck and her like, her boobs, ok, right, and then she heard this tinkle sound of these little clay statues, right, and all that other stupid crap on the shelves that used to belong to his ex-wife, in her ear, ok and then he started to..."

Lux Fitzpatrick suddenly stopped reading. She looked up at the door as it opened. Her heavy red lips stayed parted, waiting for the next word to fall from her mouth. Her cheekbones were high and her skin would have glowed with youth and vitality had it not been hidden under a thick layer of drugstore makeup. Her long mess of pretty hair struggled against an unprofessional dye job and too much hairspray. Streaks of eye shadow in shades usually reserved for plumbing fixtures hung over each eye. Lux's long legs were wrapped in plaid purple stockings; her rounded buttocks were just barely covered by a short orange skirt. D-cup breasts rode high in a brightly colored, low-cut top. If you chose not to take a second look, Lux might be summed up by the industrial term "DayGlo."

Lux's sense of shame was as underdeveloped as her sense of fashion, and therefore when the conference room door swung open she did not stop reading her opus erotica out of embarrassment, but simply because she was interested in who might be coming into the room.

The other two women already in the room were not as bold as Lux. Gripped with the fear of getting caught doing something dirty, they seized their brown bag lunches and tried to look cool. Aimee tucked her own little erotic manuscripts under an office report while Brooke slid hers directly beneath her butt. Then the pair swiveled their heads like a single terrified doe to see who was opening the door of the conference room.

Margot Hillsboro, Esq., laughed to see the frightened women staring at her as she strode into the room.

"Sorry," Margot said. "For being late, I mean."

"Late for what?" Aimee asked, tugging on a corkscrew of her black curly hair.

"Oh, for your meeting. Your club. Your Tuesday writing group thing."

A sigh of relief. She was one of their own.

"Is the club by invitation only?" Margot continued. "I was under the impression it was a literary club open to anyone in the office who was, well, literate."

Margot's assumption was incorrect. The latest club

circulating through their large law firm belonged exclusively to Aimee.

When Aimee first realized she was pregnant, she knew she needed something to distract her from the growing fear that the growing baby was going to change her life so dramatically that she would lose herself entirely. Aimee wanted company. She wanted creativity. So Aimee handpicked forty of her closest colleagues and invited them to brown bag lunch every Tuesday in the conference room and share their literary musings.

Aimee presented first, reading a short story she'd written in college about a little bird she'd rescued from the mouth of her cat only to have it die in her kitchen. She laughed with her girlfriends over her use of a particularly cumbersome metaphor and secretly wept at the realization that what had seemed, at the time, to be her great, nascent literary talent, wasn't. In the first month of meetings, everyone had at least one old poem or story to share but by the second it became apparent that the only way Aimee's Tuesday writers' group would survive is if the members started writing something new. Something interesting. Half the women dropped out.

The remaining club members put their minds to creating something fascinating to read out loud to their friends, but time was short and their complaints too similar. Even Aimee started to get bored with all the flowery haikus about blah, blah, blah and the epistles to the extreme tedium and unfairness of completing an advance degree in the arts only to discover rent and food are indefatigable ways of expressing money. When the Tuesday writers' group looked like it was about to fall apart, Aimee suggested they spend a few sessions focusing on erotic writing. When Lux dubbed the venture *The Tuesday Erotica Club,* five of the remaining women dropped out immediately. Seven said they would come and three—Lux, Aimee and Brooke—actually showed up. Margot Hillsboro's sudden, unexpected arrival made four.

"I mean," Margot said as she closed the door and chose a good seat at the conference room table, "I assumed your writers' group was open to anyone."

If Margot was embarrassed, she did not show it. Aimee liked that.

"Did you come to listen? Or did you write something?"

"Oh, I've written something. Something erotic. And I definitely want to read it," said Margot in the cool clear voice that made her ideas seem terribly important. A voice that had served her very well through law school, that rang out in meetings above the slushy baritones of her arguing male colleagues. "You're wrong," she would say boldly in dulcet tones. They had heeded Margot's advice often enough to raise her up to the position of Senior Counsel at the law firm of Warwick & Warwick, LLP.

At fifty, Margot was fit and strong and wore expensive dresses two sizes smaller than the cheap cotton ones she had worn when attending high school in a small corn-farming town in the Midwest. Like Lux, Margot dyed her hair and sprayed it. Both women wore foundation and pressed powder and mascara; however, the final effects were completely different. Maybe it was the quality of beauty products each woman had access to. Margot paid thousands of dollars a year to have her hair dyed the exact color that grew naturally out of Lux's head. Overcompensating for her sense of invisibility, Lux hung her head over the kitchen sink and dumped in a bottle of $7.95 goo that turned both the sink and her pretty auburn hair the color of a bright copper penny. Or maybe it was the quantity of products used that made the two women appear so different. Margot used hairspray to gently keep her tresses in place while Lux unintentionally created a hairstyle that could protect her skull from rupturing in the event of a head-on collision.

Like Lux, Margot Hillsboro had not been invited to join Aimee's literary club. Margot was a lawyer and Aimee a paralegal. Margot, therefore, flew above Aimee's friendship radar. Lux Fitzpatrick, as a secretary, had not been invited because she was beneath Aimee's interest. Everything about Lux annoyed Aimee, starting with her name.

Lux Kerchew Fitzpatrick was to have been called Ellen Nancy, after her mother and paternal grandmother, respectively, but Mr. Fitzpatrick was really high the night his only daughter was born, so he named her "Lux," because he liked the way the word rolled around in his mouth and "Kerchew" like a sneeze because it made him laugh. He did not consider the fact that "Lux" rhymes with, among other things, "trucks" and might someday be a burden for a pretty young girl. Her mother was not amused by the name, but changing it meant a trip into the city, a trip that was often planned but never executed. By the time Lux was out of diapers the name had stuck and couldn't be scrubbed out.

Once, on a school field trip when she was fourteen, she met an older gentleman who told her that her name meant "light" in Latin. She was pleased with the information until that same gentleman started showing up at her school, claiming to be her husband. He was quickly recaptured and returned to the ward from which he had escaped. Alone, Lux could not figure out how to confirm whether he was lying or telling the truth about her name. The people who loved her told her to forget about it, that names weren't important. The event planted a lovely seed of thought deep inside her. The idea that words had meaning lay dormant inside Lux, waiting for some sliver of sunshine to set it growing.

"I'm joining your, you know, writing thing," Lux had announced one Tuesday at lunch. When she plopped down at the head of the table in the conference room, her purple miniskirt rode up to reveal a tear high up on her blue and fuchsia striped stocking, hastily patched with a blob of clear nail polish to prevent a deeper run down the leg.

Oh, no you're not, Aimee wanted to say. Get your cheap, too-tight, purple suede skirt out of that chair and march it back to your secretarial station right now. This lunch hour is for me.

If she had said those words out loud it might have made Lux's lower lip quiver, might have made Lux slink tearfully out of the room. Or it might not have. Lux might have told Aimee to fuck herself and remained in her chair, but Aimee would never know because Aimee did not have the courage or strength to confront Lux and order her out of the club.

And so Lux, with her scribbled-upon, handwritten manuscripts, manuscripts that actually spelled out all the "likes" and "you knows" that peppered her normal speech, became a member of Aimee's writers' group. After Lux's first literary presentation (something about a dead cat that had been run over by her boyfriend's motorcycle) a new rule circulated to everyone except Lux via company email that read, "no laughing at the submissions, no matter how stupid Lux sounds." When the club whittled down to only three members, Aimee might have been grateful for Lux's dogged appearance, if only to make up the numbers. She wasn't. The close proximity to Lux's raw youth and ignorance grew more annoying every week.

Margot Hillsboro heard of Aimee's club through office gossip and quickly forgot about it until she saw the women file into the conference room holding manuscripts and emerge a lunch hour later with hugs and a few tears. I'd like a little bit of that, thought Margot. I can write, she told herself. I've made a very successful career of expressing my ideas and arguments on paper. Surely I can write something interesting and new. Margot wracked her brain looking for some thread that she could pull to unravel her great genius to the women in the writers' club. If she could just imagine some deeply tragic and personal story, she too could be on the receiving end of some of the warmth and congeniality that would seep out of the conference room every Tuesday after lunch. She was still waiting for the story to find her when Aimee's Tuesday writers' group took its erotic turn.

Suddenly inspired, the whole fantasy spilled out of her pen with Margot just transcribing it. And then, manuscript in hand, she walked boldly—Margot only knew how to walk boldly—into the conference room, interrupted Lux's recitation, sat down and joined up without actually being invited to do so.

"You wanna go after me cuz I'm almost done," Lux said and then put her nose back into her own smudgy, smutty opus.

"Yes, if that works for everyone," Margot responded politely.

"*And then, ok then when he comes, it's like this joyful, grunting noise,*" Lux continued reading her piece.

"A joyful, grunting noise," Brooke said, turning the phrase over in her mouth, judging the literary and physical quality of it. Lux eyeballed her suspiciously and then continued.

"*And then that noise is big, right and then it, I mean his coming noise, it like kind of shakes the whole room. And this girl, right, she's like kind of totally digging the way he's making noise, right, cuz she knows he knows the neighbors can hear, ok, right, ha! ha! And then it is over. The End.*"

Lux folded her story in half and promptly sat down.

"I'm sorry? That's it?" Brooke asked shaking her head as if she didn't understand.

"That's it," Lux said. "The end, I said it, the end. You going deaf or something?"

"Yep, that's it. That's the end. Anyone else have anything to read? Margot, you ready to go?" Aimee said quickly, ready to push on, push away from Lux and her oozing sores.

"Did you actually write *ha! ha!* in your story? Or was

it an editorial part of the performance?" Margot politely inquired.

Lux swiveled around in her chair and looked at Margot, trying to figure out if she meant something rude by the question. Margot had a slight smile and an open face, and after a moment, Lux decided the coast was clear.

"I wrote out the *ha! ha!*s," Lux admitted.

"There you have it," Aimee pressed on. "Thanks Lux. Anyone else have something to read?"

"Hang on. I think I missed something in your piece," Brooke said to Lux.

"Like what?" asked Lux, trying not to sound as defensive as she felt. She had pushed her way into this room for a reason. If she kept hitting back every time she believed herself attacked, she would not get the thing she wanted from these women.

"*She* didn't come," said Brooke.

"She doesn't."

"Why?"

"She just doesn't."

The older woman looked sympathetically down on Lux, so young, so pretty, so stupid.

"Your character is frigid?" asked Brooke, her perfect blonde bob waving gently as she shook her head in disbelief.

"Hell no! It's just not part of the story. It's not in like the author's *vision*, ok."

Lux started folding her manuscript again. When it was a tiny, little box that could not be folded another time, she stuffed it in her orange, fringed handbag.

"Ok," said Brooke. "But I think in your story the girl

should come too. I'm just saying it would make a better story. In the first place there's all the feminist implications, but also it's more balanced that way. I mean, if you consider the architecture of the piece."

"She doesn't come," Lux insisted.

"Why?"

"Because there are things in sex that are more important than sex," Lux said. And that was all she was going to say about it.

Brooke looked at Lux for a long time. She took a long cool sip of what Lux said and washed it around in her mouth, savoring the flavor of the thought and considering the woman who had said it. Brooke had been a debutante in New York, Palm Beach, and, for reasons she could not comprehend, Geneva, Switzerland. All those white dresses bored her. Brooke loved color. Brooke's mother considered her a pathetic failure because she had chosen a career as a painter over a well-matched marriage proposal.

Lux squirmed under Brooke's gaze. She didn't like being looked at like that. Although there was something delightful about it, there was something frightening in it too. She wanted to say "fuck" or do something stupid to make Brooke think she was less than she was, to make her stop looking. Lux pushed away from the conference room table and scribbled a set of entries in her notebook, which read:

> <u>architecture of the piece</u>—*What the fuck is that?*
> ~~Brooke a dyke?~~
> *Don't write no more ha! ha!—why?*

Lux's ears were turning red as she scribbled. Anger?

Shame? Aimee hoped it didn't explode out on the conference room table.

This is why, Aimee told herself, I didn't invite any secretaries into the club. They can't handle emotion. They have no sense of humor or irony. Aimee needed deep, intelligent emotions and personal interaction to live, but she needed them from a safe distance. Safety and distance, to her, was what art added to make pain beautiful. At the moment, she deemed it best to take the focus off Lux and move on.

"Margot, you look like you have a burning need to share with the group. Would you like to do so now before you burst?"

"Actually I would. I'm Margot Hillsboro. I work mostly with Corporate and sometimes Contracts, although I started out in Trusts and Estates."

"I'm Brooke, one of the supervisors in Word Processing."

"Yeah, yeah, we all know who we are," said Aimee dismissively. She had become a paralegal after admitting to herself she was never going to make enough money as a photographer. Brooke, an old friend from art school, helped her get the job at Warwick. As a supervisor, Brooke sat at a big desk in front of all the word processors' tiny desks and solved their problems with the computer programs or the attorneys or their work schedules.

As a paralegal, Aimee's job was very similar to that of a first-year attorney, except she got paid a fraction of the salary and had little possibility of advancement. Brooke worked part-time to augment her trust fund. This allowed her to accept last-minute invitations to parties in far away places such as Bali or Romania. Aimee worked full-time so she could eat and pay rent.

"Right. Um, I zipped this together this morning before the gym. It's just a little fantasy I've been having again, and again, and again," Margot said. She took out her manuscript and read the first perfectly typed sentence.

"There was something about his furniture that made her want to take her clothes off."

Of all the members of the nascent Tuesday Erotica Club, Margot was the best paid, bringing home a check of little less than a quarter of a million dollars a year on a 60 to 80 hour workweek. She had no dependants and was addicted to shopping. Approaching menopause she saw that there was a cliff at the end of her autobahn, a great falling off. What would she do when she no longer went to work? She was not a partner at Warwick & Warwick, did not own any piece of the business she had helped to build, and therefore she could not own or control one hundred percent of her life. At some time in the not yet visible future they were going to ask her to stop coming into work.

"You'll do the same thing you do on the weekends," her mother had advised her. "You'll stop working and life will be a constant weekend."

Margot worked through most of the weekends of her life. In her free time she looked for clothes to wear to work. Even on vacations or quick trips with a lover there was always her briefcase full of necessary distractions that she could climb into when things got dull or disappointing. The briefcase was a magic bag out of which she drew respect, a sense of self and purpose, as well as a $4,000-a-month apartment, a killer wardrobe, interesting travel, and a very good facelift. She met her lovers through her briefcase. (Opposing counsel was exceptionally delicious after the deal was closed.) The intermittent months without blood between her legs reminded her that all things do eventually slow down. The thought emblazoned a new series of entries on her to do list in a bold font much larger than all the others, which read:

Find a hobby/lover.

Try to sit quietly.

Get ~~better~~ friends.

This nagging little sex fantasy, which had been stuck on replay in her mind, the one that was clogging up other thoughts and popping up at inopportune moments became her first attempt to access new friends. She figured writing about it could kill two birds with one stone. A little private literary session with some new girlfriends would surely exorcise this fantasy for good. She was wrong.

"*It stood in the corner of his kitchen,*" Margot began reading, "*a large, fine, mahogany, Louis XIV china cabinet of exquisite craftsmanship, filled with Baccarat crystal and Limoges porcelain.*"

Lux put down her nail file.

"*She'd seen it at several late-night dinner meetings that had evolved into drinks and playful banter. And while they discussed last quarter's earnings, or bridge, she often felt distracted by her own mind as it wandered over to that big piece and wondered how it would feel to have her naked ass pressed up against it.*"

Confused looks were traveling around the room

where there should have been only an interested silence. Was her erotic obsession with furniture too freaky for them? She hadn't even gotten to the freaky part, the part where she actually hoisted her buttocks onto the protruding ledge so Trevor could make love to her. Did they not believe her old ass could fit on the ledge of a china cabinet? Or was it just too much for them? If they were so prudish, why bother making it erotic? Margot folded the carefully typed index cards into her lap. She looked up to see that Lux was staring at her.

"It's ok?" asked Margot. "I don't want to offend."

"It's perfect," Brooke said. "Keep reading."

Margot looked around the room. All eyes were upon her. They were waiting, even eager to hear the rest of her story. Margot jumped in.

"*His kitchen was a marvel of architecture and he, a master chef. One night after pâté and champagne she threw caution to the wind and her brassiere on the floor as she walked naked across the tiles and into his waiting arms.*"

As she listened to Margot's unfolding tale of sex on a precariously balanced piece of antique furniture, Lux wondered if Margot had ever been to Trevor's apartment.

2. The Belly

THE BELLY WAS GETTING in the way more and more every day. Aimee, seven months pregnant, held the door to her downtown loft open with her knee while balancing a pair of shopping bags on one arm and, at the same time, tried to pull the key out of the lock. It would not budge. It wasn't even hot. There was no reason the key should so love the lock that it would not release it. Aimee tugged. She wiggled. She swore. She called his name.

"Honey, come help me," she begged. His photography, stunning large-format, archival-quality prints, called back to her saying 'he's not here. Honey.' In the end she put the grocery bags down and with two hands, slowly worked the key free from the lock. Then she flopped on the bed and cried.

Even when the sobs subsided she couldn't get comfortable. Lying on her belly pushed acid up her esophagus until it burned the back of her throat. When she lay on her back the tears ran into her ears and the snot ran down the back of her throat until it met the acid from her esophagus. The snot should cancel out the acid, she told herself, but it just strangled her. Lying on one side crushed some nerve while lying on the other side made her feet go numb. In the end she sat down in a straight back chair at the kitchen table, rested her head in her arms and cried. No one interrupted her. Hunger and curiosity finally dried up the tears. Why wasn't he home tonight?

No note on the fridge. No email on her computer. Her side of the answering machine had only one message and it wasn't from him. His side had fifteen messages. Should she eavesdrop? Would there be some giggling voice recorded on his side of their machine that Aimee could filter through her fears to discover his infidelity? Aimee untwisted the black ringlet of hair she had wrapped around her finger then hit the button on his side of the machine.

Beep. A message to say that one job was cancelled. Another postponed. Look in the paper. There's a write-up of your last show in Philly. Can you go back to Tokyo next month? It's worth five grand a week. The repairs on your zoom lens are done. Come pick it up. I can't be home tonight, honey. I'm working late.

"Idiot," she said out loud. "You left a message for me on your side of the answering machine, you jerk. How was I supposed to hear it?"

And yet she'd gotten it. Maybe he could be random because he knew she would dutifully explore all possible locations until she found an explanation for his absence. Absences.

Aimee pushed her hair out of her eyes and hugged her suddenly double-D-cup breasts closer to her body. It wasn't just the belly growing anymore. The hair had also exploded in a rage of growth, spilling curls into her eyes just weeks after she'd had it cut. And then there were those breasts. Aimee had been pleased when her 32A bra got tight. She'd been thin and flat-chested most of her life. It was kind of cool to have B-cup breasts. Then, one morning at work she thought she was having some kind of an asthma attack. She was sitting at her desk, reviewing a contract for an attorney when suddenly she simply could not breathe. It was like there was a rubber band across her chest, suffocating her. She feared for the life of her baby and rushed off to see a doctor.

The cabdriver looked terrified when Aimee breathed the words "emergency room" through the acrylic partition, and he raced as fast as he could. The nurse rushed her into an examination room. Aimee removed her blouse and the intern immediately noticed the deep cuts across her back and shoulders. As soon as he snipped off her size 34B bondage, Aimee gasped air once more, filling her lungs to capacity for the first time that day.

"Did you eat a lot of salt today?" the intern asked.

"Pastrami," Aimee had gasped.

"It'll make you swell. All over."

Aimee looked at the broken, lacy bra in her hands.

"First baby?"

"Yes."

But not the first pregnancy. There had been a miscarriage. And the abortion. Abortions. Not yet, not yet, he'd said. I need three, no, four, no, five years and then I'll be ready, he'd said. And she agreed with him, while at the same time sometimes letting herself get off schedule with the pills. And then she would panic because he had panicked, and she would agree that right now a baby would ruin their lives. After seven years she and her body just had enough of it.

"I'm going off the pill," she told him and then said it again to make sure he heard. He said ok and they didn't discuss it any further.

He figured that after a decade of artificial hormones, Aimee would need at least two months to be fertile again. She thought it would be closer to four. Both were wrong. Aimee's body was ready within two weeks.

Her period came like clockwork for the first three months of the pregnancy. Thinner, but red and definite in its arrival. Then another month passed as Aimee waited to see if this first missed period was just stress. After three sticks of positive pregnancy tests were tossed into the incinerator, she needed a little more time to find the strength to tell him. When she finally did, he flipped so she flipped but the doctor stood quite firm. He would not abort a five-month-old fetus.

Aimee rejoiced and he sulked.

"Our careers!" he shouted at her. "What will this do to our careers?"

But it had been a long time since Aimee had a career. She had a job and an expensive hobby in which she was highly skilled. She found herself at forty years old unwilling to sacrifice her last chance at motherhood for some filament of a career in photography.

When she told him her decision he broke down and sobbed. There was a moment of sorrow and guilt that turned to stony disgust as his sobs grew too big, too dramatic, too manipulative.

"What have you done!" he cried and turned crocodile on her. Tears flowed as he rested his head at a tragic angle on the doorway of their bedroom and watched her pack. She slammed her suitcase shut and walked to the elevator. Ohmygod, ohmygod, ohmygod she kept telling herself as the elevator descended. Where will I go? What will I do? How will I live? Scarlett O'Hara echoed in her head as she descended past the fourth, third, second floor. Her heart pounded, not with fear but with a sense of her narrow escape from him. She stood in the lobby of their building wondering where she could go to get away from his relentless disappointment in the joy that was growing within her.

In a small room at the Chelsea Hotel, Aimee stood naked in front of a poorly lit mirror and marveled at her belly. And then a little goblin of fear and loneliness peeked out at her from around the beveled edges. Could she afford to be a single mother? Was she strong enough to do this thing alone? In the middle of her large and painful panic attack, he tracked her down and begged her to come back to him, baby and all. His phone call slew the goblin. It was just bad timing.

"I miss you too," she admitted.

"I can't live without you. You're everything to me. If you want this baby, you can have it. I love you. Please come home, Aimee."

He checked her out and paid the bill and carried her suitcase to the cab. When they got back to their loft, he opened the door and carried her over the threshold. He tucked her suitcase into the space between the nightstand

and the wall. He kissed her cheek. And then he disappeared.

Not suddenly. Gradually he worked longer hours, took more jobs out of town, traveled to Tokyo so often he broached the subject of purchasing an apartment there. He said this impending fatherhood-thing was forcing him to take his career more seriously. They needed security now. And cash. After years of dryly criticizing friends and colleagues for selling out to commercial photography, he dove head first into the money pool and found the waters surprisingly pleasant and a bit intoxicating. A photographer had to take jobs while he was hot, he told her as he submerged again. It could all end tomorrow, then where would they be?

Aimee stood at the enormous windows of the loft, remnants of the day their home had been an industrial space, and looked down at the city. Directly behind her, their work hung on the wall: the only two prints left over from their last year at school in Chicago when they'd shared a group show with their classmates. The big print was his and the smaller one hers.

He had big ideas. She did too, but he presented his big ideas in five-foot by seven-foot prints. She helped him pay for the paper, helped him process the huge prints. Her work was equally good, but she presented it on paper that was eleven inches wide and fourteen inches tall. She got an A in the course, and he got an agent.

She stood in front of the one print of his that had not been sold, a five feet wide by seven feet high vagina only slightly obscured by the finger inserted into it. A discerning patron of the arts would have to observe the piece for a minute or two before the angle and scale allowed the viewer to recognize which pieces of human anatomy were interacting in the photograph. There had been respectable offers but he'd refused to sell it, telling anyone who asked that Aimee was the model and he could never sell Aimee's pussy.

When the photo was taken, Aimee was wearing torn blue jeans and a T-shirt. She was standing just left of the pussy, holding a reflector board that bounced the perfect light onto the subject. How anyone could believe that this vagina, with its pale and barely curled pubic hair, could be Aimee's was beyond her. This was clearly an Anglo-Saxon vagina. All of Aimee's follicles produced corkscrew curls of various intensity. Aimee had many things, but an Anglo-Saxon vagina was not among her attributes.

What have I done to us, Aimee thought as she wandered around the loft, looking at the pictures, stopping in front of her own nude, same model shot in the same studio but with more of a holistic approach to the image. And, of course, not five feet wide by seven goddamned feet high. I was good, she thought. I was just as good as he was. Why did I give up? Staring at the walls, she knew why.

Aimee could never compete with a five by seven vagina. She could never be that bold with her work. She could never bring herself to spend the thousands of dollars that he had borrowed and spent to produce fifteen huge nudes. She had been unable to take such a large amount of resources for her own ends. What if I fail, she asked before every attempt. The thought of failure made her nauseous. The inability to consume and digest risk decimated her creativity.

He, on the other hand, could eat risk and shit failure all over the place. He had no problem asking her, his parents, and her parents if he could borrow the money necessary to produce those first fifteen magnificent prints. Standing in front of the image that had jump-started his career, it hit her hard like a blow to the chest. He put the work first. Damn everything else and all pretenses of being a good and responsible human being. He was not polite. He was bold and reckless.

He had a career and she had a job.

I could turn it around, Aimee thought. I could be bold. I could take some risks. She sat down at her kitchen table and added up the numbers, a practical action that doomed her from the start. Even with the cost of a nanny, she thought she could probably afford to take a whole year off the job, provided she lived frugally and borrowed a bit from her mother. In a year, she thought, I could certainly produce something to start me on a road to that life I always assumed was waiting for me just the other side of college. The life where I was in charge, where I decided what I would do with my day. She knew from watching him that there was a world where people did not punch in from nine to five (or ten to six-thirty in Aimee's case), a world where people owned themselves entirely. All I need is to make something amazing, that everyone wants, something beautiful that I can sell.

The air seeped out of Aimee's plan as specific facts hit it, tearing little holes in the delicate spun fabric of her fantasy. If I get out of the job market I'll never get back in. If I leave my health-care provider at forty, I might not be able to find someone to cover me again. I'm no longer one of the swift gazelles at the front of the herd. I'm slow moving tiger-bait, and I need some better defenses than just a pipe dream of how I might reclaim my life. Change is a leap of faith and Aimee demanded proof that the floor still existed before stepping out of bed. It was a fatal error.

She felt like ripping his huge blond vagina right off the wall.

She used to barricade herself in the darkroom when sorrow like this overcame her and make pictures until she felt that she was at least chipping away at a foothold in the life she had hoped for. Even now she had four or five rolls that wanted to be printed. They were calling to her to be considered and sorted and printed into photographs that everyone could see and discuss. Bring us to life, they begged her, but she ignored them. Darkroom chemicals are not good for the belly, so Aimee kept walking around the apartment.

When he said hello I should have walked away. In those early days, though, he had eyes like spotlights that made her feel so special. He had pulled her into the circle of his narcissism where it was sweet and delicious: an addictive, high-calorie, nutrient-free dessert. She should have read the contents and escaped early.

Her first clue was the diamond that he couldn't afford. He told her she didn't want it; that she was too serious for those kinds of bullshit, bourgeois symbols of female conquest. She didn't really want the rock, but those courting dances have their reasons. If he won't alter his life before the wedding, he's certainly not going to accommodate you once you're married. And change is an integral part of the compromise that is marriage. A gleeful couple of hours at city hall comprised their wedding. Then they rushed back to the darkroom to finish the prints for his show. That night when he introduced her as his new wife she did not see that their wedding had been reduced to a good piece of conversation with a gallery patron.

"Oh sure, now it's all clear," Aimee said out loud to herself as she watched the city from her big windows. That night, though, she remembered being very excited to be introduced to such-and-such patron. She hoped he would remember meeting the young bride when her own show came up.

"It was a good life for a while," Aimee commented to the city below her window. Armed with youth and passion, even their poverty seemed the stuff of great bohemian legend. Art marched on. Photographs were sold. Birthdays passed, celebrated with a round of cheap wine in Dixie cups. Then, hanging a show in a gallery, Aimee fell off a ladder and broke her wrist.

It should have been simple, but the gallery was not insured for that sort of thing. Aimee wasn't insured for anything. A week later, with her fingers swollen like baby potatoes, Aimee cried the story out to her parents. Her mother barreled into the city like bear racing down the mountain to save her cub. Two weeks and $10,000 later, the wrist was re-broken and the hand saved. Aimee was broken too. He kept pushing on, though, insisting it was a grand life. She suggested some compromises. He said they were impossibilities.

If it had been booze or football or poker he loved instead of working, she would have seen it for what it was from the beginning. Sitting alone in their apartment, she told herself, *I should have insisted on a really big ring. He would never have gotten it and then I would have known how many things are more important than me.*

With that, Aimee shoved all the thoughts into the back of her head, shut off the lights, and went to bed. She lay there in the darkness, waiting for sleep to come. She waited and she waited. After a while, she started doing the thing that usually relaxed her best. She stroked and she wiggled but tonight it just wasn't working. Her hand was starting to cramp. In the quiet emptiness of her apartment, the phone rang.

"Hi, baby. What'cha doing?" her mother asked.

Well, Mom, I was masturbating, but then I realized what I really want is lasagna.

Aimee yawned and tried to formulate an honest answer that wouldn't freak her mother out.

"I was trying to relax, but I'm starving. I'm thinking about ordering some lasagna."

"Oooo! That sounds good," her mom crowed. "I don't want to keep you from your dinner."

"Yeah, I think I'm gonna get up and eat," Aimee said. She tried to sound upbeat and easy because sadness would cause her mother to worry, and worry might cause her mother to pack a suitcase and get on a city-bound train.

"You call me anytime you want, sweetie. Daddy sleeps like a dead man so even in the middle of the night is ok."

"Hey, I'm fine. A little tired and ridiculously hungry, but just fine."

"Well, you get that lasagna then. Next time I come I'll bring you homemade."

"I love you, Mom."

"Course you do. And I love you."

Aimee hung up the phone and went back to her original problem. Did she want to masturbate or eat lasagna? She was the kind of girl who almost always chose sex over pasta. Now all bets were off regarding desire. She didn't know what was a real feeling and what was a hormonal surge; wasn't sure if he'd left her or was being responsible in the only way he knew how. She pulled up her pants, got out of bed, and phoned the deli downstairs.

Money had always been an issue. Sometimes it was the only issue they discussed. After the wrist incident, she went back to school and became a paralegal. He told her not to. They would get by.

"I don't want to get by," she told him, "I want to live. I want health insurance."

"You'll miss the freedom."

"Freedom's too expensive," she told him. "Costs an arm and a leg."

"No!" he laughed. "Just your hand!"

She laughed too, sharing for a moment the bravura of his black humor. That night they went to an opening, drank coffees at midnight, and made love at dawn. She was late on her first day of classes, but not the second or any other class day after that. She graduated with honors and took a job that required her to show up in the morning, every morning, while he continued with a life that beckoned to him to stay out all night. He'd come home a couple of hours before she had to be at work, bounce into bed and wake her up.

"Oh, are you awake?" he'd ask.

"I am now," she'd groan.

"Awake enough to make love?"

"No."

"I read that sex when you're pregnant is supposedly an amazing thing."

"Not at seven in the morning."

"Gee, is it seven?"

People who regularly fail to know what time it is should die. If they're not doing it to flaunt their freedom, then they are foisting a basic responsibility onto someone else's shoulders. Either way, Aimee came to believe it should carry the death penalty.

Aimee got up, drank a glass of milk, and wondered if the heartburn would ever go away. She polished off a peanut butter and jelly sandwich waiting for the deli downstairs to bring up the lasagna—no salt please.

The downstairs deli used to be a special treat, far too expensive to be frequented on a regular basis. Lately though, fat checks with his name on them had been arriving from far away places in envelopes adorned with colorful stamps. She deposited them in their joint account and withdrew cash to pay the rent and other expenses. She became a regular customer at the deli, ordering in three or four nights a week.

Aimee eyed the cute delivery boy but stopped when she realized it made him really uncomfortable and tipped him well for remembering she wanted seltzer (salt-free) even though she had ordered club soda.

In the film *Rosemary's Baby,* Rosemary had not assumed herself crazy when she wolfed down raw liver in the middle of the night while standing in front of the fridge. Thinking about that scene, Aimee consumed her pasta standing up and wished she'd ordered a side of chopped liver. Sipping seltzer and praying that the belly would find peace with the calories she had given it, Aimee sat down on the couch to have a good long think about her life. She promptly fell asleep.

The next morning Aimee woke up in her own bed, in her pajamas. There was a fresh flower in a vase on the night table on her side of the bed, a glass of seltzer, some crackers and a little note that said I love you. He'd been there, but now he was gone.

She sat up and puked into the little bucket she kept there for that very reason, then carefully sipped the seltzer and nibbled the saltine hoping to keep it down long enough to get into the shower. She looked out the window and searched for the joy that she so longed for. It was there, underneath a wet blanket of loss and constant indigestion. In three months she would be having a baby and he couldn't even do her the courtesy of ruining it for her in person.

3. Butts and Feet

 "SHE WIGGLED HER TOES and warm wet tongues licked at her calves. A splash of icy scotch slipped down her throat and she felt the muscles uncoil, opening for the first time in days the tibialis posterior."

"Christ! Is she writing about her butt?" Lux exclaimed.

Aimee burned and the room fell silent.

"No. I'm not writing about my butt," Aimee tried not to hiss.

"It sounds like you're writing about your butt."

"I'm not."

"There's really nothing wrong with writing about your butt," Brooke felt she needed to say.

"*My* butt is a total one way street," Lux informed them.

Aimee waited. This was not what she wanted. Maybe she should quit the club and find some kind of solace in a support group specifically geared for pregnant women. There were groups all over the Internet. I'm not ready to talk about diapers and hemorrhoids, Aimee told herself. I want to stay in the adult world for as long as I can.

"It works for me," Brooke pronounced, regarding anal sex.

Margot stared at Brooke. It seemed incongruous to her that Brooke with her WASPy good looks, white blouse, and pleated skirt would voice a vote for anal sex. Margot could not imagine it because Brooke's tattoos were all in places that didn't show when she was wearing clothes. If Margot saw Brooke naked, she would understand.

"But, Brooke, there's no prostate," Margot argued. "Women don't have a prostate gland so there's nothing nice to rub up against, up in there."

"It works for me," Brooke maintained. "What doesn't work for me is a really big cock."

Then the opinions started to fly. Margot favored the bigger the better, while Brooke and Lux nearly jumped out of their seats to express their opinion on the perfect dimensions of a penis.

"I'm not—HEY!" Aimee shouted above the noise. "I'm not writing about my butt. The tibialis posterior is a muscle in the foot."

"Ew!" exclaimed Lux.

"Now, toe sucking can be an amazing experience," Brooke said.

"No," Lux countered, "it can't.

"If the toes are clean and the foot is beautiful. I mean, it's a way of saying to your lover everything about you is delicious and I want all of it in my body," Brooke laughed.

"Kind of like swallowing instead of spitting," Margot offered.

"Exactly!"

"You guys are gross," Lux said.

"My piece this week," Aimee began again, but she was run over by Margot's shock at Brooke's preferences.

"I can't believe you don't like a huge cock," Margot said to Brooke.

"Too much work."

"The bigger the better. Ten, twelve, inches. I want it all," Margot said laughing.

Brooke pulled a ruler out of her art kit on the table.

"Ten or twelve inches?" Brook said holding the bottom of the ruler down at the bottom of her pubic bone and extended it up. Twelve inches came to the bottom of her solar plexus.

"Oh!" Margot said. "Is that what twelve inches looks like?"

"Yep. So let's agree that twelve inches is just fictitious. Ten inches and you're talking porno, bullshit, rib-breaking dick. Nine is still well above my navel and even with eight, you're driving deep in my bladder and I'm spending the next week with a urinary tract infection. Doctors, antibiotics, I don't need the hassle."

"Lemme borrow that ruler," Margot asked. Brooke handed it to her and Margot became consumed with measuring the distance between the entrance to her vagina and the beginning of her ribs. No one was listening to Aimee.

"Could I please finish my story?" Aimee asked, fuming. All eyes turned to her, but as she began to read, Lux erupted with a thought she could not contain.

"Once, my mother told me that she'd dumped her first husband because his penis was too small and I said, well, like, maybe his penis was the right size and your vagina is too big."

Silence. And then.

"What did she say?" Brooke asked.

"Who?"

"Your mother," said Margot.

"Nothing. I mean, like are you asking me if she was mad? Cuz she wasn't. I mean, she's never been, you know, competitive about the size of her vagina so, you know, she just said something like 'Yeah, Lux, maybe that was the problem.' Or maybe she said 'Yeah, Lux, could you pass me the salt now,' or something empty like that."

Lux's side story about the relative dimensions of her mother's vagina hung in the air like a neighbor's bong hit, leaving everyone a little senseless and lost.

"So," said Lux because no one else seemed capable of speech, "I think Aimee wanted to read something she wrote about her ass, right?"

"No!" Aimee exclaimed. "My piece is not about my ass! It's about coming home, having a glass of scotch, and soaking my feet in a hot tub of water."

"I thought these were supposed to be sex stories," interrupted Lux, unable to be quiet for long.

"We are writing erotic stories," Aimee said, burning, "which includes anything sensual. Not just sexual. Not pornographic."

"Although, well, actually," Brooke offered, "actually, I would define the piece I wrote this week as leaning towards the pornographic. If that's going to be a problem, I would rather sit out this round of sharing."

Lux mouthed the word "buttocks" to Margot across

the table. Margot's eyebrows rose, and she felt a giddy surprise jumping up inside her too. She sat up a little straighter in her chair.

"I'd like to hear your butt story, Brooke," Margot said.

Aimee sighed. Aimee and Brooke had been friends for over twenty years and she already knew everything there was to know about Brooke's tattooed ass. Back in Chicago, when they were free and twenty-three years old, Brooke and Aimee shared an apartment and the occasional lover. Aimee had spent too many evenings sitting naked in the overstuffed chair next to the bed, feeling left out, watching Brooke writhe in delight with the lover they were supposed to be enjoying together.

"Aimee!" Brooke had insisted, "you gotta try it."

"Why?"

"It'll change your life. You'll totally rethink everything you know about sex. But not with Dave."

"Why not with Dave?" Aimee asked. He was her then current boyfriend and seemed like the perfect choice.

"Because literally and figuratively, Dave is a big dick. You need a sensitive man."

They'd settled on a guy Aimee knew and liked who was delighted by the girls' invitation to enter Aimee's rectum. He was gentle and kind. To ease the event, he brought over an excellent bottle of red wine and a large tube of some water-based lubricant. He did everything right and yet it was one of the most startling and unpleasant sensation Aimee had ever experienced.

Brooke said she'd just picked the wrong guy to do it with. Aimee quit having threesomes with Brooke. She just couldn't compete with that willing, yearning rectum.

"I don't want to hear a story about Brooke's butt," pronounced Lux. Aimee didn't want to hear it either, but perhaps she could use the issue to get Lux to leave the group.

"We're not censoring Brooke's piece. I can guarantee you won't like hearing it. You're welcome to skip the rest of the meeting if you think it would upset you."

Lux sat down and shut her mouth.

"Shall I read it now?" Brooke asked.

"Actually I haven't finished with my story," Aimee began only to be interrupted by Lux.

"So Brooke, how pornographic is it? Mildly pornographic?" Lux asked.

"No, Lux, it's a down and dirty, up the butt, wildly pornographic story. If you don't like it, you don't have to listen to it," Brooke informed her in scathing tones, which had no effect on Lux's determination to understand the full range of Brooke's story before hearing it.

"In your story, does anyone, like, act really mean to anyone else in it?" Lux asked.

"No."

"Does anyone get abused? Or physically hurt?" Lux asked.

"No."

"Does anyone have to do, you know, something against their will?" Lux asked.

"What interesting questions," Margot said.

"I got nothing against the sex parts," Lux said defensively, "but I don't like to hear about people getting their feelings or their bodies hurt, all right? Especially when the girl gets her feelings hurt just so the boy can feel better about his self."

There was a quiet in the room as everyone thought about Lux for a moment. Lux had interesting and well-thought-out ideas about how she liked her pornography to unfold.

"It's just a dirty little story about me seducing my mailman," Brooke reassured her.

"Oh, well then," Lux said by way of invitation.

Brooke opened her paper and began to read.

Aimee sighed, losing out once again to the excitement of Brooke's butt. She should have said something, but then things might have gotten unpleasant and that wasn't worth the remaining three paragraphs of her footbath and scotch description.

As Brooke began to read, Lux pulled out her notebook full of words that interested her. Words she wanted to know more about.

"*Enrique rang my bell,*" Brooke began. "*I threw on a bathrobe and ran to the door. 'Who is it,' I asked trying not to sound as lascivious as I felt. 'Mailman,' he said. 'And I've got a package for you.'*"

Lux laughed and wrote down the word "lascivious" in her notebook.

"*With my bathrobe on the floor covering only my ankles, I opened the door a crack, just enough that he would see what was waiting inside. 'Do I have to sign for this package?' I asked. 'Oh yes,' he said. 'Would you be interested in bringing it around to the back door?' Enrique's' eyes bulged out of his head, and I knew he was a virgin to that sort of invitation. I opened the door, and he slid into my house.*"

Lux gasped, but not about what was about to come in through Brooke's back door. Brooke would have kept reading her story, but Aimee quickly swatted her across the back of the head.

"Margot," Trevor said as he opened the glass door and leaned his handsome head into the conference room. The hair was gray and the face lined, but Trevor's spirit was light and fun.

Margot felt her usual belly spasm of delight at the sight of him. A mantra ran through her head, reminding her, "He's so cute, he's so sexy, he's so nice." Although "nice" had been the death-adjective of earlier passions, Margot, at fifty, craved "nice."

"You're supposed to have completed all the manufacturing contracts for the Peabody Christmas catalogue," Trevor informed her. "Crescentia Peabody is sitting in my office right now, waiting to sign. What are you all doing in here?"

"Book club meeting," said Lux with a winning smile.

"Really? I didn't know you had a book club. What are you reading? Are you open to new members?"

"Girls only," said Aimee.

"You wouldn't like it," Brooke warned him. "We read girlie things."

"I like girlie things," Trevor said with a smile.

"But you're not invited," Lux informed him.

"Fair enough." Trevor laughed as he held the door open for Margot to rush through and off to her meeting. But Margot did not get up from the table.

"The contracts are all on my desk, Trevor," Margot said, trying to be cool. "I'll be there in just a minute."

"A minute is too late. I need you now. Mrs. Peabody's a bit, well, 'rigid' would be a polite way to describe it. Let's get this thing signed and done with before she starts to pick at it."

Margot looked at her friends and sighed. She abandoned the Tuesday writers' group meeting, ran through the conference room door, raced into her office, grabbed the contracts and then sprinted back to Trevor's office. She moved with remarkable speed for a woman of fifty, hobbled by a tight pencil skirt and spiked heel pumps.

If I can get this contract signed quickly, Margot thought, maybe I can catch the tail end of Brooke's story.

Oooo! Tail end! Good pun, she told herself as she stood outside of Trevor's office and collected herself. Contracts in hand, Margot brushed the image of Enrique and Brooke out of her mind, straightened her blouse and entered Trevor's office.

Crescentia Peabody and her personal assistant Barbara, both looking like comfy Connecticut housewives, were sipping tea and chatting with Trevor.

"Ah! Here she is," Trevor said a bit too loudly upon Margot's entrance.

"Hot off the press!" Margot said gaily, waving the contracts in the air. "The contracts for your Christmas clitoris."

The clients stared back at her, their matching pink-lipsticked mouths each forming a little round "O" of surprise.

"Catalogue, Margot," Trevor said.

"What?"

"Christmas catalogue."

"Didn't I just say that?"

"No, I believe you said 'clitoris,'" Barbara said.

"Oh, thank goodness," said Crescentia, "I heard 'clitoris' too and I thought for a second that I was hearing wrong, but if you both heard it too, well actually, I'm relieved. I mean that it wasn't just me."

"Oh. Well," said Margot in that cool clear voice. "My apologies. I meant catalogue, not…the other word. Shall we get on with it then?"

4. *Housing*

*L*UX RETURNED TO HER desk after the meeting of The Tuesday Erotica Club to find an email from her attorney regarding her fifty percent share of a detached single family home in Queens. Her aunt, a prostitute (or "who-ah" as Lux's mother, in her Jersey accent, referred to her sister-in-law) had chipped in with another working girl and bought it many years ago when real estate values were so much lower. The two women had quietly used it on the side for well on twenty years. When they retired, they rented it to other who-ahs.

Lux, knowing full well where the diamonds came from, had loved her aunt the who-ah. As Lux was the only blood family member who visited the woman in the hospital, Lux inherited her aunt's fifty percent share of the house and the rolling rent the house was earning. The rent money was delivered by hand in a white envelope to her attorney's office on the first of each month. Half went into Lux's account. In recent years, that account had grown to more than $30,000. Lux never saw the white envelope or the actual money, usually presented in a stack of overused twenty-dollar bills, faded from the touch of too many hands, carefully counted and all facing the same way.

Lux read the email from her attorney quickly and made an immediate decision. The other prostitute was dying and would gladly sell her half of the house for $20,000 provided she could get the money quietly, quickly, and in cash. Was Lux interested?

"Yeah," Lux typed into the computer. "Will she take a check?"

"No. It's got to be cash only," her attorney wrote. "Can you get me the money by Thursday?"

"Yes! Tell her I said thanks."

"Drinks later?" the attorney had written back. "To celebrate your home ownership?"

"Not tonight," Lux wrote. "Busy."

Lux smiled, imagining her aunt's best and often only friend taking her $20,000 cash and going one last round in Vegas before calling it quits with the world. It was good of her to give Lux the house and Lux would make an effort to do something good back before the old lady left for Vegas and beyond.

Even though it was now all hers, Lux couldn't live in the house. Her mother would have a major fit if she knew Auntie Who-ah had given it to her and a very different fit if she knew Lux had so much cash at her disposal. Now that the house was one hundred percent hers, Lux planned to clean it up and maybe sell it. Or maybe she'd rent it by the month, instead of by the hour. Maybe she'd even tell her mother about it.

Auntie Who-ah thought Lux's mother had a tendency

to fawn on powerful people and take an untoward interest in controlling the power of others, rather than claim and hold both power and pleasure for herself. Auntie Who-ah did not use this exact language. She told Lux that her mother had a "blow job personality."

"Yeah, sure," Auntie Who-ah had told a younger Lux. "When his dick is in your mouth you rule his universe, but what happens when you take it out? And you gotta take it out if you're gonna ask for anything at all. I mean, anything for yourself. And that, baby girl, is what is commonly called a Catch-22."

Lux, at Auntie Who-ah's insistence, had been careful not to cultivate a blow job personality. If she wanted something, she got it for herself.

Lux left her inner city high school unable to spell, understand complex thoughts, or string a sentence together on her own. However, she had attended faithfully and this put her in the top of her graduating class. Her parents expected her to quickly get into the business of having babies, but Lux had access to good birth control and did not like any of the big dogs that wanted to slobber on her face. She scraped the money together to take a college course load that was really just four years of high school crammed into two, minus the obnoxious and destructive kids who had made learning impossible for everyone else. Lux had done well enough to obtain an associate degree. That led to work in Manhattan as a secretary. She was amazed at the paycheck, got a small apartment with friends, and bought lots of clothes. When she inherited her aunt's house and the rolling rent that came with it, she saw a light at the end of the tunnel.

"Yeah, yeah, you could do that. It's a good idea," her aunt's septuagenarian attorney had wheezed. "Live at your mother's house. Don't buy anything that's not necessary. Save all the money you make. Buy an apartment. Start renting it out and you'll double your income. You'll own your own little business. Then you can marry me, I'll retire, and we'll have lots of kids. Ah! Ha! Ha!"

They laughed and drank and planned for Lux's brilliant future. Now Lux worked hard and tucked away all the money, but she did not move back to her mother's house.

"Trev," Lux asked, over eggs and orange juice. "When I talk out loud, do I say "and then" a lot?"

"Hadn't noticed," Trevor said as he stretched and scratched the broad expanse of his well-muscled, slightly grayed chest. "Anything in there about me?"

Lux slammed the notebook closed. The kitchen in Trevor's three-bedroom, rent-controlled apartment needed a paint job. Lux had never thought about things like that before. He said the apartment cost him almost nothing because his parents had lived here until his father died and his mother's Alzheimer's became too intense. He had been able to hold onto the lease, but because of the low rent it was almost impossible to get the landlord to do anything. Lux was thinking about how low rent on a roomy apartment could make your paycheck feel bigger than it actually was when her eyes fell on the mahogany china cabinet.

"Trevor, that thing in the corner of your living room, the one with all your wife's glass and crystal stuff inside."

"The credenza? The one where we…last week after the basketball game?"

He looked up at her over the top of his morning coffee to make sure she was smiling. She was grinning broadly.

"Yeah, that was fun."

"What about it?" he asked.

"Whadd'ya call that clay stuff inside?"

"The porcelain is Limoges and the crystal is Baccarat."

"No shit. Have you had it a long time?"

"It was my great grandmother's."

"It's not a particularly rare piece of furniture though, is it?"

"Actually, I think it is."

"Oh."

A crinkle of concern passed over his little bunny's face, worrying him deeply. Was she going to leave him because of his grandmother's credenza? Lux was young and beautiful and full-spirited. She needed him in a way his ex-wife and their grown children never had. She was wowed by his limited knowledge of the world outside the five boroughs of New York City, by his willingness to take a stab at the Sunday crossword puzzle, and his ability to spell polysyllabic words. He had been to places like Europe, in fact had lived in London for part of his junior year in college. He rented an apartment in Manhattan and had paid to send two children through school all the way to the end of their undergraduate degrees.

Trevor was quite handsome and still strong. She wasn't crazy about gray hair, but, so far, he had not hit her. She loved that he never put her through unpleasant tests in order to prove her love and devotion to him. He never asked her to ride the A train from Far Rockaway to Harlem wearing a very short skirt and no underwear. In Lux's eyes, these things made Trevor the supreme silverback, alpha male gorilla, the best boyfriend she had ever had. Trevor did not think he could live without that reflection of himself racing back towards him from her dark green eyes.

The fact that she was the secretary to one of the partners in his firm wove a small ribbon of concern through their relationship. He insisted they keep their affair hush-hush. He made up a list of rules for her. The most important rule was never talk about their relationship at the office, not even to make dinner plans. Never enter or leave the office at the same time. Never go out after work together with people from the office. And never, ever bring their relationship into work with them. Lux agreed and their deception added to his excitement. He felt like he was cheating just a little. Lux didn't mind. He was a secret worth keeping.

"Has that, ah, Margot lawyer from work ever come over here to this apartment?" Lux asked Trevor, trying to be nonchalant about the question.

"Margot? Hillsboro?"

"Yeah."

"Hundreds of times."

"Really?"

A passion flared up in Lux. She had to have him right now. She kissed him and pulled open the sash of his terrycloth bathrobe.

"We'll be late."

"I know," she said.

"I can be late but you have to be there by nine."

"It'll be fine," she said.

"If we do this I'll have to cancel my tennis game and come home after work for a nap," he said. "And we have theater tickets tonight."

"I promise it will be better than tennis," she said as she flicked her pink, sateen robe off her shoulders and stood naked in front of him.

Shazam!

She loved that it only took nudity to get him going. No dancing around, no promises of tricky positions. The moment Trevor saw Lux naked he got an erection. Every time. It was a glorious thing for both of them. She became important, and ten years fell off Trevor's shoulders.

Hickies were for kids but Lux still wanted to mark Trevor as her property, to protect him against that Margot Hillsboro and her correctly punctuated fantasy about sex on Trevor's furniture. First there was the preamble of the best oral sex Trevor could remember, like a velvety vacuum cleaner tugging the head of his penis higher and higher, making him feel so strong and important. This was quickly followed by a bump and grind, then penetration so deep and fulfilling tears came to his eyes at the thought that it might stop. When he couldn't hold on for another minute, Trevor, an apartment dweller all his life, howled as he came and damn the neighbors. The clock ticked 8:45 when she rolled off him. She ran to grab a quick shower, leaving him on the kitchen floor in puddles of sweat, semen, and happiness.

"My wallet, my wallet," Trevor motioned to his wallet when Lux came back in dressed for work. As he lay on the floor waving feebly to the wallet that lay in his pants across the room, something deep in Lux turned sour and horrified at the gesture. She gave him the wallet with trembling fingers, then turned away as he struggled to one elbow and dug out some cash.

"What?" he said.

"I gotta go," she answered.

"I know. But here, take a cab, darling, you're so late as it is."

Lux looked at the languid outstretched hand urging her to take $20 to pay for the cab.

"I'm cool. Gotta run."

Lux dashed out the door with an uncomfortable, dirty feeling. Trevor knew he had done something to insult her but couldn't imagine how his reminder to take a cab could be misconstrued as mean. He didn't want her to be late for work. He didn't want her to be unhappy or troubled in anyway. He was crazy for her.

Lux tumbled into the office ten minutes late. They noticed. A disapproving scowl was followed by a brief lecture on dawdling.

"I wasn't dawdling," Lux said, knowing that if you defend yourself it just got worse. She should have just smiled a beggar's smile and kept quiet. But still, the word "dawdle" is best used to describe a distracted child or someone who can't seem to focus on the goals at hand, and Lux was definitely not dawdling this morning. Of course, the truth, "I was fucking Trevor's brains out on the floor of his kitchen so he would be too tired to look at other women," was not appropriate either.

While the lecture rolled off her back, she thought about the way she'd raced out of Trevor's apartment, heart pounding, feeling her life was not her own. If the clock ticked to 9 a.m. and Lux was not in her seat, Mr. Warwick behaved as if she was stealing from the firm. His look, as if Lux was something small and dirty under his shoes, created a knot of rage somewhere between Lux's stomach and her chest. I gotta escape this ownership, Lux told herself. I gotta belong to me and just me. I'm gonna make a ton of money and buy myself back from all this.

The lecture flowed on. Lux was an ok secretary. It's true she couldn't spell and had no sense of grammar, but she was substantially cheaper than the perfect automaton who had retired with a good company pension after thirty years of service. Lux would probably move on or be fired before she became vested. With an eye on the bottom line, Mr. Warwick jumped into the twenty-first century and learned to type his own emails. Any substantial documents were sent down to Brooke in Word Processing. Word processing and copyediting were billable to the client; a secretary's salary was not. Lux did his filing, kept his schedule, answered his phones, and occasionally picked up things like lunch, dry cleaning, or theater tickets for him. It paid really well compared to what Lux originally expected to get out of life, and right now collecting money was the key to the kingdom. As the lecture receded, Lux settled into her desk and flicked on her computer.

"Can I take you shopping at lunch?" came an instant message from Trevor.

"Can't today, baby. How about Saturday?"

Today at lunch Lux had to go to the bank, withdraw $20,000 and deliver it in person to her lawyer. When she handed him the money, he would present her with the full deed to the house in Queens. Lux wrote a checklist of everything that would happen to the house after this afternoon's transaction. It looked like this:

1.) Get rid of the girls.

2.) Fix it.

3.) Sell it.

Those girls could get ugly so she would tell them that the house was being painted—something it desperately needed. After painting there would be plumbing and roofing to keep them out of it. Lux would schedule the work to go slowly, giving the girls plenty of time to find other, better places to ply their trade. Lux would have the landscaping redone and all the crappy old furniture hauled off to the dump. Then, with absolutely no money left in the bank, Lux would sell it. From her own obsessive perusal of the real estate sections, she figured she could get serious money for the house. Cash down, that house could translate to a decent Manhattan apartment with a small enough mortgage and maintenance compared to the income it could generate. Lux was about to acquire her first major asset.

I'm on the road from slavery to freedom right now, Lux thought.

After the big brouhaha of being late, there was nothing to do at the office that morning. If she owned herself, Lux would be able to put her head down on her desk and catch a little nap, but she didn't. In spite of the fact that there was nothing to do, Lux needed to look busy. She pulled out a notebook and started to write.

Making love to him on the kitchen floor was like, it was like something good. It was like feeling, ok, the girl was feeling like she was all chained up ok, and then, she broke all the chains, ok, and then she flew up into the air, ok and then she inflated like a, like a big balloon, ok and then...

Lux stopped writing and chewed on the tip of her pen while she reread her work.

"It's stupid," Lux said out loud and then looked quickly around to make sure no one had heard her. She crossed out all the *ok*s and the *like*s and then read it back to herself. Still stupid. Sex this morning with Trevor was not like balloons or breaking chains. He was just the best man she'd ever had.

He was the best man she had ever had, Lux wrote on a clean sheet of notebook paper. Ok, I believe that, she told herself. Now, why is it true? Go on girl, make a list.

He was strong and he was gentle, Lux added to the paragraph, *and he saw all the things that were right and wrong about her all in the same breath and time, and from the very first time she touched him, right, she knew it was right, ok, and it was forever. With him there was no fear. And her old friends would laugh at her, right, because he was an old guy but I don't care. I really like him and what he can teach me.*

Lux quickly tore the page out of the notebook, got up from her desk and marched right into her boss's office.

"What are you doing?" Mr. Warwick asked.

"Shredder."

Lux fed her first truthful writing into Mr. Warwick's shredder and felt greatly relieved to see it come out on the other side as strings of confetti.

Worse than laughing, her old friends had congratulated her when they found out she'd scored a bed in a Manhattan apartment with an old guy who bought her things.

"Oh baby, you got yourself a sugar daddy," her friend Jonella had crowed loud enough to wake the baby in her arms.

"Suckin' old cock to make da rent!" laughed Carlos, once her true love, now Jonella's baby's daddy.

"Fuck you both," Lux said, laughing along with them. "It ain't like that."

"You screwing him?"

"Yeah."

"Screwing him good?"

"'Think so."

"You living in his house?"

"Mostly."

"You paying him rent?"

"No."

"He buy you things?"

"Yeah."

"Then it's like that."

Lux's mother had given her an earful about Trevor.

"Get it girl, you get it and grab hold as tight as you can," Lux's mother had whispered to her, urging her to get some kind of commitment out of Trevor, something that would hold up in court.

"Get yourself pregnant, fast," her mother hissed at her.

"It's not like that, Mom," Lux insisted.

Lux's mother smiled like they had a secret together, a secret that boiled down to her mother telling her you're not worth shit but you got lucky with some fool who's better than you. Lux tried to weigh her mother's opinion against what Auntie Who-ah might say.

Ride it till it don't please you no more.

"Hey, Lux! You here today or still at home?" her boss asked, standing over her desk and holding a stack of papers.

"Here," Lux chirped. She slammed her notebook shut and hid away her thoughts.

"I need these filed. First pull the bills and alphabetize them for accounting, then make a copy and see that they go into the client's files. When you're done, come see me. I'll be finished with my correspondence by then, and I'd like you to print and get them out into the mail, except for the ones that go by FedEx, which I have noted in the address. Oh, and some go out by fax, you'll just have to ask me which ones are faxed. Lux?"

"Yeah, I got it. File, then mail, then FedEx, then fax. Not a problem at all."

"And make reservations for six people for lunch, ok?"

"Done."

"I haven't told you where or what time."

"Ok, where and what time."

"Tomorrow at one o'clock at someplace with a sushi bar. Got that."

"Yep."

"Can you say it back to me just so I'm sure you've got it?"

"Tomorrow at one at someplace with a sushi bar."

"Good. Thanks. Come see me when the filing is done."

"Right."

Like a relief from pain, sensation spreads across his body and into mine.

Lux said the phrase over again to herself as she alphabetized the bills and thought about the way Trevor's orgasm had kicked off one last spasm of pleasure in her. The phrase danced around in her head, and Lux groped around her desk for her notebook. She couldn't find it quickly enough and ended up grabbing a Post-it Note and scribbling the sentence on its sticky yellowness so she could read it again later and give it some thought from a distance. As she was pasting the Post-it into her notebook she got a sudden urge to call Aimee.

"Aimee," Lux said into the phone. "Can um…"

Suddenly it seemed so stupid. Aimee hated her.

"Who is this?" Aimee asked on the other end of the line just before Lux hung up.

Lux picked up her notebook, put down her alphabetizing and went for a walk that just happened to pass by Aimee's desk.

"Hiiiiiiiiiiiii," she said with one hand on Aimee's doorway trying to pretend her existence was wholly accidental.

"What?" Aimee asked.

"I guess I want to thank you for letting me into your book club."

"Writers' group."

"Whatever."

"In a book club you read published works. A writers' group brings writers together to read each other's work."

"Right."

"And..."

"And I'm really enjoying it."

"I'm so pleased," Aimee said without looking up from the papers on her desk.

There was more to say. Lux wanted to whip out her notebook and show Aimee her sentence, her first good sentence. A sentence she had written all by herself. A sentence that pleased her because it said something real and yet did not embarrass her. I wrote a good sentence, Lux thought and longed to say. Can you believe it? Because I never thought I ever could but here it is, a good sentence and ok, it's only a short sentence, but it's my first real sentence and I want to show it to someone who knows something about sentences.

"Is there something you need?" Aimee asked, unaware of what was bubbling up in Lux. All she saw was an annoyingly young woman in blue high heals and loud purple stockings jumping from foot to foot in the doorway of her office.

"No, I just wanted to say, like, ah, I guess, thanks."

"Right. I gotta make a call," Aimee said as a way of saying get the hell out of my office. Lux understood the full meaning and backed out of Aimee's doorway. She hurried back to her desk to finish the filing and faxing and make the reservations for someone else's lunch. Sushi, she reminded herself. He wants sushi.

5. *Gossip*

AIMEE AND BROOKE ALWAYS wore black. Occasionally they threw in a little white or, on festival days, a red handbag or gloves would finish off an outfit. And so it was that when the two of them sat together on Aimee's white couch it was hard to tell where Aimee ended and Brooke began. Margot, sitting across from them, wore a peach silk pantsuit by Chanel and rather demure 8mm pearl earrings. Underneath her black smock, Aimee had outgrown her DD-cup bra and was wearing an absurdly large white cotton bra that unhooked over each breast to reveal the nipple: a nursing bra. Brooke wore a large pair of hollow, hammered silver bangles that sounded like giggles when they clinked against each other. At that moment, Brooke's bracelets and all the girls were laughing.

"…and then, ok, like and then he said, like ok."

Brooke was falling off her chair with the hilarity of it all.

"She doesn't even have a name! She's got an adjective!"

"Oh, Aimee, she has got to go," Margot said laughing too.

"No!" roared Brooke, "She's priceless! We have to keep her!"

"I'm sure she'll drop out," Aimee said, trying to control her laughter not for the sake of Lux but because it hurt her belly.

"Should we stay on the erotica or try something different?" Margot asked, pleased to be part of the group and yet slightly uncomfortable. Margot hadn't had any girls as friends since seventh grade. She was afraid of girls.

"I was Queen Bee of my seventh grade clique," Margot told her first shrink, "and was instrumental in driving a sniveling little girl named Juliet so low on the social totem pole that she just dropped off the ladder and out of school. Not a major tragedy. I mean, this girl Juliet, she favored knee socks and plaid skirts anyway. She enrolled in the local Catholic school and was just fine. With no one to pick on, however, the popular girls suddenly turned on me the way a wildfire can suddenly turn. Oh how they turned on me! On me! Their leader!"

Since he had nothing in his own background to compare it to, Margot's shrink sat quietly in his chair trying to imagine what it might be like to have one's own prescription for demoralizing another child shoved down one's own throat. The guilt on top of the pain had ruined the taste of "girlfriend" for Margot forever. She didn't trust girls, and she didn't trust herself.

"Oh no, let's stay on erotica," Brooke said.

"Let's try poetry. That should scare Lux away," Aimee said.

"Poetry?" Margot shivered. "That'd scare me away!"

"What if we spent a few sessions writing about something she doesn't know anything about?"

"Debutante balls?" suggested Brooke.

"You're the only one of us who's been to a debutante ball," Aimee guffawed.

"The closest I ever came to coming out is when I had sex on the front porch," Margot admitted.

More vicious giggles rocked Aimee's abdomen and some pee leaked out into her underwear.

"No stop! No more laughing! You're killing me!"

Aimee struggled up off the couch and waddled into her bedroom to change her underwear, blaming Lux for making her wet her pants.

"What are you doing in there?" Margot called.

"None of your business," Aimee called back to her. The choice of underwear was painful to Aimee. Pre-pregnancy she preferred the thong for a variety of reasons that went way beyond questions of panty lines. Now her large collection of racy, lacy undies lay unloved in the back of the drawer beneath the newly purchased cotton crotch nylon jobs that washed well but looked like something her granny would recommend for comfort and durability.

The window in her bedroom was open. Someone, somewhere in the city had done something disgusting which sent an unknown horrible smell up through Aimee's bedroom window and into her nose.

"Hkak! Hkak!" A gurgle rose from Aimee's throat as she raced for the toilet. On her way to the bathroom she began to puke. Moving forward, Aimee was running into the puke that was spilling out of her mouth. She had a choice: either stop running and puke on the floor or continue racing towards the bathroom in an effort to get a percentage of puke into the toilet with the rest falling onto her clothes. Neither one was an acceptable alternative for the other, but it was all she had to choose from. Aimee stopped and puked on the floor.

"Hey!" Brooke called from the couch. "You ok?"

"Fine."

"You don't sound fine."

"I am though."

Aimee took a great wad of toilet paper out of the bathroom and wiped up the puke. There was too much and in the end she had to use a towel. Aimee wrapped the contents of her too-delicate stomach up in a fluffy white towel. She gritted her teeth and tossed the once-lovely towel into the trashcan rather than risk puking again when she washed it.

He should be here to wipe up my puke and wash the towels, Aimee thought, but that thought lead to other more dangerous thoughts. Those kinds of thoughts had to go out of her mind, or *she* would go out of her mind. It was all a symptom of the way her life ended as soon as she got pregnant.

Aimee brushed her teeth and put on clean granny underwear. Her pregnancy was unfolding like a cross between some horrific, destructive hurricane and kidney stones, but in the end she would have a baby and that thought made it bearable.

"Aimee, this is a great apartment," Margot was saying as Aimee returned to the living room.

"Thanks."

"What do you pay?" Margot enquired.

Such questions are considered rude everywhere in the world except their city where affordable housing was a problem for even a rich girl like Margot.

"Four thousand."

"Mortgage and maintenance?"

"Rent."

"Can you buy it?"

"When it was a reasonable price we didn't have the cash."

"Wow, yep, me too. I've got a great two-bedroom that I should have bought back in the early nineties. I had the cash, but it just didn't seem worth it back then."

"Listen, thanks for the beer," Brooke said as she gathered up her coat and bag, "but I gotta catch a bus."

"You should move into the city," Aimee said.

"Yeah, I should," said Brooke in a noncommittal way that did not reveal how lazy Brooke had become or how she could not imagine that a life that had been so wild in the city at twenty would end up so quiet in the suburbs by forty.

"Margot, how about a movie?" Aimee asked.

"I'm a gym rat every other night for at least two hours," Margot said. "It keeps me sane and thin. If you can wait until the ten o'clock show, though, I'll see anything. I'm an entertainment slut, any movie, anytime, anywhere."

"Ten's a little late for me to get started. I've been conking out by eleven every night," Aimee admitted.

"Another time, then,' Margot said. "What kind of movies do you like?"

"Sci-fi, action adventures," Aimee said, and the other women laughed at the absurdity of her answer.

The chitchat continued as the women walked to the door and rang for the elevator. There were quick hugs and promises to go to the theater together. On the way down Margot and Brooke discussed throwing a baby shower for Aimee. Margot thought a luncheon at a local restaurant would be pleasant and appropriate.

"What's her husband like?" Margot asked Brooke as they reached the street.

"He's a good guy. Obsessed with his work. Handsome, tall. Used to drink too much but stopped. Actually I haven't seen him since, gee, for a while. Gets a lot of work shooting rock bands in Tokyo."

"He's a photographer?"

"No, Margot, he's an assassin. Duh! Of course he's a photographer."

Brooke gave Margot's arm a quick shove at the shoulder. They laughed and hugged and promised each other another evening of giggles and beer. Margot walked away feeling good about her new friends.

Alone in the apartment, Aimee dialed his cell phone. It rang and rang. "Listen, don't come home, ok," Aimee said out loud to the ringing phone. "Why are you hanging me up like this? Just tell me that we're done and I'll move on and…oh!"

His phone picked up and asked her to leave a message.

"…ah, hi. It's me, babe. Bunch of checks came yesterday. I deposited them. That account's getting kind of full. Maybe when you come home we should clean it out and buy an island. And, ah, I love you. Bye."

It was clearly a *Lord of the Rings* night. There was a small theater that Aimee could walk to and catch a cab back. It had been showing all three parts of the *Lord of the Rings* trilogy, back-to-back, twenty-four hours a day for almost two years straight. Aimee and her husband started going last summer just to get out of the heat. Now that she was alone, Aimee would go too often and escape into Middle Earth.

She loved the enemies the best for they were so clearly evil. The evil in Aimee's life was like cancerous tumors that couldn't be killed without destroying some of her own flesh too. She loved the glory of the battles; the way the actors threw their full selves into smashing and hacking at evil until major body parts were severed from the whole. So much easier to hack and destroy than to save or change. And so she went repeatedly and sat in a dark theater for the vicarious thrill of watching unquestionable good destroy undeniable evil. She loved the heroism of the characters and the great hunky actors. She lamented that in the whole of the trilogy, only Frodo removed his shirt.

I'm a geek, Aimee told herself as she always did when she walked this familiar path into a funkier neighborhood where the theater stood. I don't know why I fixate on these heroic boy-stories when the only person who ever flew in to save me when I was in distress was my mother. Passing a local bar, Aimee glanced through the plate glass window. She was nauseated by the sight of two happy patrons inside the bar making out like a couple of teenagers.

The woman, to Aimee's suddenly prudish eye, was practically licking the guy's face. Aimee scowled at them and then returned to the scolding of her inner critic: I should be celebrated by my society as a creator of life not shuttling off to movies by myself. I should be home cataloging something, reading one of the arts journals that come to the...Christ! Oh my god! What *was* that?

Aimee turned on her heel and walked back to the plate glass window in front of the bar. She would recognize those purple stockings and blue pumps anywhere. She traveled up the entwined bodies, mentally separating the parts into his and hers, and sure enough, home-dyed auburn hair bobbled on top, tangling itself into some poor old fucker's thick head of gray hair. When's she gonna come up for air, Aimee wondered. Girls in their twenties must just need less oxygen than normal women. They probably store the extra air in the uplift of their pert bosoms the same way a camel stores water in its...Christ! Is that Trevor?

She looked closely. It couldn't be Trevor. Aimee took a step forward. She'd worked with Trevor on several problematic briefs. He was low-key and kind of boring as far as Aimee was concerned. The kissers were coming up for a breath and a sip of their drinks. Aimee leaned in. The guy's hair was messed up like he'd just dragged himself out of bed. The Trevor Aimee knew always appeared well pressed and prepared for work. This guy's lips looked a tad raw and swollen from having so much spit and lipstick rubbed across them. As the man looked over and smiled at the girl who was probably Lux, Aimee had to admit, this was definitely Trevor.

"Ew!" Aimee said out loud. "Trevor and Lux? Gross."

Aimee turned on her heel and scurried all the way to

the movie theater. She paid for her ticket and raced to the bathroom where she washed her face like someone whose eyes were on fire. She tried to put Lux's troubles out of her mind. It was none of her business if the girl wanted to ruin her life. Aimee made sure she emptied every drop of liquid from her poor cramped bladder, shoved as it was into the shrinking space between the growing uterus and her spine.

Sitting on the toilet, Aimee laughed at Lux. Trevor was at least fifty years old, not to mention a middle-level cog who was never going to make partner.

"Stupid girl," Aimee said out loud as she wiped and wondered if they'd had sex.

Aimee left the bathroom and felt the full blast of the theater's excellent air-conditioning. The cool air was saturated with the smell of cheap hot dogs and buttery popcorn. She swayed for a moment at the bathroom door. She desperately craved a pop culture opiate, something to wash away the day, but suddenly could not will herself to enter the lovely old theater lobby. I've already got my ticket, she coached herself. I just have to walk through the lobby. After the lobby it's a free fall and I've escaped my life until I have to show up for work tomorrow at ten. I already have the damn ticket! If I can just walk through the lobby, I won't have to think about anything until tomorrow morning. I could burn through a lot of time.

Aimee told herself it was just the smell as she turned right and bolted for the big glass doors that lead to the street. The smell of the hot dogs is too much. I wouldn't be able to concentrate. I need to go home right now. The adventure in Middle Earth was over for Aimee, at least for the night.

Aimee's chin was wiggling, spasming with tears that she wanted to hold on to until she got back into her own apartment. She sucked it all into herself and did her best not to waddle as she ran from the theater.

She paid the taxi driver too much and sprinted into her building where she sat on the couch and admitted to herself that her husband had left. It all crashed in on her.

She wanted to get up and make something. That always made her feel better. She wanted to write something tragic and cathartic about her present situation but then she'd have to read it in front of Lux. Her writers' group had been ruined by some tarted-up, pert-breasted, red-haired, twentysomething idiot. They'd have to get off the erotic bent immediately. How could Aimee listen to Lux go on about anything sensual while picturing her wrapped around saggy old Trevor?

What the hell did Lux see in him? He was old and not rich. And Lux! She was a dodo! Not exactly a trophy with her loud wardrobe and her lowly status. It was all wrong.

Aimee grabbed her knitting bag and tried to concentrate. It was so nice at the knitting store surrounded by other clacking needles and charming conversation, but in Aimee's real life knitting was impossible. Still, Aimee needed to make something. Since all passageways to the comfort of creating were temporarily closed to her, Aimee picked up the phone and started to make some mischief.

"Hey Brooke, Aimee here. You there? Call me back as soon as possible! You will not believe who I saw sitting in this bar around the corner. Kissing! Are you there, Brooke? I'm at home. Call me as soon as you get in."

Aimee hung up the phone and sat quietly for a moment, wondering if Margot Hillsboro might be interested in gossiping about Lux's sex life.

6. Belleview

ARLY SUNDAY MORNING, LUX extracted herself from Trevor's bed and let herself out of his apartment. He planned to take her shopping later that morning, but first she had a nagging errand that had to be run. She did not, under any circumstances, want Trevor to join her, so she slipped out before he awoke. She skipped down the front steps of his apartment building. Her first stop of the day was the bakery at the end of his street, then onto the subway.

Lux walked up the long hallway looking for the room number the nurse had given her. She shifted the cake box from one hand and to the other and worried that he would cry because it was not chocolate. She tried not to look into the rooms as she passed. The displays of human weakness in blue hospital gowns juxtaposed against the kindness of cheerful visitors started her head spinning stories that she did not know how to purge.

She entered room 203 and, as the nurse said, found him in bed C. He was sitting up, happily chatting at his neighbor in B. When Lux entered she drew the green curtain around his bed.

"Is that cake?" he asked before hello.

"Yeah, Daddy," Lux said, "the kind you like."

"Black and whites?"

"No, Daddy, carrot cake. You love this kind."

He lay back against his pillow and thought about it, trying to remember when he had loved carrot cake. He couldn't find any notation of such a fact anywhere in his brain, but then, there were so many holes that sort of information could slide through.

As a young man, he had wanted to be anything other than a fireman. Unfortunately, his own father insisted that all males living in the Fitzpatrick home would grow up to be firemen. His heart wasn't really in the job. One afternoon his disregard and his hopeful, wandering mind got him trapped under the wrong beam at the wrong time. He lived through the collapse of the building, but a broken back put him on permanent disability and prescription painkillers.

In some ways he was a grand success. He was alive and walking in spite of his injury. He was cheerful in spite of multiple surgeries, constant pain, and limited mobility. He had survived a sadistic, controlling father. A gentle man, he broke the cycle of father-child violence that stained his ancestors for generations prior. His disability payments, combined with the illegal sale of some of his more interesting prescriptions, had fed and sheltered his family of six. He truly loved and cared about his children. When her first grade teacher quietly suggested to him at a parent-teacher conference that Lux might be retarded, Mr. Fitzpatrick adamantly insisted that everyone immediately stop smoking pot around his beloved daughter, at least on school nights.

In some ways he was a great dad. He was kind and usually at home. He loved to play games and always wanted to make brownies. He was open, available to talk and happy to help his children through their problems. Unfortunately, most of his advice was strained through the colander that was his brain. When Lux was being bullied on the schoolyard, he advised her that even if someone hits you first, you can never, ever hit back. But spitting is ok.

He was currently hospitalized for a bleeding ulcer. The prescription pills helped him with the pain in his legs and back, but they ate out bits of his stomach. He tried to compensate, experimenting with a combination of illicit and prescribed marijuana. For years nothing worked. In pain and despair he began to waste away. When Lux was in third grade he finally solved the problem. In a linen closet in their home, under specially ordered hot house lights, he grew a small, but widely praised crop of Cannabis, subspecies Indica. These highly hallucinogenic buds eased his pain, but contributed to his fear that Lux was in danger of swallowing her tongue. To combat the latter, he kept her home from school for a whole week, staying with her constantly and feeding her soft foods that he insisted on preparing himself. Lux remembered it fondly as one of the best weeks of her life.

"How you feeling, Daddy?" Lux asked as she sat down next to his bed.

"Good. You?" he replied.

"A'right," Lux told him. "Job's ok. And I got a boyfriend."

"Sounds like you're heading straight for the stars."

"Yeah well, why not, right?"

Lux's father smiled and patted her hand.

"And how are my boys?"

"Ian's still in Utah. Sean's up for probation and they let Joseph out early. He's home now, which is really nice. Mom's so happy. You wouldn't believe it could happen, but he got even more muscley this time," Lux said.

"And how's my little Patrick?" he asked with a soft smile.

"Uh, well, his fur is growing back."

Lux smiled and her beloved father beamed back his great pleasure.

"All good news then," he said.

"Yep," she agreed. "Listen, Daddy, I came by cuz I wanna ask you something about your sister."

"Which one? The whore or the housewife? Or the lesbian?"

Mr. Fitzpatrick only had two sisters.

"Estella."

"Whore."

"How'd she get to be that way?" Lux asked.

"It's like when you hard-boil eggs. Some are hard to get out of the shell and others just slide right out," Lux's father pontificated from his hospital bed.

Lux thought about it for a while.

"Well, wuzzat mean? That she was just like that?"

"Yes. Because that was what she decided to do after my father kicked her out of the house for having a baby at sixteen with a guy who wouldn't marry her. Navy fucker just passing through town. She coulda scrubbed floors or picked a guy who woulda married her, like your mom did. Decisions. Decisions."

"She had a baby?" Lux asked. Lux had never heard anything about Auntie Who-ah having a baby.

"Yeah. She gave it away. I used to like to pretend I was her give-away baby cuz she would come bring me ice cream and patch me up when your grandfather got crazy on my head. I heard from the lesbo that she died with no money and no friends."

Lux knew that Auntie Who-ah had died with substantial money and property to her name. She had left bequests to several charitable organizations and one grateful niece. She gave good advice like, be strong and true to yourself. Lux could imagine Auntie Who-ah would bring ice cream and comfort to a frightened little boy, but could not imagine Auntie Who-ah, who had always told her to make sure she did the things that made her happy, would have allowed a crappy family and an unwanted pregnancy to force her into prostitution. Lux told her semi-conscious father that she doubted his story.

"She wasn't like that," Lux said.

"Sure, when you met her she wasn't like that no more. It's easier to tell the world to go to hell when you got lotsa money," he told Lux and then for his own amusement he added, "or a permanent disability check."

Lux waited until the giggles subsided. She wanted to tell him about the house she had inherited from his sister. He would not disapprove of it the way her mother would, but he would take it away from her. Not all at once. A little loan at a time would slowly bleed away her money. Still she wondered if she should give him something when she sold the house. He was happy and kind and his body hurt him most of the time. Lux sat quietly and wondered if she could give him $1,000 in pain relief without raising the suspicions and outstretched palms of her mother and brothers.

While Lux tried to figure out how she could safely encode her love and generosity, a nurse came in and jabbed a syringe into the tube that lead into his arm.

"What's he getting?" Lux asked.

"Morphine," said both the nurse and her father at the same time. The nurse reported it as if it were a fact. Her father mouthed the word as if it were a special dessert topping and he a very good boy.

"Listen, Pumpkin," her father said in a very serious tone, "I been meaning to talk to you about something, but I don't know how to say it, so I'm just gonna say it. I don't like that boy, Carlos, you been seeing."

"We broke up," Lux said, and her father's face broke into a happy smile.

"Problem solved," he mumbled and drifted away into the sweet relief of chemical sleep.

7. Paint

AFTER HAVING A BEER and a giggle with Aimee and Margot, Brooke caught the 7:10 p.m. train to Croton-on-Hudson, where she kept her studio. It was a beautiful room with old wooden floors and big windows. It had been redesigned just for Brooke, to her specifications. The light was perfect. Brooke had been painting there for years and created some of her most significant work under its roof. The only drawback of the studio was that it used to be her parents' pool house, and therefore gently reminded her that most of her comforts and independence came not from her work as an artist, but from the successful investments of prior generations.

Brooke let herself into the main house, walked into the kitchen, and opened the Sub-Zero fridge. She pulled out the roast beef, the mustard, and yesterday's focaccia and started to make a sandwich.

"Oh! I didn't see you there," Brooke said to her mother.

Her mother was sitting in the dark in the kitchen, smoking a cigarette and thinking too much about Brooke.

Like her mother, Brooke was beautiful, blond and naturally thin, with long legs and porcelain skin. In low lights they looked like twin sisters, although the mother did not have a medieval dragon tattooed on her lower back with claws that stretched over her buttocks and a tail that curled into the inner thigh of her left leg.

"I'm glad you've come. Bill Simpson wants you to go with him to the Muscular Dystrophy ball on Saturday. You should call him tonight."

"This Saturday?" Brooke asked.

"No, Bill Simpson's ball is on the twenty-fifth," Brooke's mother explained.

"Hmmm," Brooke said, trying to picture her jampacked social calendar in her head, "did he say what time it started?"

"Oh, he didn't say at all. I heard about it from his mother. You should call him tonight. Bill turned out to be such a handsome man. And he seems to love you so much."

"Yes. He does."

"Are you going to call him?"

"Of course."

"Tonight?"

"I'll call him tomorrow, Mum."

"You should have married him when he asked you."

"I didn't want to get married so young."

"It's amazing that he's hung around so long. Waiting."

"Yes, Mummy, it is."

"But I haven't seen you two together in several months."

"I know," said Brooke.

"Have you two broken up?" her mother asked.

"No, just kind of slowed down," Brooke said.

Brooke's mother wanted to ask why. Ten years after the fact she still didn't understand what happened to the big wedding she started planning the moment her beautiful daughter, Brooke, began to date Eleanor Simpson's handsome son, Bill. The event was long past due, and now Brooke was talking about slowing down. What is my beautiful girl doing wrong? What is stopping her from finding a good husband, Brooke's mother thought.

"Carole will be coming around with the kids tomorrow," Brooke's mother said, instead of saying what was going on in her head. "Can you stay?"

"Yeah, sure."

"It's Emma's birthday."

"I know that."

"Seventh."

"Wow, that was fast."

"You got Emma a blue plastic purse and a matching belt. For Sally, you got her a Barbie. You know, a consolation prize for it not being her birthday. I wrapped them already, but since you're here you can sign the cards."

"Thanks, Mum."

Brooke's mother waved her diamond-crusted hand to indicate that it was nothing.

"Do you want to see the latest pictures of the girls?"

"No way! I'll see them tomorrow in person and give them both a big hug."

Her mother seemed disappointed.

"I mean," Brooke said, "why don't you give me the

pictures and I'll take them into the studio to look at while I prep."

Brooke took an envelope of snapshots and a quick kiss from her mother out with her to her studio. Brooke's cell phone rang. Aimee. But tonight Brooke wanted to stay focused on her mission, so she turned the ringer off and slipped it back into her purse.

"Aren't you going to call Bill?" Brooke's mother asked again.

"I will, Mother," Brooke promised.

It began when her mother called his mother because Brooke's date for some cousin's debutante ball had gotten ill at the last minute. As it turned out, Bill was also a cousin of this cousin and already had his tux pressed in anticipation of the event. Bill arrived at Brooke's parents' upper Fifth Avenue mansion modeling the perfect picture of a respectable, posh, New York teenage escort. They were drunk and having sex while her corsage was still perky. Throughout high school they were inseparable. Both of their mothers assumed a wedding would follow college, but that assumption became a hope as Bill finished law school.

"She's too 'arty' for him," some people gossiped.

"She's too 'old money' for him," others contradicted.

"I heard he offered to marry her ten years ago but she was too interested in her career to bother with marriage back then. Bet she's sorry for that now," ran the most unpleasant of the stories.

Brooke ate the roast beef sandwich while flipping through photographs of Emma and Sally, her sweet and pretty nieces. Darling blond girls, age seven and three, caught in various poses of merrymaking with their mother, Brooke's younger sister. Tucked in with the photos was a check for $1,000 drawn on Brooke's mother's account. The check was for no reason except that Brooke's mother thought that Brooke was failing to enjoy life to its fullest. Brooke tucked the check into her pocket and began to pull canvases from the rack.

She didn't marry Bill after college because at twenty-two he was the only man she had ever slept with, other than her riding instructor. She told him that she still had oats to sow. She figured if he really loved her they would settle down together when they were both ready. At thirty-seven, she was ripe and ready. She wanted children. She wanted them with Bill, but by then Bill had other things on his mind. He asked her to wait for him to figure a few things out. She waited in the way beautiful, smart, rich, talented girls wait. She focused on her art and saw other men. Still her heart, and, by extension, her womb, waited for Bill.

Five years slipped away and by forty-two, Brooke figured that sweet, chubby babies would only be hers if she got a commission to paint cherubs on a church ceiling. There had once been plentiful tears about the children she did not have, but Brooke had put aside that hope.

Sometimes she was sorry she did not marry Bill in her twenties. Other times she would not have traded those years of freedom and paint for anything. What pained Brooke consistently was what would become of the children she had brought into the world: the unhung canvases stacked in the pool house going bad from neglect.

She pulled one of her creations from the rack. Her mother, sitting on a lawn chair near the pool on a too-hot day, wielding a cocktail and a cigarette; the whole image shimmered like an oasis-mirage in the desert. Brooke looked long and hard at the canvas. Tonight was the night, but that was not the painting to start with. A self-portrait was likewise spared and returned to the rack. A picture of her parents' living room and the dog sleeping on the couch. She would begin there.

Brooke pulled out a large tub of gesso and began annihilating the dog and the living room and the moment captured from another lifetime. Suddenly a wail sounded from outside the window.

Her mother, holding a tray with two gin and tonics stood outside the glass door shouting.

"No! Stop! I loved that dog! What are you doing?"

Brooke opened the door and let her in.

"Relax," she said, grabbing a drink off the tray.

"I love that painting!"

"It's a good one," Brooke agreed as she continued to white it out and send it back to oblivion.

"Why?" Brooke's mother demanded, horrified and with tears.

Brooke gestured to the rack behind her, full to over-flowing with canvases. Good canvases. She had a keen eye for character and each painting stared back as if it was speaking, cut off in mid-sentence. She painted people, dogs and trees, and other representative images. Representative images had not been in fashion for many years. Brooke knew it going in but had followed her heart.

People liked her work. Over the years she'd sold many canvases and received many commissions, but no one wrote about her work, no one ever resold her paintings. And so she had remained unimportant.

"Canvas is expensive," Brooke explained to her mother.

"I'll pay off the rest of your debt," Brooke's mother announced.

"It's not the money, it's the space," Brooke said. "I can't stand to see them stacked up like this, like firewood. Mum, I can't add another beautiful baby to this stack of shit we have hidden away here. I tried making really small paintings but that wasn't for me. And I don't want to stop painting, but I want to stop accumulating canvases that no one sees. When I stop painting I feel all backed up, like I desperately have to drain the spit-valve of my mind but you know, then it comes back to the I'm-tired-of-creating-things-no-one-sees, so I decided that I would paint over the stuff I have. So I can keep making shit without having to make piles of shit."

"It's not shit," her mother whispered.

"Stuff," Brooke corrected herself. "I don't think it's shit either. No one thought it was shit. They just didn't think it was gold. With no one looking at them, they're kind of dead, these things I made. You wouldn't keep your dead children stacked up like this and that's how I'm starting to feel about them. They're great, big, dead, unloved children that I made and at least this way I can recycle them back into some kind of life. Jesus, Mummy, don't cry."

Brooke's mother was sobbing into her gin and tonic. "It's my fault."

"Yeah, ok, I mean, if you want it to be."

It worked. She laughed.

"It's not a question of fault, Mum. It's just that I picked a field with a very small winner's circle. And I'm not in it. I'm not even close to it anymore."

They sat in silence, both suffering from Brooke's failures. Brooke's mother sat quietly while Brooke whited out three or four canvases, scraped down the rough spots, preparing them to take paint again.

"Thanks for the check," Brooke said after a while.

"Buy yourself something nice," her mother said warmly. Brooke smiled although she knew that there was nothing on a store shelf that would satisfy her. The way her mother said that, the way her face caught the light captivated Brooke and for a moment, filled with the pleasure of a new adventure, she thought she would paint her mother looking mournful and loving at the same time. But Brooke hesitated. There were so many wonderful paintings of her mother. The house and the rack were filled with them. She would paint the little girls, the nieces. She would give it to her sister as a gift. She would make it beautiful and happy, knowing such a painting would find a home on a wall of her sister's house with lots of lovely admirers to consider it and give it life. Brooke fumbled for the packet of snapshots and began working.

Her mother disappeared. The room disappeared. The yellow of a little niece's dress started whispering gently to Brooke like a lover, saying "More blue in me, more blue, sweetheart. Let the shadows lay, perfect, perfect, I'm lovely." Brooke worked until her legs started to hurt and her stomach rumbled. Somewhere in the studio lay a half-eaten sandwich and a bed waiting for Brooke to flop into it, happily exhausted.

The painting was well on its way. The little nieces looked as wonderful in paint as they did in life and her sister would swell with the pleasure of seeing her babies saved forever in their moment of loveliness. Carole would hang the canvas somewhere where everyone would see it first thing when they walked into the house. And when Brooke and her sister and their mother were all dead and long gone, maybe the two nieces would argue about who would get the lovely painting of the two little girls they had been.

The older one would win. She always won. And she in turn would hang the beautiful painting of her lost daffodil-yellow self somewhere where people could still admire it. She would die. Everyone dies. She would will the lovely yellow painting of the little girls to one of her own grandchildren and on and on until the owner might forget exactly who the two girls were, but he or she, this fictitious progeny now only distantly related to Brooke, would still love the way the yellow in the little girl's dress was making love to the blue. And then Brooke would live forever.

"If that is what I have," thought Brooke as she fell asleep, "I'll have to make it be enough for me."

8. Atlanta Jane

STILL GLOWING FROM A two-hour workout, Margot waved to the doorman as she sashayed into the elevator. At the last minute a stranger jumped onto the elevator and so Margot rode all the way up to the top floor and then back down to the lobby. When she first signed the lease, Margot loved that the elevator doors opened directly onto her apartment. Twenty years later, it made her feel anxious and vulnerable. Now, she would ride up and down the elevator until she was the only person left in the car, and only then would she put her special key in the slot that showed her initials.

Recently, she had wanted to build an additional door, or interior vestibule, something that needed to be unlocked between her private apartment and the public elevator, but the owners would not allow it. That had been a shock. In her heart Margot believed the apartment belonged to her. All her things were there. In fact, the actual ownership of the apartment had changed hands four times in the twenty years Margot had been renting it. She swore the next time the rent went up she would find someplace where she could have total control.

Finally alone in the elevator Margot slid her special key into the slot marked "M.H." and the elevator jerked skyward. Once her key was in the door, the elevator would not stop until it reached her apartment. On the long ride up she rested her shopping bags on the floor and flipped through her mail. Bills. Bills. Bullshit and bills. And one large ivory envelope with Trevor's last name above an unfamiliar return address.

Margot dumped the junk mail into the trash, placed the bills on the counter in the kitchen and then tore open the large, ivory envelope.

You are cordially invited, the invitation began and after lots of well-thought-out, old-fashioned words, it ended by informing Margot that Trevor's eldest son was getting married at a Long Island synagogue at 8 p.m. on Saturday in six weeks' time. Very nice. An excellent excuse to buy a new dress.

When their youngest child left for college, Trevor's wife dropped fifteen pounds and got a fashionable new haircut. She chucked her old wardrobe right down the incinerator. And then the swan flew away, taking with her the summer cottage in the Catskills. Margot held Trevor's hand through the divorce.

Once, over Chinese take-out in his apartment, Trevor had leaned over his mu shu chicken with the intention of kissing Margot on the lips. She was just about to laugh at something on the television and therefore at the same moment he put his mouth on hers, she exhaled a huge, garlicky guffaw. Their first moment of intimacy felt like getting too-spicy mouth-to-mouth resuscitation.

"Christ Margot, I think you may have popped my lung," he laughed.

"No, not popped," she countered. "Just over-inflated. But let me hold on to you because you're in danger of spinning all around the room like a big balloon with the lips suddenly untied."

They flopped back on the couch and wiped the laughter from their eyes and the kiss from their mouths. Margot reached across and held his hand but Trevor did not attempt the kiss again. There would be plenty of time for that, Margot thought. *Our friendship will find that kiss again, soon.*

But the invitations for take-out and videos dried up after that evening. Margot was busy at work and they still had lunch together. She hadn't really noticed their distance until she, after registering the full meaning of the word "peri-menopausal," called him. She left some tears and a request for company on his answering machine. She got a response by email two days later. *Sorry you're blue,* he wrote. By that time though blue was no longer her color. She was black and red by then and so their friendship burned up to a little ash. Maybe the wedding would rekindle it.

Margot put her take-out dinner down on top of her briefcase and looked at the ivory invitation. She thought about weddings. In all her life, Margot had only received one marriage proposal, from a boy named Bobby Albert.

Bobby Albert was blond and strong and probably stupid, although in her youth and inexperience, Margot didn't recognize the latter. She planned to lose her virginity to him, maybe even in the back of his father's truck. As long as there was a clean blanket to lie on, she wanted him. She didn't, however, want him in the cornfield.

It would be hard for anyone meeting Margot Hillsboro today to see her as a fuck-me-in-the-back-of-a-pickup-truck girl, but in those days she was a small-town girl named "Allie Hillcock" and the pickup truck would have worked just fine.

Thirty-four years ago, before she changed her name, Margot desperately wanted to have sex with Bobby Albert. She couldn't wait to pop the snaps on her cheerleader bodysuit and feel him touch her body. She was making a beeline for that pickup truck, but the feeling came over him too quick and all her plans to make love in a way she could paste into a scrapbook got lost in the corn. They were kissing and she was pulling him back to that truck, but he just couldn't move another step without having sex. So she lost her virginity to Bobby Albert in a cornfield.

Not a high summer cornfield, either. It was an early autumn cornfield and all the stalks had been cut. No corn at all. No cover for anyone who might look out and see Margot's skinny legs splayed out or Bobby Albert's white ass pumping up and down. After he came, Bobby Albert asked Margot Hillsboro, nee Allie Hillcock, to marry him.

Allie Hillcock said no. He'd ruined her deflowering fantasy, trashy in hindsight but very important to her at the time. She felt violated.

"Like he raped you?" her second therapist had asked her.

"No. We were definitely on our way to having sex. In the truck. He violated my idea of what that sex should be like. My first taste of sex and it made me feel cheap and insignificant. I was discount, bargain-basement sex. Not worth the extra few feet to the truck bed. I was devastated at the time. I couldn't bear to be myself anymore and so I changed."

"And do you think you changed for the better?" Margot's third therapist enquired.

"I think so," said Margot, "but I still can't understand why anyone would ever want to get married."

Margot had met Trevor's son a few times while he was at Yale, and then once again after she'd pulled a little string to get him a good internship. Margot thought he was a nice boy, cut from the same cloth as Trevor except that the boy was still bursting with the beauty of—

Youth. Trevor hasn't taken care of himself as well as I have taken care of myself. That's why the boy in his youth is so remarkably more handsome than the father, Margot told herself.

"Let's take a look at what Mr. Ping put together for dinner," Margot said out loud to the take-out bag. She ate asparagus and eggplant while flipping through a Bergdorf's catalogue looking for the perfect gown.

She ate her vegetables slowly, but dinner was still over and done with too quickly. She wanted to eat more or have a drink, wanted to go back to the gym, wanted to rot in front of the TV set, but Margot was too controlled to allow any of that to happen. Eating more would result in her becoming too fat. Back to they gym? Too thin. TV made you too stupid. Was it too late to go out to the stores? In a department store or a boutique, Margot felt calm and in control.

Her unquenchable, unachievable desire to change her skin caused her closets to literally burst their hinges. The swollen closets in Margot's apartment held an outfit for every occasion. She had stunning eveningwear that actually got worn to company parties. When a black-tie charity event came up, Margot could be counted on to buy a whole table and invite her colleagues to join her partly because she was truly charitable, partly because she wanted an excuse to get a new dress. She had suits, both formal and casual. She kept her cashmere sweaters stacked in the zippered plastic bags that her linens had come wrapped in. Amidst all this wonder and spectacle, Margot owned only one pair of blue jeans and one pair of flat shoes.

When the closet doors would no longer shut on the great beast of her wardrobe, Margot culled and cleaned and gave away, which put her on a first name basis with the people at Goodwill. Recently, Margot discovered the vacuum bags that would suck all the air out of the spaces between the clothes she shoved into them. This reduced the storage requirements of her wardrobe and Margot hailed it as a miracle of modern science.

Margot stood in front of her magnificent closet. She looked at her watch. It was not too late to go out shopping, but even that pleasurable sedative was growing oppressive.

There was always the briefcase, but Margot had already sworn off using work as an opiate. After her landlord refused to allow her to build that interior door, home furnishing magazines turned sour and Margot gave up the narcotic of redecorating her apartment. She wanted to work on something that was hers, something she could own. But for all her money and pleasure, she didn't own anything real. Margot sat at the table and looked out the window, waiting for a sign that told her she was ready to begin creating her next life. Preparation, for Margot, was everything.

A departing lover once screamed in her face, "You're an anal-retentive control freak." He might as well have told her the color of her own eyes.

"Yes! I know!" Margot had raged back. "If you can't deal with it, piss off!"

Preparation was good and he failed to understand why she was not about to teach him. Kissing prepared her for heavy petting, which lead to sex, in the same way high school prepared her for college, which gave her the skills to succeed in law school. At fifty, Margot was ready to start creating something that would carry her through years seventy to the end. It wouldn't do for Margot to arrive at seventy and say, "Oh, golly, look where I am. Now what?" Like everything else in her life, seventy would flow gracefully from waves that had been generated at fifty.

She crossed to her computer and flipped it on.

As an attorney, words had been her bread and butter. Words had lit the pathways of Margot the girl, Margot the student, Margot the lawyer. It was only reasonable to assume that words could light the way of Margot the gracious old lady. Margot sat down and began typing.

At ~~50 49 50~~ 55 Trevor was still a hot, sexy ~~stallion stud~~ man and when he leaned over and kissed her..., Margot paused, momentarily concerned about the name. She'd use a universal replace to change it later.

...when Trevor leaned over and kissed her, the earth moved, but that was just the beginning. Kissing her left an open invitation for her to kiss him back. And kiss she would. Oh how she was planning to kiss this man! Her obsession with health food and aerobics paid off when she, even at fifty, could drop her dress to the floor with the lights still on and not worry about the best angle to approach his bed. Full on was best for her, and she strode across the room, tossed aside the covers and took his strong, rigid penis in her...

Penis? No, Margot thought, penis is too clinical. What's another good word for penis? Always a planner, Margot opened a clean screen in her word processing program and proceeded to make a list of synonyms for "penis." The list looked like this:

Penis, Pecker, Peter, Putz, Package, Pud, Rod, Dong, Shlong, Ding dong, Thing, Wang, Weiner, Weewee, Z-Z, Peenee, Wrench, Sausage, Shmuck, Salami, Johnson, Joy stick, Groove thing, Genitals, Cock, Club, Hammer, Manhood, Harry and the Boys, Pipe, PP, Prick, Raoul

She erased "Raoul" because it really only applied to a specific weekend she had spent with a particular man in Brazil. Then she had the computer sort the list into alphabetical order and saved it in a file easily accessible for later use. Pleased with her effort she made the same list for "testicles," "breasts," and "vagina." An hour later,

and her homemade thesaurus in place, Margot felt prepared to continue writing.

*Trevor lay back on his couch and while her hands enter-
tained Harry and the Boys, Margot let her mouth find his…*

Margot stopped writing again. It was ok to call him
Trevor but she felt too giddy writing about a character
named "Margot." Maybe Ellen. Alma. Jennifer. Atlanta.
Margot erased everything she had written and started again.

*Atlanta entered the room and Trevor's heart stopped. She
~~walked strode~~ leaped across the room and landed on top of him
where she began tearing at the bedclothes until she got to his…*

I'm a frigging sex-lion, thought Margot. Sounds like
I'm going to doink him and then eat him. Sitting alone in
her apartment, Margot giggled out loud as she typed.

*… until she got to his…skin and then Atlanta started
with one light finger to trace down the line of his chest. As she
got closer to the line of his belt the tension across his chest,
among other exciting things, was growing thicker and
Atlanta started to…*

Wait. What about the name *Atlanta Jane*, Margot
thought. Ooo! I like that. I'll make it a western when I
eventually add the story part to the sex part. This could
be good. Very good. Who do I know in publishing that
owes me a favor?

Margot erased the last few paragraphs. She considered what it might be like to be a woman named Atlanta
Jane and then she began again.

*Atlanta Jane slid gracefully across the room. Trevor couldn't
keep his eyes off her beautiful, full breasts. As she got closer, his
hands followed his eyes. He touched everywhere, running his
hands down her back and over the muscled humps of her buttocks.*

Muscled humps? Yeah, why not, she thought as the gray world slid away, replaced by whatever color she chose to add to her story.

With his hands on her ~~butt~~, ~~ass~~, ~~rump~~, butt, Trevor pulled Atlanta Jane into the warmth of his body. He rolled her onto the bed and slipped the strap of her thin, silky camisole over her shoulder, then down and off her body. He started kissing those upturned nipples while she stroked his shoulders and urged him lower.

The phone rang. Margot was lost in her creation but her hand, after so many years on the job, automatically flipped the phone up to her face.

"Margot Hillsboro," Margot said instead of hello.

"Margot? Aimee. You are *not* going to believe who I just saw licking Trevor's face in a bar downtown!"

9. The Last Good Meeting

"*LIKE RELIEF FROM PAIN, sensation was sweeping across his body and into mine.*"

At the first sentence, Brooke looked up from her magazine. Lux's hands shook a little as she read.

"*The gym doors, you could hear them opening but it was too late to care. With Carlos moaning and hitting the wall with his fist I just went crazy with him, under him, until it was over. He hugged me and kissed my neck, which was a soft thing to do and not like him at all. And as I started to pull down my skirt, Mr. Andrews, who taught social studies, was standing over me and Carlos, and he said to me something like he wouldn't tell on us if he could take a ride too. Which was such a stupid thing to say, you just couldn't believe how stupid it was. Mr. Andrews was an idiot because we weren't children. As soon as he said something like that to us he sure as fuck couldn't report us to no one. He'd say he'd seen us and we'd say what he said to us. I mean, what we were doing was against the rules but what he said was worse. I told him I wouldn't fuck his ugly ass if it came with a full guarantee of graduation for me and all my friends. Couple of weeks later*"

Carlos and his friends, they jumped him and beat the shit out of him. Off campus, of course. And then he quit teaching. The end."

Lux slammed her notebook shut and hugged it to her chest.

"It's stupid, right?" she asked.

"It's not," Margot said quickly.

"It's not stupid at all. I liked the part where Carlos beat him up," said Brooke. "It's like chivalry is not dead."

"How do you mean?" asked Lux.

"Carlos defended your honor."

"Ah, no," Lux said with an undertone of *you're an idiot.* "Carlos likes to beat up people who won't report him to the police."

Lux was surprised to hear the laughter that greeted the simply stated truth about her crazy ex-beau, Carlos. Being with Carlos had been a real drag, and they were a bunch of rich, well-protected, psycho-bitches if they thought something like beating people up was funny. Still, Lux had a need for these women so she tried to be cool.

"Right. So, what's so funny?" she asked.

"It wasn't funny. Not at all. It's horrible. But what you said was surprising, so we laughed," Brooke said.

Margot said nothing as she returned her carefully typed index cards to the zippered portion of her handbag. The western erotica of Atlanta Jane seemed stupid and small compared to the life that Lux had lived. And, even though she had instructed the computer to change the name of Atlanta's sexy, gray haired playmate from "Trevor" to "Peter," dressed him in buckskins, gave him a monstrously large phallus and a tattoo of a wolf, it was still another fantasy about Trevor. No one would know, but Margot could not read her erotic story about Trevor out loud to the woman who sucked on the real thing.

"How can you be sure it was Trevor?" she'd cross examined Aimee last night on the telephone.

"It looked like Trevor."

"It may have looked like him, but are you one hundred percent sure it was him?"

"Geez, you're tough," Aimee laughed.

"And the girl?"

"The one licking his face?"

"Allegedly licking his face. You say it was Lux, but all you really recognized was her skirt and stockings."

"And shoes."

"Ok, and shoes."

"Blue shoes and purple stockings."

"It could be a trend. You were in the Village, after all."

"It was Lux and Trevor. I just know it."

"But there's no proof."

"Gee, Margot, that old man-young bimbo thing really rubs you the wrong way."

"Why do they go for young women?" Margot had asked Aimee the question but before Aimee could answer, Margot went on about the suppleness of her own fifty year old ass and the firmness of her never-suckled breasts. There was a little hitch of plastic surgery here and there, Margot admitted, but that made the whole package even better.

"And on top of it, I am a great lay!" Margot had roared to Aimee. "And after the sex I make a mean conversation!

And I can pay half the cost of any place you'd like to go!"

All this time, Margot thought she was inches from Trevor's bed, when in fact that slot was already filled.

"I don't know what you're so mad about," Aimee had laughed. "Didn't he have a wife or something?"

"No, no they're divorced, two kids, five years ago. Not pretty, but done," Margot informed Aimee.

"What should we do about it?"

"What do you mean?"

"About Lux and Trevor."

"Well...nothing. I mean, well, what *can* we do about it?"

The best revenge scenario Margot could conjure from her own imagination was pulling Trevor aside and having a heartfelt conversation about the dangers of sexual harassment, real or perceived, that might follow a failed office romance. Don't shit where you eat, dance with the girls who carry the coffee, and so forth. She composed a quick email to Trevor while on the phone with Aimee.

"Should I send it?" she asked Aimee.

"You owe it to him as his friend."

Aimee sounded so sure that invasive intervention was a good idea, but as soon as Margot hung up the phone the email, which read *have lunch with me to discuss ramifications of social interactions with subordinates,* suddenly sounded like sour grapes from a neglected vine. Margot wished she could get it back. Still, such an email was sure to get a rise out of him. And Margot wanted to have lunch with Trevor again, even if the meal started out with an apology.

"Look, Trev, I have no proof it was Lux. I have no

proof that it was even you," she planned to begin the conversation, "but a man in your position has to protect himself from these crazy girls. And what better protection could you possible have than a skilled, mature, strong, naked attorney such as myself?"

He would laugh. She would laugh too and the ice that had formed over the top of their relationship would break. Trevor would never choose a girl like Lux over her. Although this Lux, the Lux standing in front of Margot right now, trembling a little as she read a handwritten story, looked kind of beautiful if you could see past the overlay of her poor choices. She was certainly interesting, and aggressive, and maybe even smart.

"So, um, what'd you think of my, like, story," Lux asked.

"It wasn't like a story," Brooke said. "It was a story. A real story."

"Really?"

"It was a really good start," Margot told Lux.

"Really?" Lux beamed with pleasure. Her face positively glowed with the warm blood that was rushing to her cheeks.

"Yeah," Margot said looking at the manuscript in Lux's hands. It was torn, scribbled over and punctuation was an optional condiment sprinkled in here and there. Still, an interesting story.

"Who's this Carlos?" Brooke asked.

"Old boyfriend."

"Trevor know about him?" Aimee asked casually.

Lux giggled, then turned worried. Margot's heart sank at Lux's reaction. It wasn't Aimee's crazy imagination or bad eyesight or any of the other reasonable excuses she had told herself. The girl in Lux's stockings and shoes was Lux. Trevor had found someone else.

"How do you know about Trevor? We're really, you know, discreet and shit."

"Saw you at Bar Six on Grove Street Thursday night."

"Oh."

"You didn't look particularly discreet with your lips wrapped around his face," Aimee pointed out.

"Well, I mean, discreet in like the office. I mean, he's got all these friggin' rules of how to behave to each other. No eye contact in the hall. No personal email messages, except in code. I'm a like, sex spy. It's kind of fun, though, you know."

"Lux, he's gotta be thirty years older than you," Aimee interrupted.

"No way. Just twenty. I'm twenty-three, he's like, forty-three. He said, I think forty-five or something."

"He's got an adult son who's getting married next month. Trevor's youngest kid is at least twenty-five."

"Oh. So? Ok, duh, so he's older than me. So what?"

"A lot older," Aimee insisted. "Margot, how old is Trevor."

"Fifty-four in August," Margot said quietly.

"Wow. He looks good," said Brooke, wishing it would stop being the Tuesday Gossipy Stupid Club so she could read the next installment of her latest creative obsession entitled *Enrique Rings the Back Door.*

"So listen, is it my turn to read?" Brooke asked.

"Go ahead," Margot said. "I don't have anything."

Brooke pulled her manuscript out from under her art kit and started to get all tingly at the thought of *Enrique* and the carnal delights his medium-sized penis was about to deliver to his favorite postal customer.

"If he's fifty-four when you're twenty-three," Aimee couldn't help showing off her math skills, "that means when you're forty-three, he'll be seventy-four. And wrinkled and old, old, old."

"Yeah. So?" Lux said.

"I'm just saying, he's too old for you," Aimee said. She had helpful, concerned woman painted all over her face and "nice" dripped off her words.

What the hell does she care who I bop, Lux wondered. In the eleventh grade, Lux got in a fistfight with her best friend, Jonella, over the attentions of that same Carlos who one year later would become Jonella's baby's daddy. She'd broken Jonella's nose without denting their friendship, and since then Lux moved bravely through the world without worrying about some hurt feelings between girlfriends. Busted feelings and noses could heal. It's best to say what you think.

"Whassup Aimee? You want to fuck Trevor?" Lux demanded.

This is much better than *Enrique,* thought Brooke as she choked on a laugh. Brooke loved that Aimee positively recoiled from Lux's attack, looking both amazed and insulted.

"NO! I'm just saying that there's a bigger price you pay for hooking up with an old man. I mean, the money and the lifestyle may seem great to a girl like you; may seem worth closing your eyes to the wrinkles and the softness, but in the end you gotta be careful not to get tied down to an old man lover."

A girl like me, thought Lux. Of all Aimee said, that was the one phrase that stuck hard and drew blood. The rest was bullshit.

"Trevor is a great lay," Lux said.

"Why do I find that hard to believe," Aimee replied.

"Umm, because you're dried up and ugly maybe? I heard your stories, girl. Sexy stories about your feet? Why you ain't got no man in your story? I see this all the time, you know. Girl get pregnant; girl get dumped. You're not so far from my neighborhood," Lux told her.

The words shot out, causing the muscles in Aimee's neck to bunch into painful knots.

"The big difference between me and you, Lux, is I won't do it for money."

When Lux brought her hand back, Aimee's pregnancy, in equal measure with the distance across the conference room table, stopped her from slapping Aimee hard across the face. Instead Lux lunged across the table, throwing her body down on top of it and traveling far enough across the table's surface to reach up and grab a hunk of Aimee's curly hair. Then she pulled.

"Ah! Ahhhhhhhhhhhhhhhhhhhhhhhhhhhhhhhhhh," Aimee wailed.

In her twenty-three years of life, Lux often had motive, opportunity, and need to sell herself. It was a matter of deep personal pride that she had only taken money once and for something that, at the time, had seemed like a very good reason. (Prom dress.) To say the experience left her feeling empty could not describe the great void that had howled through her sixteen-year-old body. She'd never done it again.

Here was this Aimee girl in her clean, small world accusing Lux of sleeping with Trevor for money. Lux knew she was taking something from him but it wasn't cash, never cash.

Aimee did not know what kind of line she had crossed, but clearly she had sent a barb too close to an ugly welt that had not healed on Lux. No one called Lux a whore because she had made a great effort and sacrifice not to allow herself to become such.

Aimee's curls wrapped tight around Lux's thin fingers. Lux had intended to give a yank and let go. It was to be a warning shot, not a full engagement, but she hadn't counted on the texture of those corkscrew black curls. Even when she let go the angry fist, Aimee's hair stayed locked around Lux's fingers. Lux started to shake her hand trying to free herself from Aimee's curls. The more she shook, the more Aimee screamed.

"Ok, ok," Margot said and tried to sound soothing. She jumped up and grabbed Lux and tried to hold her still. She didn't realize how small Lux really was across the back until she wrapped her arms around her upper body. Margot could feel Lux's heart pounding underneath well-defined ribs more like a caged tiger than a trapped bird. Margot tried to keep her quiet while Brooke jumped in and did her best to quickly unravel Aimee's heavy curls. The last bit of hair was still caught on the cheap silver ring Lux wore on her right hand.

"Ok, ok, almost there," Brooke said as she unwound the hair from the ring. Lux was shaking with rage.

"You can let go of me now," Lux told Margot. Even though she knew Margot had yet to do anything hateful to her, she could not stop herself from spitting the words. She wanted to say sorry when Margot jumped back, embarrassed to have held onto Lux's body for a little longer than necessary. But while she was thinking of the words to form that apology, Brooke twisted the last bit of hair free. Lux bolted for the door.

"Bitch," Lux said as she grabbed her notebook off the table and swung open the door. "Stupid, stupid bitch!"

With a bang, Lux was gone. Aimee was furious.

"Did you see what she did to me?" Aimee asked.

Margot grabbed for a tissue although Aimee was not crying.

"Psycho! Idiot! Fucking crazy girl! She pulled my hair! Do I have a bald spot, Brooke?"

"No, no," Brooke said calmly. "I think the shock of it was the worst part."

"And I don't think she intended to pull that hard," Margot said.

"Why? Why would she do that to me?"

"Well, honey, you shouldn't have called her that," Brooke said.

"Yes, I think you went too far," Margot clucked an agreement.

"WHAT? Called her what? What did I call her?"

"A prostitute."

"Never!"

"You accused her of selling it," Margot agreed.

"I did not!"

"You did."

"So what if I did? Clearly it hit a soft spot! Whore. Fucking-psycho-slut-tramp."

Among her duties as supervisor of the Word Processing Department at the law firm of Warwick & Warwick, LLP, Brooke was responsible for making sure the correct spacing followed every period on every piece of paper produced by the firm during the hours of her shift. She did this for spending money and to ensure she did not drift too far away from the real world. Sometimes on the weekends she put on a very short rubber skirt with very high shiny heels and went out to play psycho-slut-tramp in the city. She had never played prostitute.

"Well," Brooke said, "I'm gonna guess that 'whore' is a kind of verbal line in the sand of Lux that one does not cross and still keep one's hairdo intact."

"She attacked me."

"She pulled your hair," Brooke said.

"I want her fired."

"And when the managing partner asks 'What were you ladies doing in the conference room,' what are you going to answer?" Margot asked. "Oh gosh right, we were reading dirty stories in the conference room during our lunch hour. It gets a little messy."

In the silence that followed, Aimee thought, it must be terrible to live in fear of the suggestion that one might become a whore.

"I used to be nicer," Aimee said.

"You're still nice," Brooke tried to comfort her.

"I used to be kind and flexible and generous. What's happened to me?" Aimee asked, hoping her friends would help her make up an excuse for her bad behavior. She would accept any reason except the truth. Her man had dumped her while she was pregnant. The pain had turned her brittle and cruel. Her friends offered no sweet lies to soften the moment. In fact, they all turned away from her, and each woman focused on her own thoughts.

"You know," Brooke said, even though she knew it would make Aimee mad, "if Lux could turn that rage into words instead of gestures, she could transform into something amazing."

Having said that, Brooke and Margot spent the little bit that was left of their lunch time consoling Aimee and agreeing with her that Lux was crazy and what she did was way out of bounds, totally wrong, and unacceptable.

"Thanks," Aimee said. "I'm sorry. I never should have let her into the group."

She assumed they were on her side, but the room was silent as Brooke and Margot failed to heartily agree with Aimee's assessment of the situation.

"Brooke, you coming? I'll walk you to your office," Aimee offered.

"No, I'm going to sit for a minute," Brooke said. She was moved by the image of Lux's rage and wanted a quiet minute to figure a sketch that might someday become a painting. She did not want to lose the way the red hair had flown back and Lux's mouth became wet and hard with anger. Margot was perfectly polite in a business-friend way as she said a quick good-bye at the door.

"Should we set another meeting?" Aimee asked. "Same time next Tuesday?"

"Mm, send me an email," Brooke murmured into her sketchbook.

"Call me when I'm sitting at my calendar," Margot said as she disappeared down the hall, high heels clicking against the fine marble flooring.

Aimee got up and wandered down the hallway. She wondered if they would come back next week. Margot seemed personally offended by the whole event. Brooke would always be her friend. They'd been naked together too many times for that to ever end, but Aimee was sorry to lose Margot. She assumed their relationship would diminish into one of those business friendships that have no real loyalty or even affection. They would smile at each other and make some jokes to pass the day at the office, but that's all.

Aimee walked back to her office, feeling like she had allowed her pain to ruin a really good thing.

10. Children

ARGOT GRABBED HER MESSAGES and returned to her office, feeling sorry that The Tuesday Erotica Club was falling apart so spectacularly. This is why women can't be friends, she said to herself as she sat down at her desk. We get catty. We get mean. We pull hair, literally and figuratively. We have no boundaries. This is why I never had women friends. They're scary. I don't need them. In her big stack of messages, she saw that there was one from her little brother, Amos. How strange, Margot thought.

"Mosy?" she said when he answered his phone. She could hear the tractor in the background and figured he was right in the middle of harvesting something or other. "Everything ok?"

"Nope," he said in the monotone he used to indicate joy, sorrow, and all points in between. "I got some trouble and it's heading your way."

Amos, like all of Margot's younger brothers, was startlingly handsome until he spoke. It wasn't just the monotone. His obsession with the health of his cows and crops and the second coming of Jesus all managed to dull the blue of his eyes and the cut of his washboard stomach. Still, he was a good man and as long as he stayed outside her apartment, Margot loved him very much.

"Ohmygod! Is Pop ok?" Margot asked as panic rose.

"He's fine. It's me," Amos intoned.

"Oh, Mosy! What happened? Are you ill? You can't be ill. You're never ill."

"Oh Allie, I'm about to die!"

When her brother said "Oh Allie," he was referring to Margot herself. Her brothers had never accepted her name change and "Allie" had a way of transporting her back home, very quickly. Those same syllables also made her hit the brakes on the ride, not wanting to get sucked back into all the things she had already escaped from. Her brother's monotone declaration of impending doom made her wish she had not returned his urgent phone call.

"You can't believe what happened. Adele left me," he said.

"Oh, you poor thing," Margot said, picturing the bright and pretty little sexpot Amos had married fleeing the confines of her brother's farm. "And right in the middle of summer too."

"And she took the kids."

"Oh dear."

"And she got on a train."

"Poor Mosy."

"And she's headed to New York," her brother said and let that last fact hang in the air until Margot got the full effect of her sister-in-law's sudden travel plans.

"FUCK!" Margot said.

"Miss Allie Potty Mouth! I do NOT want you talking that way around my kids."

"Kids!"

"Right."

"She's coming with the kids?"

More was said, much of it potty mouth on the part of Margot. And yet, the fact that her sister-in-law was, even as they argued, bulleting her way straight to New York City with her young children in tow could not be denied.

"When will she get here?"

"Four hours."

"FUCK!" Margot said again as she hung up the phone. There was a weekend sale at Henri Bendel's and a by-invitation-only sample sale at one of the design colleges. She'd worked hard to wrangle that invite to the college. And she had a ticket for the ballet. She flew out of her office and interrupted her assistant.

"I know when you started here I promised there would be no personal business, but I find I have an emergency personal favor that's easy to execute, and I would so appreciate it if you would do it for me," Margot said to her assistant.

"Whatever you need, Margot," her assistant said as he looked up from the novel he was reading. For a minute, Margot wondered if she could impose on this nice young man, an actor, to entertain her family this weekend. She wondered if she would be more willing to impose on him if he was a woman and she was a man. Could she at least ask him to go collect her kin from the train station, as they were coming in unexpected and in the middle of her business day?

"Could you," Margot began, paused and then continued with, "see if you can get me four more of these ballet tickets. The four new ones should be together, but they don't have to be anywhere near this one I already have."

"Sure. No problem."

"And I guess I'm gone for the rest of the day. Errands and then the train station, but don't hesitate to call me on my cell for any reason whatsoever. Ok?"

"You got it," he said and, sliding a bookmark into his novel, started to work on her tickets.

Margot raced to the grocery store to fill her empty refrigerator with the kinds of foods she thought her sister-in-law and the kids might like, such as mayonnaise and cheese that came in individually wrapped slices. Then she grabbed a taxi to the station and got there before their train pulled in. She stood on the platform and tried to remember the names of her nephews, three interchangeable faces with an identical river of green and yellow boogers rolling between nose and upper lip. Her sister-in-law, Adele, had been a beautiful, lusty virgin on her wedding day. Then within the first four years of her marriage, she gave birth to three children. She must be huge by now, Margot thought, with breasts like watermelons. Margot kept her eyes peeled for a woman the size of a house, towing three small snot machines.

"Aunt Allie?" asked the little boy standing right in front of her.

"Oh!" Margot gasped at the angelic face that was a perfect replica of her brother at his most beautiful. She looked around for Adele, but all she saw was little boys.

For a moment Margot panicked that Adele had sent the boys alone.

"She goes by Margot now," said the tallest of the boys in a high, tired woman's voice. Margot looked twice before she had to admit that the dull, skinny thing in the blue jeans standing behind the three healthy, glowing boys was her once bodacious sister-in-law, Adele. It looked to Margot like Adele's life force had been sucked into her children.

"How are you, Margot?" Adele began wearily. "I'm so sorry to impose on you like this. I just got up too early this morning and started looking through a magazine while I was cooking breakfast and the next thing you know I was, I was, was, was."

Adele couldn't say it, but clearly the next thing she was, was on her way to the station with her children. Given that Margot was probably the only person Adele knew on the other end of any train line, Margot became her destination.

"Come on. Let's get a cab. You tell me all about it back at the apartment."

In the taxi back to the apartment, all three boys kept their noses pressed against the windows, looking in awe at the city and occasionally glancing at their Aunt Margot, as if they could not believe someone they knew lived here. Clean and snot-free, they were quite charming.

"They're so well-behaved," Margot marveled as her three nephews hunkered down in front of her big TV set.

"Well, the television is on. And they're shell-shocked from the trip," Adele said. "It's a little scary for them."

"And for you?"

Adele's silence seemed like a good point for Margot to jump in.

"So, Adele, why are you here?"

That morning, Adele woke up early. She set out a fine breakfast of coffee, milk, toast, bacon, and eggs for all of her responsibilities. While they ate, she began leafing through a woman's magazine that made it seem, to her at least, like every other woman on the planet was living in search of the perfect orgasm. In comparison, Adele suddenly believed her life was cow poop molded into a constant cycle of laundry, cooking, and cleaning. In Adele's world, a woman fell exhausted into bed every night, sometimes in her clothes, sometimes without even scraping the debris of three small boys and a blithe husband off her blouse. In some other place in the world, women were rating their orgasms on a scale of one to ten and suffering to wear high-heeled sandals studded with rhinestones. And so that morning, instead of driving carpool, Adele decided to escape her life, taking with her only the few things she absolutely needed to live. Those few things were named Harry, Eric, and Amos Jr.

"I dunno, Margot," Adele said dully. "I'm usually fine as long as I stay away from women's magazines. You know, the glossy ones where everyone's getting more than you ever will. Amos says they're an agent of the devil and today I'm thinking he might be right."

"Oh dear," Margot said as she opened a bag of cookies and placed them on a plate. Adele reached out to take one, but before her hand reached the plate three small boys swarmed the kitchen and gobbled up all the cookies.

They were hunkered down back in front of the TV before Margot could blink.

"They're growing boys," said Adele, the shrinking woman.

Margot suddenly began to think in magazine ads. The sidebar that would best apply to Adele might read: *What To Do When Your Clitoris Has Fallen Off.*

"I hope you'll let me and the boys take you out to lunch," Adele said sweetly, "and then we'll be on our way back home."

Margot thought of her weekend plans, the lovely sales and shops she could visit if she agreed with Adele's plan and set her on her way right now.

"Actually, I was planning on shopping," Margot began, "at the toy store this very afternoon. And I can't imagine what I would buy without some children there to point out the good things."

Adele looked relieved. And exhausted. And small and sexless.

"I'm thinking lunch and a nap for you, while me and my nephews take a walk."

"Oh, I don't think you can handle three on your own," Adele said wearily, "especially not in a toy store."

"Of course I can," said Margot with a glance to the three angels on the couch. "Let's get you set up for a little rest and rejuvenation while the boys and I tear up the town."

Margot had used the phrase "tear up the town" as a metaphor. Standing with three small boys in the middle of a large toy store, she felt it literally. Adele was right.

She needed reinforcements. She couldn't call one of her many business colleagues. This would be an inappropriate imposition. She needed to call a friend, and since Margot only had two to choose from, which number to dial wasn't a hard decision.

"Aimee," Margot wailed into her little cell phone, hoping the crumbs and smear of chocolate that now covered the mouthpiece would not interfere with reception. She explained the situation, promised it would be good practice for Aimee's own future and then tried not to beg when she added, "can you come help me now?"

"Of course I will," Aimee said, really glad that Margot had called her. She put her phone down, forgot her own troubles, and dialed Brooke's extension.

"Margot's in deep doo-doo with three boys in Times Square," she told Brooke, using a tone she hoped sounded fun-filled and not at all urgent. "She needs our help."

"Margot's in a bar in Times Square?" Brooke asked.

"No. Toy store."

"What the heck's she doing in a toy store?"

"Let's go find out."

"Mmmmmmmm, ok," Brooke said, game for any adventure that had three boys in it. Aimee waited to explain to Brooke the true nature of Margot's crisis until they were already on the subway and Brooke was, in some way, already committed to going.

"What the heck," Brooke said, and then with a warm squeeze of Aimee's hand added, "let's go save Margot."

The little one was weeping over a hand-held electronic toy that cost more than a medium-sized television set. It wasn't so much the cost of one, for Margot, but their insistence that if the little one got it, the other two had to have it too. Margot was going to just give in and drop $700 more than she had intended to spend that day when the older boy let it slip that Daddy didn't approve and would not be pleased if they came home with even one of this particular toy.

When Aimee and Brooke arrived, they saw the three boys crowded around Margot, each explaining their separate, urgent needs. They stopped a few feet away and watched the disaster unfold.

"But! But! It's so cool!" the little boy squealed again. "I'm sure Daddy will like it once he sees it!"

"I really gotta pee!" the middle boy said for the fourth or possibly tenth time.

"What do you mean you don't have any breakfast bars in your purse?" the eldest inquired, loudly and clearly insulted by the thought.

"I don't think we should separate," Margot said. "If one of us has to pee we all need to head over to the ladies' room."

"I'm NOT going into the ladies' room," the eldest boy informed her.

"Well, you guys can't be in the store alone, and they'll arrest me if I go into the men's room, so I think we're going into the ladies' room all together," Margot told him.

"I'd rather sit in the barnyard and eat shit than go into a ladies' room," the boy screamed at her.

"Potty mouth! Potty mouth," the other two boys started shouting and pointing at their eldest brother like

Donald Sutherland in the final scene of *Invasion of the Body Snatchers.*

"So, this is motherhood," Aimee said to Brooke.

"Don't be frightened, honey," Brooke said. "This is like sneaking into a horror movie at the grisliest scene."

"I'm up for the challenge. Let's rescue Margot before she loses a body part."

Smiling broadly, Aimee and Brooke strolled over to Margot and her darling demons.

"Hey there, why don't you let me take you to the bathroom," Aimee said, kneeling down and using her most gentle voice.

"Stranger! Stranger!" the little one screamed as he clung to Margot's leg, nearly tripping her.

"No, no, Eric, this is my friend Aimee. She can take you to the bathroom. It's ok," Margot promised.

"I don't want to go to the bathroom with her," the middle boy said. "I want to go to the bathroom with HER!"

Margot and Aimee turned to where the boy was pointing. Brooke, surprised, smiled brightly.

"Ok, who needs to pee?" Brooke offered.

All three boys raised their hands.

"I thought you wouldn't go into a ladies' room," Margot asked the eldest of her nephews.

"Well, not with you, Aunt Allie," he said, smiling at Brooke.

"Who is Aunt Allie?" Aimee asked.

"Me. I'll explain later," Margot sighed.

"Well then," Brooke said as if it were the most exciting destination in the city, "let's go to the bathroom!"

They traveled as a large, cumbersome crowd across the toy store. Even though the destination had been agreed upon, and even though they sought it with some urgency, it still took twenty minutes to cross the floor to the ladies' room. On the way, they picked up and put down three teddy bears, a stack of Yu-Gi-Oh! cards, ("incomprehensible," Margot declared), a bag of balls that lit up when they bounced, and one lone clothes hanger that the middle boy used to pretend he was Captain Hook, until he accidentally hooked it into the mouth of his elder brother.

"Break it up! Break it up!" Aimee called as they began a fistfight in front of the ladies' room. She had lost the silvery sweetness of her first greeting and was now talking in the sort of voice that might belong to a harried teacher, a hockey coach, or maybe an arresting officer. She was pleasantly surprised when the boys responded quickly and respectfully to her growled command. They stopped trying to kill each other and waited silently for their next orders. Cool, Aimee thought.

"Now, who has to pee?" Margot asked.

No one answered.

"Didn't you have to pee, Eric?" Margot asked the middle nephew.

"I'm Eric," said the youngest.

"I'm so sorry," Margot said. "Harry, you said you have to pee."

"Yeah, I did, but I don't have to anymore."

"Did you wet your pants?" Margot asked her voice filled with deep dread.

"I am NOT a baby," Harry said, offended to his core.

"Then you still have to pee," Margot informed him. "Pee doesn't just disappear."

"No, I don't have to go anymore."

"Yes, you do," Margot explained. "The urine is still in your body. You have to get it out."

"Maybe later," he said.

"Later you will be in a panic and we won't be anywhere near a bathroom. After all the work we put into getting across the store and over to the bathroom, I think you're going to pee now," Margot informed him, but he stubbornly dug his heels in and would not enter the bathroom. Margot looked up at her friends, pleading for aid.

"If you don't pee," Aimee told Harry, "no toy."

Harry quickly entered the ladies' room, followed by his two brothers.

The other women already in the bathroom were unaffected by the arrival of three little boys and their female escorts. This was a toy store, after all, full of bleary-eyed parents trying desperately not to lose the bodies and souls of their media-saturated children. Margot crossed to the sink. It came up to her knees. She bent down and washed her hands, surprised by how dirty they were. Still, she felt that a crisis had been averted.

"I need help," Eric informed her.

"Doing what, dear?" Margot asked as she looked down at the boy.

"Peeing," Eric said as if the situation was obvious and Margot stupid.

"Ah," Margot replied thoughtfully, "and exactly what would that entail?"

"I can't get it started," Eric said and Margot felt a

cold, wet sweat start to creep across her body.

"And, and how, how am I supposed to, ah facilitate that?" Margot stuttered.

"You mean you don't know how to do it either?" Eric asked, his voice rising into panic.

"Well, I ah, well, I usually sit there and it just happens," Margot said worried that the boy has some strange urinary tract condition that no one had thought to mention.

"But before that. I can't do the part before that!" he wailed.

Margot racked her brains trying to think what came before peeing in the act of peeing. And then: Aimee to the rescue.

"He probably can't get his pants undone," Aimee intervened and Eric nodded. "Come, I'll help you."

"You're a natural, Aims," Brooke said as Aimee helped Eric undo his button.

Mission accomplished, bladders emptied, the boys filed out of the ladies' room. Margot felt a deep sense of triumph. Everyone peed. Everyone washed. She had successfully maneuvered her nephews in and out of a bathroom in a toy store; although without the help of two other women, the whole event would have been a disaster.

"All right now," Aimee said when they regained the glittery, pulsating floor of the store. "You have fifteen minutes to pick out a toy. If you haven't picked out a toy in fifteen minutes, a toy will be picked out for you, understand?"

"And there's a $100 total limit on whatever you pick out," Margot added.

"On your mark," Brooke said, "get set, go."

"I'll take the little one," Aimee shouted as the children suddenly scattered in different directions.

"I got the middle," said Margot as she ran off after Harry.

In a time frame that reasonably resembled fifteen minutes, all the children had picked out their toys and Margot was on her way to the register, ready to drop about $350. Eric, the youngest, had managed to exceed his hundred-dollar limit but the other children had not yet noticed. The extra fifty bucks was well worth the fact that they were now on their way out of the store.

"This would break me of shopping," Margot declared to Brooke as she signed her credit card slip.

"What are you planning to do with them tonight?" Aimee asked.

"Ballet," Margot said.

"Are you crazy?" Brooke almost shouted.

"No. Why? You don't think they'll like it?"

"Well, maybe their mother has better control of them," Aimee said.

"Well, actually, I'm sending her to a masseuse and facial while I take the boys to the, oh Christ, you're right," Margot said, "I'm dead."

"I'll come with you," Aimee offered and then she looked at Brooke.

"Yeah, why not. I'll come too."

Adele was asleep when they arrived. With the help of her friends, Margot got her nephews washed, brushed, and changed for dinner.

"How does she do this all by herself?" Margot

whispered before she woke Adele to inform her that a car would arrive within the hour to take her, alone, across town for an evening at a spa and salon.

"Really?" Adele asked as tears came to her eyes.

"Really," Margot said. "And then tomorrow we'll look through my closet and see what fits you."

"God bless you, Allie," Adele said. "How were the boys?"

"Perfect," Margot said, "as soon as I got two additional adults to come help me, everything was under control."

While Adele went off to rediscover herself and her body, Margot directed her party of nephews and girlfriends down the elevator. She led them into an Italian restaurant that was within walking distance. It was a place she often went for a quick, simple meal. The waiters made much of the boys and suggested dishes they had never heard of. In the end, after several sour faces, plain pasta with butter was specially prepared for Harry and Amos. Eric, the youngest, was excited when Brooke read "Squid Ink Linguini" on the menu and insisted on ordering it, even after Brooke informed him it was like thick, black spaghetti. When it arrived, Eric ate all of it and declared it the most delicious meal he had ever chewed. At the ballet, Harry and Amos quickly fell asleep, but Eric, thrilled with the dancing and an opportunity to see girls in their underwear, sat wide-eyed and at the edge of his seat.

"That was really cool. Thank you very much, Auntie Margot," he sighed contentedly as he fought sleep in the cab ride back to Margot's house. "And thank you also, Auntie Margot's friends."

"Ok," Aimee whispered over Eric's sleeping head, "I'm in love. I could do this. It was hard but really, I could do it every day. I can't wait to do it every day. How about you, Brooke?"

"I had fun," Brooke said wistfully. "If I'd played my cards differently with Bill I would have had at least two kids, I think, maybe three. I suppose I could do it alone, but it's just too hard to do alone, even with lots of money. Well, it's not going to happen for me, so I'm not going to worry about it."

"I had a great day," Margot whispered to her friends. "I'm glad that we did it but I'm glad that it's over, and I would not do it again for a million dollars. Tomorrow I'm going to work, a place where no one asks for my help in the potty. And on Saturday, I'm getting a facial, a massage, and a manicure, and I'm having my legs waxed. Then I'm going shopping. For me, whatever I might have missed, the occasional visiting nephew more than makes up for it."

Margot, Aimee, and Brooke rode on in silence until Margot said a very quiet "Thanks for your help." Brooke and Aimee smiled back, glad of the company and the adventure.

Arriving at Margot's apartment, they realized the sleeping children were far too large and heavy to be carried by women in high heels. Grumbling and growling, the boys awoke and made their way into Margot's elevator. They tumbled into the apartment, where a fairy princess who looked vaguely familiar greeted them warmly.

The sleepy boys could not be bothered to notice that their mother had, temporarily, regained the sheen of the head cheerleader/prom queen she had once been. Adele wiped down the boys' faces with a wet cloth, handed a toothbrush to the elder boys and actually moved the brush over and across the teeth of the youngest. Margot, Aimee, and Brooke were amazed to see little Adele actually lift each one of the sleeping boys and carry them from the bathroom to the couch, where she stripped them of their slacks and shirts and shoved them into pajamas. Then she assembled their lank bodies on the couch for sleeping.

"Oh, hi Mommy," one of them murmured before falling back to sleep.

"How were they?" Adele asked.

"Sweet as pie," said Brooke, and Adele beamed.

"It's all over so quickly," Adele said, and Margot, assuming Adele meant the pleasure of her afternoon alone, responded, "Well, Adele, you come back anytime you want."

Adele meant that her beautiful boys were growing up too fast, but she didn't want to hurt poor, lonely, barren Aunt Allie's feelings, especially since she had been so kind to her and her children. So instead Adele just smiled at her sister-in-law.

"Thank you, Allie. I just might do that," Adele said.

11. Pumps

$\mathcal{E}$ARLY THAT MORNING, BROOKE stopped by her parents' house to pick up the dress Bill Simpson bought her to wear to the Muscular Dystrophy ball. It was a hideous ivory-lace concoction with a high neck and a low back. Lately all the dresses had been ivory or blush or white.

"I think he wants to marry you," Brooke's mother said as she regarded the ugly dress on the hanger.

"He wants someone to be a bride," Brooke said. "I'm not sure it's me."

"How do you know it's not you?" Brooke's mother asked.

"Well mother, I was naked in bed with him last night and I rubbed and I danced and I sucked but nothing came up. Aren't you glad you asked," Brooke said.

"You girls put too much emphasis on S-E-X," her mother told her. "He probably drank too much."

"It's possible," admitted Brooke. Although sex with Bill, drunk or sober, used to be an amazing thing. He was long, thick, passionate, and perfectly matched for her body. In the past few years, though, an occasional problem with premature ejaculation had morphed slowly from disinterest to impotence. Their passion had fallen away like the continental shelf—Atlantic, not Pacific. Like the beach that lay in the backyard of her parents' estate in Florida, Brooke had luxuriated in the warm ocean of sex with Bill for quite a distance. Then, suddenly it was over, and she was out to sea.

And yet he still loved her. He called her almost every day. He still sent ugly dresses for her to wear to charity balls.

"Maybe he has a blockage in his plumbing," her mother suggested. "Daddy went to a cracker-jack urologist and…"

"If I hear a single detail of Daddy's urological issues I will fall on the floor and blood will spurt from my ears," Brooke warned.

"Well then, I'll just give you the doctor's name and phone number. I'll even print it with my left hand so you can't recognize my handwriting. This way you can pretend you got the information from someone else if you like."

Her mother flipped open her address book searching for that last urologist who had done such good work for them.

"So you think Viagra is an appropriate gift for the man who has everything?" Brooke asked her mother.

"Beats another cashmere sweater," her mum answered casually.

While her mother scribbled down the doctor's name, Brooke took the dress out of the bag and spread it out over the couch.

"Well, you should at least try it on," her mother said, handing her the slip of paper. Brooke stared at the doctor's phone number, wondering how she would broach the subject of diminished sex drive to Bill without insulting him.

Brooke followed her mother up the stairs and into her private bedroom. Brooke had never thought it odd that her parents had separate bedrooms. She had always considered it an issue of decorating. Her mother's bedroom, with the floral peach wallpaper in the same pattern as the floral peach bedspread would certainly cause her father to drop his masculinity at the door. Her father's bedroom was brown with lots of leather. On Christmas mornings or when they were sick in the middle of the night, Brooke and her sister went there first, knowing that they would probably find both mom and dad asleep underneath his brown plaid comforter. And yet her mother felt she needed this separate bedroom to make her own for the days and nights that his presence in her house and life was just too overbearing.

Brooke closed the door in case one of the maids wandered by. Then she flipped the dress off the hanger and slid it over her head. Brooke's lucky genes gave her an ultra-fashionable body without even trying. She was as long, thin, and straight as a girl could be without actually being a boy. Bill's latest purchase flowed down and settled in on her body, making her look even more flat chested while showing off her well-muscled back. Brooke did a half-hearted twirl around her mother's flowered bedroom then plunked down on the bench at the end of the bed.

"At least he always includes a gift receipt," Brooke's

mother drawled from her comfy spot on the bed pillows. And then, "Your darling boyfriend has no taste at all."

Brooke's mother's impish little giggle began to swell into a big fat, unladylike laugh. The laugh grew louder and Brooke noticed that her mother had started to cry.

"Poor Eleanor," Brooke's mother whimpered.

"Poor Eleanor? I thought you didn't like Bill's mom."

"I don't. What I actually meant, darling, when I said 'poor Eleanor' is that I'm fucking furious that her perfect son has ruined my daughter's life."

With that, Brooke's mother downed her G&T, slipped off the bed and sashayed down to the library for a refill from her husband's bar.

"I'm sorry, dear," she began when Brooke entered the room. "It's none of my business how you ruin your life."

"Mummy," Brooke began, but her mother refused to turn around and look at her. Her mother was suddenly entranced by the light as it refracted across the cuts in her glass, so Brooke strode across the large room until she was standing right in front of her mother, blocking the sunlight as it came through the window. Her mother tried to continue to avoid Brooke's gaze by taking a long, deep sip of her fresh drink.

"Look here, Mother," Brooke said with some force and authority, "Bill Simpson did not ruin my life. The tattoos did."

Gin and tonic squirted through her mother's nose.

"I love you, Brooke," she laughed. "God, how I love you. And I always wanted the very, very best for you. I'm so sorry your life is shit."

Brooke stood there for a while, her jaw dropped and

her eyes blinking. Her mother looked like a cat caught peeing on the good rug.

"My life isn't shit," Brooke finally said.

"Well, I didn't really mean shit. You know, dear, I shouldn't touch gin. It makes me too honest. I mean, not honest, but well, you know what I mean," her mother slammed and then backpedaled and slammed again. "It's just that I'm so sorry so many things didn't work out for you. The painting thing and the marriage thing. You're so alone. I'm just so sad that you have nothing to show for your life."

"I'm very happy, Mother."

"Don't try to fool me, Brooke," her mother said gently. "Why won't you take Granny's apartment on Fifth? You live in that horrible one-bedroom thing you call an apartment. You don't even have cable!"

"Cable!" Brooke exclaimed. "Mummy, I don't even have a TV. And when did you become so, so...American."

It was an odd choice of adjectives. Brooke's mother reacted to it by jutting her head forward and throwing her hands up in the air. The woman could trace her ancestors back to the Mayflower. Any more American and she would be native.

"Maybe 'American' is not the right word," Brooke conceded. "When did you become so acquisitive?"

Again, the hands shot into the air, this time indicating the three-acre mansion filled with more crystal than the White House.

"Not exactly what I mean either," Brooke agreed. "Aren't you the woman who told me 'Prozac is for women who can't afford to travel'? I'm not saying I got everything

I wanted. Sure, my life would have been different if I had married Bill the first time he asked me. We would have kids by now, and I would need the space and so I'd probably move back into Fifth Avenue. I wish my paintings were getting written up in journals and magazines. I wish people were watching me, so I could feel like I was creating for an audience. I'm sorry I don't have children. I'm sorry I'm not famous, but all the rest is pretty fucking good. My life is a great time. It hurts me, Mother, that you insist on mourning the loss of things I never really wanted."

"Do I?"

"Oh yeah. So I didn't marry Bill in my twenties. It was the right choice for me. I just wasn't ready for monogamy."

"Darling, I'm not talking about monogamy," said Brooke's mother. "I'm talking about marriage. A pledge of love and support from a man. I'm not a particularly monogamous girl either, dear."

"Mummy, I don't need that kind of support. I have a trust fund. I love to paint."

"But don't you want this?" Brooke's mother made an expansive gesture with her glass, indicating all that was under the roof of her own house.

"Are you kidding? I want this at least once a month, which is why I come to visit you so often. And when you die it will be very nice if you and daddy leave me the greater percentage of it since you think my life is such shit without it. Until then, none of it will fit into my comfortable little single-girl apartment. Until then, I travel and play and fuck and eat and paint and play and work just a little and have a really good time. So quit crying for me."

"Are you happy?"

"Wouldn't you be?"

Brooke's mom killed another gin and tonic. The honest answer was no. She would be terribly unhappy with Brooke's life. It had been a long time since she had really loved her husband and yet could not imagine divorcing him. She loved her house and her children and her position. She lived in dread that one of his flings might turn his head away from the security of their détente and cause him to seek a divorce. Although much of the old money was hers, she believed all would crumble if he left her; that in spite of her own substantial address book, without her husband she would be alone in the wide world. She could not imagine where her daughter found the strength to face life without a formal contract with a man.

She stood on the good rug and regarded her daughter. The sting of "Your life is shit, dear" was starting to dissipate, and Brooke looked peaceful.

"Everything's fine with me, Mummy," Brooke said.

Brooke's mother was certain Brooke was lying in an attempt to keep her from worrying too much. Bill is probably having an affair, she thought. All the signs are there. Well, if Brooke can't talk about it yet, I shouldn't push her. Then she found a decent smile that she could bring to the surface of her face. Once it was in place, she gave it to Brooke.

"Well then, for goodness sake, let's return that horrible dress to whatever matronly shop Bill found it and go into the city and find something decent for you to wear."

"He does have the worst taste, doesn't he?"

Bill's bad taste had a price tag of over $5,000. Cash in

hand, Brooke and her mother had themselves chauf-
feured into the city. Brooke directed the driver to drop
them on a corner in a fashionable shopping district full of
darling boutiques. They started up the street fondling
fabrics and being fawned on by stylishly malnourished
men and women working for a small percentage of sales.

They blew in and out of the little shops that presented T-shirts like priceless museum artifacts. They were
looking for a gown that could be pulled off the rack and
onto the dance floor without alterations. It would be
impossible for most women, but Brooke had the just
barely female body all those just barely male designers
created for.

She looked great in everything, but a ruby Lanvin
ready-to-wear gown with a daring plunge made her look
like both a girl and a goddess. The shopkeeper promised
to press it, wrap it, and send it on to Bill's house. Brooke
and her mom continued down the other side of the street,
spelunking for the perfect pair of shoes and matching
evening bag.

"Too glittery," her mom declared when Brooke discovered a gorgeous pair of ruby pumps. "And the satin
slingbacks go better with that dress."

The shoes Brooke really wanted, plus the Lanvin creation, left her only $20 for the matching bag that cost
$625.

"Get the slingbacks, and I'll pick up the bag," her
mother offered, pouting a little at the thought that
Brooke might pick the glittery pumps in spite of her offer
to pay. The scene had played out hundreds of times in
Brooke's teenage years, with her mother holding the

power of the credit card over her daughter's desire to look different from every other white-gloved debutante. Brooke lost the battle so many times that one more pair of slingbacks when she really wanted pumps didn't seem too terribly important. Still, a little frown of disappointment wriggled over Brooke's mouth. Before she could give into the slingbacks, Brooke's mom felt a great rush of pity and guilt for her daughter.

"What am I saying," Brooke's mother suddenly said. "You want the pumps. And glitter is so right now. And I love the bag. And you should have what you want. Come, let's ring them up quick and we'll still have time for a coffee. I'll phone the driver to pick us up at the café and then he'll drop you at Bill's when we're done."

The perfect ruby pumps and the matching crystal purse were paid for, wrapped, and deposited in a shopping bag. Brooke and her mother dished their neighbors as they sat around a tiny table and sipped tiny ten-dollar coffees and shared a $6 blueberry scone.

"Call me and tell me what everyone wore," her mother sang as Brooke got out of the backseat. She called, "Have a great time" as the car pulled away. Brooke swung her packages across the sidewalk and into the cool, dark lobby of Bill's Fifth Avenue digs.

12. The Space Between Two Worlds

THE GIRLS WERE OUT. The roof was fixed. The old, used condoms that once littered the backyard were dug in under the new landscaping. Hopefully the new owners wouldn't have a dog. Lux hired Carlos to paint the inside, telling him a friend of a friend from work owned the house and needed a good painter for money under the table. She paid him decently and felt good about it. Then she sold the house.

The realtor had named a ridiculously large amount of money as the initial asking price. Lux dropped it by $20,000 and the place sold for $60,000 over asking price after only sixteen hours on the market. She turned around and bought a two-bedroom apartment in Manhattan that needed serious work.

"Yeah, hey," Carlos said on the phone with the baby crying in the background, "it's me. If, like, you know, those bozos from work ever need ah, you know, someone to lift and shove stuff for them again, call me ok. Under the table, right?"

"Yeah, different people," Lux said as she traced her

finger up and down the chipped paint in Trevor's kitchen, "but they got a place in Manhattan that needs a little work and they want to let me, you know, be in charge of it. Decorate and stuff."

"You gonna paint the whole place purple?"

Her realtor instructed her to paint the walls "Irish Linen" which are fancy words that mean beige.

"You want the job or no?" Lux said in a hurried voice, worried that Trevor might emerge from his shower while she was on the phone with her ex-boyfriend talking real estate and paint.

"Yeah, yeah. When and where?"

The kitchen was trashed. Lux ordered new cabinets and Carlos hung them. She saved the old sink and planned to scrub it and have him reset it into the new counter. Carlos had a smooth hand with the plaster and patched up every last one of the holes in the ceiling and walls in just one day. They rolled up the carpet and found bugs and a hardwood floor. Carlos had a buddy who worked for a guy who had a sander, and the buddy wasn't opposed to borrowing the sander and the varnish and coming in and redoing the floors on a Sunday for an all-cash price. Carlos worked like a dog with Lux coming in on the weekends to sweat it out with him.

"No, no, see, last week my mom was sick," she told Trevor. "This weekend my girlfriend from high school's got it and I'm watching her baby so she can, you know, rest."

It took six weeks for the flu to make its way through

all of Lux's old friends and family. On the last weekend, Jonella came in and helped Lux clean up.

"I woulda painted it purple," Jonella said while they rested.

"Yeah, me too," Lux agreed as she watched the muscles on Carlos' back twitch and flex under his shirt.

"Take your shirt off," Jonella instructed him.

"I ain't that hot," he replied.

"Yeah, but we are," Jonella laughed.

He laughed like a gorilla grunt and dropped the sweaty T-shirt on Lux's head.

"Now the pants," Jonella said.

"No."

"Aw, come on, baby."

"I got work to do."

"So?"

"I ain't got no underwears on."

"Oh," said Jonella.

"Show's over then?" asked Lux.

"Yeah, he don't wanna get no paint on his dick."

"I don't blame him."

"Fuck off the both of you crazy sluts trying to get into my pants."

He pushed the roller up the wall, covering over all the dirt and stains, leaving a blank canvas for some tenant to make their own.

"How's work?" Jonella asked as she scrubbed out the sink.

"Sucks," Lux said, wiping down the refrigerator. "How's motherhood?"

"Sucks," Jonella reported, "but the baby's good.

Carlos went back living with his mom which is ok, cuz, GOD, is he an asshole, or what?"

"Oh yeah, Carlos is an asshole."

They laughed and Jonella punched Lux in the shoulder in a friendly fashion that would leave a bruise.

"When you gonna have one?"

"Baby?"

"Yeah."

"Nah, not me."

"I'm gonna have another one."

"You pregnant again?"

"Nah, just planning."

"With Carlos."

"Carlos the Asshole? No way."

"With who then?"

"Someone I ain't met yet."

"What's Carlos gonna say to that?" Lux asked and, by way of reminder, held up her own mangled little pinky finger, four years healed but still looking kind of bent and broken.

"Carlos loves the kid, but he don't want to love no more babies cuz ah the money. So when I get pregnant I'll let him think it's his until he's ready to piss his pants and when it turns out to be not, he'll have a fucking celebration and fall down and kiss my big ass."

The plan seemed reasonable to Lux. Still she feared for her friend.

"What if it goes different and he gets mad?"

"It won't."

Carlos wasn't so tall, but he was very strong and wiry. He didn't have much that you could take from him. He was as comfortable in jail as he was in Queens. There was no civilization, no restraining order to hold him back once he got it in his head to make something happen. In the tenth grade Lux had been his best girl and Jonella had been his second-choice girl. He kept his harem in line with punches and slaps, but only once had he broken a bone, the little bones in Lux's pinky. He twisted it until it fractured.

Soon after she graduated from high school, Joseph, Lux's biggest brother, was also released from prison. After inspecting his baby sister's crippled little finger, Joseph invited Carlos over to the house and informed Carlos that Lux was now free to do what she liked. There had been lots of shouting, hitting, and blood, most of it falling out of Carlos' head. Although the fighting went on for a long time, Carlos and Joseph were friends, so it ended fairly amiably.

"Yeah, well fuck you then," Carlos had shouted.

"Yeah, fuck you too," Joseph shouted back. "And don't forget I need a ride tomorrow."

"Yeah right. I'll be there."

"You better."

Joseph let the screen door slam behind him as he walked back into the house. Lux was sitting at the kitchen table, her palms pressed close to her ears. She had been listening to the rumbled ocean sounds echoing in her head from the pressure of her hand, drowning out the crunching sounds that she knew were either Carlos hitting her brother or Joseph hitting her lover. Joseph smiled at her, sitting there at the kitchen table looking like a frightened mouse. He pushed his finger into the new bruise on Lux's cheek and said, "He ain't gonna fuck wit you no more." Then he sat down on the couch to drink beer with their mother. With Lux out of the picture, Jonella had Carlos all to herself.

"I think next time I want to have a girl," Jonella was musing, a funny smile caught in the corner of her mouth.

"You don't have any money," Lux reminded her.

"So?"

Lux didn't say anything.

"Money comes," Jonella continued smiling as she thought about the full and good way pregnancy made her feel and the sweet, wet smell of her baby's skin. She wasn't going to be stupid and have six or eight babies like some of the girls she knew. But one, or maybe even two more wouldn't make much difference in her mother's house.

"We ain't never gonna be rich, so why not have what I want," Jonella announced.

Jonella surveyed the kitchen. The parts she'd worked on were sparkling clean; other parts weren't so good. Jonella redid the work Lux had attempted.

"Good thing you're doinking that rich guy. You'd never keep a job in the real world."

Lux excused herself to the living room where she rolled up the tarps and pulled the painter's tape. When the last of the work debris was cleaned up, the apartment suddenly transformed into something real. Lux's future.

Jonella swept the floor, telling Lux about this old friend or describing something the baby did, who got fat, who got troubles. By the time they got to the bedroom, the old friends had run out of things to say. The two women sat on the radiator, watching their ex-lover roll paint onto the walls.

Carlos was a good, clean painter. He'd never have done it—not for all the money in the world—if he knew the apartment was Lux's. If he found out he'd probably track her down and break her other fingers. It was unlikely he would ever discover that Lux owned the property because Auntie Who-ah's almost-dead attorney had set up an S corporation to avoid paying income tax. Her new apartment was in the name of a company she had dubbed "Trevor Holdings." The only way Carlos would know she was the real owner is if she told him.

Carlos finished the last stroke of clean beige paint. He carefully laid the roller down on a piece of newspaper and stepped back to consider his work. Pleased, he unbuttoned his pants, turned to the women, and stepped naked out of the pants.

"Ok, now I'm ready," he said.

The girls' giggles were throaty and not at all high-pitched.

There were hard, raised red keloid scars across Carlos' arms and torso, some accidental, some intentional. On his bicep was a tattoo, well-drawn and executed with extreme detail, depicting a rooster hanging dead by a noose. Carlos, who was not completely lacking in humor, liked to rub his hand over the tattoo and tell people he had a well-hung cock. His body was rock hard and one time, on a hot day, Lux had kissed him while he was eating a peach. That was the kiss that stayed with her, the sweet taste of fresh fruit mixed with his lips and sweat, the kiss that came back to her when he stood there laughing at them, daring Jonella and Lux to come get it.

Jonella jumped and Carlos caught her. They had no doubt that sex was good and bodies were fun. Lux held back.

"Wassup, baby?"

"It's you, Carlos, she don't like you no more."

"No I think it's you, cause you got fat or maybe she done gave up the dyke."

The rhythm was coming from within and Lux watched as Jonella and Carlos danced it into each other.

"Girl, don't listen to him, you ain't fat at all," Lux called by way of encouragement when Jonella dropped her overalls. Jonella, her lips lingering on Carlos' nipple on their way to his crotch, waved at Lux, her fingers beckoning, arm dancing like an entranced cobra to a sweet beat.

I'll come up behind her and rub my breasts on her back until she goes down on him and then I'll have Carlos' hands and mouth all to myself until she mounts him. Lux was choreographing in her head. In front of her Jonella had already pressed Carlos to the floor and was pushing herself on top of him. Lux's entry ramp was coming up soon. She had to jump off the radiator fast or she was gonna miss it. When Carlos flips her over and comes at her from behind, Lux planned, then I'll come up and just shove my boobs in his face. Lux stood up and the moaning started.

"Baby, baby, baby. Oh baby. Yeah baby."

"Oh bayyybe."

"Mmmmbaby"

The ship was sailing on without her but Lux still couldn't move. Lux, hanging between two worlds, watched Carlos' golden back turn shiny with sweat, and joy turn Jonella's face beautiful. Her head fell back and twisted as Jonella started to lick the air like she was looking for something to roll around in her mouth. Lux thought of that peach-sweetened kiss.

Lux watched her friend's face change from thoughtful to blissful and back again. It was as if she was in turn wowed by a terribly deep thought and a moment later, conversing with God, then back to a math problem, then pure religion, then complex geometry as her brow furrowed and relaxed in shorter and shorter cycles each rising in intensity. Math/God; Math/God; Math/God. And as Carlos pumped her harder and harder: God, God, God, God.

Lux knew Carlos, out of a desire to control and not out of generosity, would make sure Jonella came first. The things that made him an amazing lover were the same things that made him a terrifying boyfriend. Carlos took deep pleasure in controlling women.

"No, no no nononon."

Jonella always denied the pleasure at first. Carlos loved that about her. She tried to escape the wave. It was too big, it was too much, but Carlos chased her, flicking his thumbs over her breasts, sucking on the nipples. Between denial and acceptance came confusion.

"No baby, yes yes baybee no! oh no!"

Carlos looked up for a moment and saw Lux, clinging to the radiator, her mouth slightly slack and one hand wrapped around her own breast. He winked at her.

When they were finished, Lux knew, when the room came back into focus and the buttons that connected them came undone, they were going to ask her questions about why and make fun of her for watching them. Carlos would assume she was waiting for him, waiting to have him all to herself like old times. It was in his wink. He told her he was saving something just for her.

Lux slid off the radiator. She clicked the locks and ran all the way to the subway. She arrived at Trevor's apartment breathing hard. She found him sitting on the couch in his bathrobe, talking on the phone. She immediately ruined his plans to catch a movie with an old friend.

13. Standing Naked on the Rabbi's Toilet Bowl

MARGOT KNEW HER DRESS for the wedding had to be perfect. And turquoise. Margot looked great in turquoise. In the end she found a slinky sheath, cut on the bias to drape in that amazing way that bias-cut fabric drapes. Spaghetti straps and clingy fabric would require the perfect underwear, which was really a girdle, though the salesgirl called it Supportive Panties.

"It keeps you all tucked in," the salesgirl at Macy's told her. Margot judged the girl to be about twenty-three years old and two hundred and thirty pounds.

"I'm wearing one now," the girl announced proudly. "Takes a good ten pounds off my hips."

"Oh," Margot said, finally filling the space left open after such a remark, "good for you."

Margot bought the girdle in spite of the shocking sales pitch. On the evening of the wedding she tried to slip into it after the shower but found that the latex fabric would not slide up if her skin were even the slightest bit damp. That was all right. There were other things to do.

Margot put on her makeup and shoes and was doing her hair when the phone rang.

"What are you wearing?" Brooke asked.

"Right now just my shoes," Margot told her.

"Hmm, you'll be cold tonight in the air-conditioning." They laughed.

"Do you know what Lux is wearing?" Margot asked.

"Haven't talked to her since the hair pulling debacle in the writers' group," Brooke said. "Whatever it is, I'm sure it will be startling."

More laughter as they concocted possible Lux combinations in fuchsia and purple with bits and bobs of cheap, fake jewelry. Margot, sitting naked on her living room couch waiting for her nails to dry, drew a scene for Brooke's amusement that featured Lux, at this very moment also getting ready for Trevor's son's wedding, hair dryer in one hand and a can of extra-glue hair spray in the other.

Margot planned to stand next to Lux as often as possible. She planned to speak wittily and clearly and jut out her hip at seductive angles while her bold yet tasteful turquoise dress promised a sensual body beneath. Trevor didn't have to know anything about the girdle.

Makeup applied, hair coiffed, nails done, shoes on— there was nothing left to do but get the girdle on.

"I gotta go, Brooke," she said. "I'll see you at the wedding."

It was time for Supportive Panties. In her hand it looked tiny. Like a little girl's summer short set except the tube top was attached to the pants. Margot took off her shoes and slipped her feet into the legs. The fabric stretched up her hips and then stopped. As Margot jumped around the room, tugging and praying, her turquoise dress, which she had thrown across the bed, slipped to the floor. Margot pulled, Margot swore and still the rubbery girdle, which might be useful next Halloween as a dominatrix costume or in the summer if Margot went scuba diving, would not slide up her skin.

Margot hopped into the bathroom and looked for something to make it slide. Body oil would smell nice but might bleed through to the silk of her dress. Hand cream? Margot considered her magnificent array of products. Creams, gels, scents, soaps, none of it would do. Then she saw it. An inexpensive bottle of the perfect solution! A full body dusting of baby powder finally got the latex flowing up the hips and over the breasts.

"Thank the goddess!" Margot gasped.

She breathed out and then could not breathe in.

"Oh my," Margot said, having second thoughts about her new underwear. It was slimming, but terribly uncomfortable. Still, breathing aside, Margot felt wonderful and packed tight. As she leaned over to snatch the dress where it had fallen to the floor she realized there would be no sitting down tonight. The fabric would bend and flex easily but all the extras of Margot's body (internal organs and such) had no room to shift as her body bent. Her posture would be perfect all night, her back ramrod straight, her stomach sucked, and her breasts at attention because Margot risked passing out or damaging a kidney if she attempted the very tricky sitting down maneuver.

Who needs to sit at a party? I'll just dance all night, she told herself. She was going to look fabulous, if she could figure out how to bend low enough get the turquoise dress off the floor. In the end, in a modern dance maneuver that might be described as "Worm Burrowing Across Carpet," Margot slid into the turquoise dress. She managed to limbo herself back onto her feet, and then headed out to conquer the world.

"I'm going to Long Island. I'd prefer to take the FDR to the Triborough," Margot told the taxi driver, and was pleased with his grunt of third-world macho disgust at her bossy tone and wanton appearance. He did as she instructed and turned the cab towards the FDR.

"What are you doing, lady?" the cab driver asked when he could not see her head in the rearview mirror.

"Nothing," Margot said, stretched out across the backseat of his cab so that she could continue to breathe.

The night was warm and she carried only the thinnest shawl and a small clutch bag set with real turquoise stones. If it got chilly she would borrow Trevor's jacket. The cab drove up to the address in the invitation.

"Are you getting out?" the cabbie asked.

"Of course I am. Just give me a minute."

Margot waited until the car in front of her unloaded and drove off.

"I'll need you to open the door for me, please."

The driver looked in his rearview mirror and saw no one. Crazy half-naked lady, he thought but he got out of the car and opened the door for her. Margot slid herself like a body on a slab, feet first out of the cab. She tipped the cab driver extra because, although his eyes had bulged, he did not laugh.

There were drinks and hors d'oeuvres before the ceremony. Margot, looking around for Lux, bumped into Brooke and Aimee just as Brooke was tipping a bottle of vodka into her glass.

"This is fabulous!" Brooke announced loudly. Clearly it was not her first tip. The vodka was frozen in a block of ice that had been carved into a bucket. The bucket had small metal pivots on either side that were set into a stand, allowing even the most inebriated guest to continue pouring frozen vodka into a glass by just putting a few fingers of pressure on the neck of the bottle. All around the ice, penguins fashioned of hardboiled eggs and olives cavorted on a mountain of Crisco and slid into an ocean of caviar.

"What's Lux wearing?" Margot wanted to know.

"Haven't seen her yet," Aimee said.

Trevor's ex-wife waltzed by.

"Hey Candice!" Margot waved and got a glare in return.

"What was *that* about?"

"About enough evil energy to fry her eyeballs," Brooke laughed.

"Margot, I think that woman hates you."

Good, thought Margot, let her hate me. I hope she has reason to.

"Lot of people from work," Brooke commented as they filed into the hall for the ceremony.

"Oh god, is that Lux?" Margot asked suddenly.

"Rabbi's secretary," Brooke said.

"I didn't know Trevor was Jewish," Aimee said.

"He's not," Margot informed them. "The bride is."

"The ceremony's starting," Brooke said as she helped herself to a little more of the penguin's stash of frozen vodka.

"Well, let's go in," Aimee said.

"Hold on, one more dip in the caviar," Brooke begged.

"You've got a black smudge of it on your mouth and, oh god, Brooke, look at your teeth," Aimee said, digging in her purse for a pocket mirror.

Brooke wiped her face and did a quick swish around her mouth with the last bit of her frozen vodka.

"Where's the ceremony going to be?" Brooke asked.

"In there," Margot said.

They spoke in lower tones as they entered the festooned sanctuary.

"So, where's the reception?" Aimee whispered.

"Right here," Margot said. "There's another room over there."

Margot pointed to the back of the synagogue, to a wall with accordion pleats.

"Bar mitzvah room. Wall pulls back. Full bandstand. Rotating disco ball and everything," Margot said.

"Cool religion to keep a rotating disco ball on hand for significant events," Brooke said.

They quietly took their seats on the groom's side. The synagogue had been decorated with long ropes of Pepto-Bismol-pink garlands of over-dyed roses and ribbons that made it impossible to enter the pews from the inside aisle. You had to go around to the outside or be strangled by flowers.

"It's very Long Island Jewish Princess," Aimee

whispered to Brooke and Brooke said "Shush!" with a slight giggle.

Brooke and Aimee and Margot sashayed to the center and found seats close to the flower garlands. The music began and the hall grew quiet. The flower girl entered, eyeing the guests suspiciously and dropping a single petal from her large basket of flowers every ten feet. An aunt and an uncle passed by, and then a slightly bewildered old lady, looking lovely in a lavender gown, stopped in the middle of her trip down the aisle as if she had suddenly forgotten where she was going. The pink chain-link of roses on either row of seats afforded her only one destination, the rabbi smiling at her, waiting to marry someone.

"But I'm not Jewish," the old lady said to Margot who was standing at the end of the row.

"No dear, Teddy is marrying a Jewish girl. This is Teddy's wedding," Margot replied.

"Teddy?"

"Trevor's son."

She looked at Margot blankly and reached for her hand. As Margot struggled to get to the other side of the roses, Trevor suddenly appeared and led his mother down the aisle. Thank you, he nodded to Margot over his shoulder, and her eyes filled up with tears.

"Wow," Brooke whispered. "Put me down before I get there."

"Shush!" Aimee and Margot ordered at the same time.

Trevor managed to anchor his mother to something and make it back in time to walk his son down the aisle.

Teddy's look of nervous excitement was nothing compared to the pained looks on the faces of his parents. Too much family all in one place put the happy event on overload.

Teddy, Trevor had confided to Margot, would never settle down. Certainly would never marry. He'd been living with a graffiti artist when his parents' marriage fell apart. Suddenly he was in an MBA program and then engaged to this very traditional girl from Long Island.

"I don't like it," Trevor told Margot when she asked about the wedding. "She's too ordinary for him."

Trevor looked brave, and Margot wanted to reach out and touch the sleeve of his tux as he walked by, but those enormous pink roses put a stop to any contact. When all were assembled, the lights got a little lower and the strains of the bride's processional began. Then suddenly the lights went out. A moment later a sharp spotlight hit the back of the synagogue, revealing the bride standing there alone dressed in blinding white. Trevor's mother gasped.

"Christ on a crutch!" Brooke whispered. "It's Wedding Gown Barbie."

Still overwhelmed by the effect of the spotlight and the as-if-by-magic appearance of the bride, neither Margot nor Aimee criticized Brooke's outburst. If the bride heard, she wasn't showing it through her dazzling smile, freshly bleached for the occasion.

The bride's dress, a bright white bias-cut sheath with spaghetti straps, fell all the way to the floor. Still, the bride had insisted on getting a full leg and deep bikini wax which had stripped her bare all the way from the tiny hairs on her big toes to the thick and curly hairs that grew in the cleft between her vagina and thigh. She should have gone to the salon the day before but Teddy had dragged her to some art show in the city. She'd rescheduled a full wax for 8 a.m. but slept through it. Canceling her meeting with the rabbi, the bride raced out at the last minute to the salon for the total hair-ripping treatment.

It was a mistake. She was horrified by the little, raised red pinpricks that covered her legs, toe to vagina, wherever a hair had been yanked out. She had intended to be sexier than hell that day but ended up looking like a plucked chicken. As the hour of her wedding grew closer, the red welts faded, but a slight burning sensation kept her from putting on pantyhose. Therefore, under her dazzling white bias-cut sheath with spaghetti straps, the bride was barely wearing a simple white thong.

Margot noticed first but Aimee said it.

"My god, Margot, she's wearing the same dress as you," Aimee observed after the ceremony as they strolled into the bar mitzvah room for dinner and dancing.

"Who?" asked Margot, as if she didn't know.

"The bride."

"No way. Hers is…"

"White," Brooke informed her.

"What can I say? She has excellent taste."

Brooke, Margot and Aimee were seated at Table 11, with other friends from the office. There was no little ivory card with Lux's name spelled out in calligraphy on the table.

"I think I'll just take a lap around the party before I

sit down," Margot told her friends as they made themselves comfortable at the table.

The room, which may not have been so beautiful in daylight, looked elegant in the darkness. There was, as Margot had predicted, a slowly spinning, mirrored disco ball in the center of the room that splattered jeweled patterns of light across smiling faces of well-wishers. Margot stood. She would stand all night. She was pretending to listen to the band when Trevor came up from behind and hugged her.

"Thank you."

"Oh!" she exclaimed at his warmth. "Thank you for what?"

"My mother."

"Oh yes. Of course. I would have done more but—"

"—the flowers."

"Yes," she said

"Very sturdy roses."

"Ridiculously sturdy. You all right?"

"Ah. Sure. My ex-wife is as angry at me now as she was when we were married. I'm not sure why we bothered to get a divorce."

"Dance with me," Margot said, not caring that it was a non sequitur.

"Oh yes, please," Trevor answered, and took her in his arms.

He put his arms around her waist. She nestled a hand in the collar of his tux as they swept out onto the floor. Margot wore high heels almost every day of her life, so she could glide gracefully in the spiked shoes that brought her almost up to his height. He felt a warm, strong body beneath his hands and did not know that a fraction of the effect was created with spandex and rubber. For a moment they roamed the dance floor like a single tiger stalking the jungle. The father of the groom has limited responsibilities on the night of the wedding, but Trevor and Margot danced right into one of them.

"May I cut in?" the bride asked. For a moment Margot looked at her blankly, hiding her outrage at being bumped out of heaven by some twenty-three-year-old vixen in a bias-cut sheath. Then Margot graciously stepped back and watched Trevor sweep away this young girl and her nearly identical dress. Margot smiled and looked relaxed while planning her escape.

Brooke and Aimee waived her back to the table but she couldn't go sit down with the girls and start drinking because she couldn't sit down. Watching Trevor dance away, Margot's smile grew a little rigid, and she stepped out of the hall. She looked around the synagogue, searching for the bathroom.

The ladies' room was filled with cousins and flower girls and young bridesmaids. No one was pissing, they were just lounging by the mirrors, gossiping about boys and twirling their hair. One girl was smoking and showing off a new earring that was stuck through her eyebrow. Margot thought about making her way through the crowd in the ladies' lounge and hiding in a toilet stall, but there too, she would have to sit down. There would be no solace in the toilet tonight.

Margot prowled through the synagogue, smiling a frozen smile at friends and strangers alike. She looked through the window into the locked Hadassah Gift Shop, pretending to be interested in cups and candlesticks and books about Hanukkah. I would buy the candlesticks because they're pretty, thought Margot shopping in her head. And I like those braided candles. Everything else was a little too fifteenth century retro to really interest her. Then her eye fell on a door behind the gift shop that looked like it lead to a different bathroom. Margot tried the door and found it unlocked.

A dressing table with a mirror was the focal point of the room. The mirror was surrounded by a ribbon of lights, like those in a backstage dressing room. The bride's street clothes were thrown around the room and Margot noticed that the bride, like Margot, wore size four slim, Gap jeans. Margot looked at herself in the mirror and wondered at the difference between twenty-three and fifty.

Nothing. More money, more power, more peace. What have I lost? Margot made a list in her head.

1) Giddiness.

2) Poverty.

3) Inexperience.

4) The ability to make the wrong choice quickly.

5) A wide-open playing field full of bad options, dead ends, and heartaches that obscure the right paths.

6) An inability to focus.

7) The possibility of wasting fifteen years discovering that one has married the wrong man.

Nothing worth keeping on that list, Margot thought. I'm at least twenty-five years older than this woman that Teddy is marrying. In those years I've gained so much; surely I've lost something too. Margot looked at herself in the lighted mirror. She had to twist and lean to see her face, but declared to herself that there was very little difference between the flashing white of the bride and the deep mature turquoise of her guest. She pulled out the chair and tried to sit in it, but the bondage of spandex was stronger than Margot's will. She just couldn't bend it.

There was a door at the other end of the room, slightly ajar with something shiny on the other side. A larger mirror, Margot hoped, full-length and well-lit. Opening the door, she flipped on the lights and found a small private toilet, with a door leading to another room. Margot entered the bathroom and poked her head into the room beyond. The rabbi's private study. And this must be the rabbi's private bathroom, Margot thought. Well, semi-private bathroom, as he obviously shares it with the brides during their weddings.

Clearly the brides dominated the décor, as the tiny room was wallpapered pink and one whole wall was taken up with a floor-to-ceiling mirror. Margot stood there and looked at her whole self. She thought she looked fabulous and young. Still she was unsure. Of late, Margot had grown increasingly farsighted and she had not brought her glasses. She stepped back to get a more focused look. And then another step brought the toilet up under her knees. She stepped up onto the toilet to get the full effect and scrutinized her loveliness for signs of decay.

The body is perfect, Margot declared. The face, unlined after an excellent facelift. Her plastic surgeon had recommended she gain a little weight, that at fifty she had to choose between a tiny tush or a fuller, younger looking face. Her dermatologist suggested the same, telling her that the creams he could recommend or prescribe needed to be augmented by better, if not simply *more*, nutrition. But after so many years of dieting, Margot found food hard to swallow. When her primary care physician gave her the lecture about brittle bones and a potential dowager's hump, Margot managed to slide an extra pound or two onto her frame. The effect on her face had been lovely.

So what is the big deal about young flesh, Margot asked the mirror. Why would Trevor want Lux when he could have me? The physical difference is in millimeters, Margot told herself as she pictured the bride's thin arms stretching out of her spaghetti straps. The skin on those arms had a tiny fraction of an inch more fat in the skin and less on the muscle. The bride's freckles are a few millimeters smaller than mine and a few shades browner. Ok, so she has girlish freckles and I'm starting to have the spreading stain of age spots. Her hair is longer (no big deal) and shinier. Margot covered the gray of her hair well but could do nothing about the thick, wiry texture that had replaced her own once-glossy mane. But that was just hair. Everything else was totally camouflaged. And the twenty-three-year-old bride had a little pouch of a belly sticking out, while Margot's belly was flat as spandex.

Suddenly Margot pulled the turquoise bias-cut sheath off her body and dropped it to the bathroom door. She stood on the rabbi's toilet in her modified dominatrix girdle and started to shake just a little. She suddenly felt stuffed and fake. If she took a lover home tonight they'd have to go in separate cabs so he wouldn't see her laid out on the back seat like a dead fish because she could not bend enough to sit down. And he'd have to give her at least a half an hour head start so she could strip her girdle off before he got there. Either that or make spandex tug-of-war into sexual foreplay.

Margot started to wiggle and shake and tug the girdle off her breasts. The right boob popped out like a rounded hunk of Styrofoam bobbing up to the surface of a lake. Struggling to free the left mammary, she started to slip off the toilet, the spikes of her shoes unable to balance on the curve of the toilet seat cover. As her legs flew out from underneath her, the left breast popped out, sporting red ribs where the spandex had dug in. Margot cried out when her tailbone, unprotected by fat, hit hard on the seat.

"You ok in there?" a girl's cheerful voice cried out from the bride's room.

"Fine!" Margot called back as she locked both the doors into the room. Sitting was better anyway. She could slide the rest of her bondage down her body. The waist rolled off easily and, although the tush required a bit of bump and grind, it was Margot's feet that clung hardest to the girdle. It finally came off, turned totally inside out with both her shoes trapped inside it.

Breathing and sitting comfortably for the first time all night, Margot smiled. She snatched her dress off the floor and flung it over her head, glad of the tousle it made of her hair. No more hair spray, Margot told herself. Let it fly and be free. Margot reapplied her lipstick and put on her shoes. She was ready to get out there, sit down and have a good time. She stepped back onto the toilet to look at the full effect of her transformation and began to weep.

14. Phone Sex

" 'SO, WHAT ARE YOU *wearing?' David asks.*

'*Nothing,' Grace says even though she has on jeans and a T-shirt.*

On the couch, Grace reaches down the front of her jeans.

'*So? What are you doing to me now?' she wants to know.*

'*I'm pulling your body into mine, and I'm tracing my hand along your inner thigh. Do you like it?' he asks*

'*I love it. Tell me about my breasts,' Grace says.*"

"I thought the group decided to move away from erotica and was writing about technology," Aimee interrupted.

"It is about technology," Brooke answered, looking up from her manuscript.

"How is it about technology?"

"They're having sex on the phone."

"Oh. I get it. I didn't get that, Brooke. You have to make it clearer in the first paragraph or I'm just confused," Margot said.

"Confused? Really? About what?"

"Well, I'm wondering why he's not touching her," Margot said.

"Didn't I make that clear?" Brooke asked.

"Not to me. Aimee, did you get that it was phone sex?"

"No. Not at the beginning," Aimee agreed, although that wasn't the point she was trying to make.

"I mean," Margot continued, "I thought it might be something, some barrier between them, because he was touching his penis and she was looking out the window."

"Actually," Aimee said, "I liked that part."

"He's holding his penis and she's looking out the window doesn't just scream phone sex?" Brooke asked.

"Nope. Not for me," Margot said.

"I thought when he said, '*What are you wearing,*' that it was such a classic phone sex line that the situation was understood," Brooke said.

"Oh yeah, that's a phone sex line," Margot said, thinking about it. "But you know, Aimee and I still both missed it, so maybe it's not enough of a clue. I think we would enjoy the whole piece more if the phone sex thing was clear from the beginning. Although I like the idea of burning desire at odds with physical limitations yet they manage to get themselves off with what they have at hand, no pun intended."

"I guess I could spell it out."

"I think you should."

"Can you really get off on phone sex?" Aimee asked, wondering if there was some possibility of reaching across her belly and the miles to Tokyo. Sex had held them together through poverty; maybe sex could work its magic against his sudden prosperity.

"Yeah. I mean it's not the best. I suggested phone sex

to this guy I had in Paris and he answered '*ma sex n'est pas si long*,' or roughly translated, 'my penis isn't long enough,' you know I mean to cross the Atlantic. It was funny at the time. Why is everyone so quiet?"

Lux did not stand apologetically at the door and wait to be invited in. She opened the conference room door, entered, and sat down.

"Sorry I'm late."

They had not spoken to Lux since the hair-pulling episode. She called in sick the Tuesday prior (and had, in fact, been looking very run-down and tired lately). She never did show up for the wedding, according to Brooke, who had stayed drinking and dancing as late as the syna-gogue would allow. Aimee had grown tired and split around 11 p.m. Margot disappeared before dinner.

Lux sat down at the conference table and took out her notebook and a pencil.

"Good to see you," Brooke said.

Aimee glared at Brooke. Aimee had said she didn't want Lux in the writers' group anymore. She thought it was too dangerous. Lux was too dangerous. Lux didn't know how to behave. And so they decided to stop invit-ing Lux. They would continue to meet, but not tell Lux when and where. And yet, here was Lux taking her place at the head of the table. Brooke looked very pleased.

"Um," Lux said, "thanks. I, ah, haven't had a chance to write anything cuz I've been busy with something and Brooke said you'd switched to writing about technology so I'm gonna have to think about that for a while but I, you know, I'm gonna listen if that's ok."

"Why didn't you come to the wedding?" Brooke asked Lux.

"What wedding?" Lux replied, looking at them blankly.

"Saturday night. Teddy's wedding," Brooke pressed.

"I don't know anyone named Teddy."

"Trevor's son, Teddy," Margot said it a little too loud, as if Lux should know. And a second later Lux understood. Trevor had a son named Teddy and Teddy had gotten married over the weekend and everyone in the room, except Lux, had been invited.

"Oh right, Teddy," Lux said with unusual composure. "Why would I be invited to Teddy's wedding?"

Well you're fucking his dad, aren't you, was the thought Margot did not share with the group.

"Don't feel bad," Aimee said.

"Why should I feel bad?"

"I mean, it's just the way it goes." Aimee kept talking even though she had nothing to add.

"Just the way what goes?"

"Just the way men are," Aimee said flatly, although the words were thick with meaning. Lux wondered if Aimee was doing that thing called "irony" that she'd been reading about. Irony was a tricky thing, and Lux was struggling to understand it.

"Ok, so who's presenting today?" Lux said, also flat, but devoid of irony. She just wanted to get on with it.

"Brooke," Margot informed her. "Something about Grace and David and they're about to have sex."

"I thought we moved on to technology," Lux said.

"Phone sex," Margot and Brooke said at the same time.

"Ok, I'm just not quite ready to give up the previous topic," Brooke said defensively.

"It's all right by me," Lux said.

"You're barely a human being."

Aimee said it and, although it seemed like a non sequitur to the rest of the women, it flowed perfectly from the line of thoughts in Aimee's head that went from (a) she doesn't belong here, to (b) she never once apologized for what she did to me, to (c) Trevor's fucking her but didn't invite her to his son's wedding and she doesn't even *care*.

Lux sighed. She looked out the window and wondered if this writers' group, which had been so full of promise, was going to fall apart or become a stupid waste of time, just like everything else. Aimee's furious comment bounced off Lux because Lux did not doubt that she was, in fact, a human being. She immediately understood that Aimee hated her (but who cares), wanted her to leave the room (which she would do when she was good and ready), and that there was no danger of physical violence. That meant, to Lux, that she could do as she pleased. So Lux sat in her chair and stared blankly at Aimee, waiting for her to say something interesting, something that had meaning.

"You're an idiot!" Aimee started. "How can you let him use you like that? How can you have so little concern for yourself, for your body. He's just using you for sex."

"You think?" Lux said laughing. Of course Trevor wanted her for sex. Every man she'd ever known wanted her for sex. What did Aimee think she and Trevor were doing together? Washing windows? And suddenly the ball dropped for her, but on another subject entirely. Is this what was meant by irony?

"No, I think he loves you," Aimee answered, using irony too subtle for Lux to understand. "Yeah. I think he's so lonely after his divorce that all he wants is to get married again and you're the perfect wife number two because you're so young and beautiful and full of life. You can give him that second family that he's longed for now that his children are grown up and out of the nest. He loves you because you're so special, Lux, and all he wants is to make you his very own."

Lux's blood ran a little cold at the very thought of it. Belonging to someone was slavery as far as Lux knew, and she was doing everything possible to own herself. Just yesterday morning Trevor had grilled her about where she'd been all weekend, wanting to come help her take care of her sick but fictional friend. He wanted to know why she was so tired when she came back to him on Sunday night, who she'd been with, what she'd done.

"Aimee," Brooke said, cautioning her old friend against pushing Lux too hard.

"Yeah, that's enough. Let's call it. Maybe we'll get together again next week," Margot said.

"I'm sorry," Aimee reflected. "I'm just being honest. So the poor girl doesn't waste her time."

Margot, planning a quick exit, gathered up her things. She didn't want to look at anyone so she kept her eyes glued to the table where they raced over Lux's open notebook. There she saw a list of words written in Lux's childish scrawl:

Louis the 14th—some french king
pat-ay—some kind of food? or drink???
To throw caution to the wind—not giving a fuck
brazeer—a fancy word for bra
la-siv-ee-us—(sexy? dirty?)

Ha! thought Margot, she's using us for vocabulary insights. She'll never find the meanings of those words until she learns how to spell them. Someone should help her with the spelling.

Aimee pushed passed Margot on her way out the door, leaving Brooke and Lux alone in the conference room. Brooke smiled at Lux.

"Sorry," Brooke said. "She'll get over it. I'll have a talk with her."

"Forget about it. It's not important."

"Yes, it is."

"What? That some girl don't like me? I got my own road."

Brooke looked at Lux and decided to do whatever she could to become Lux's friend. Not because she thought she could help Lux, but because Lux was so damn interesting. Because Brooke visualized everything in the world as graphics that might lead to paintings, she imagined Lux's naked body in the lower right-hand corner of a large canvas, her skin glowing against the long red ribbons of stories that flowed freely and luxuriously from her head, becoming everything else in the painting, from the red couch that she reclined on to the roses in a glass vase on a table.

"You, ah," Lux started, "do you want to read your thing to me?"

"Nah." Brooke sighed. "The mood's gone."

"Yeah."

"I'm sorry about Aimee," Brooke said.

"Yeah, whatever. I crashed her club, her personal art party and she's pissed. Whatever, I needed to hear the words."

"Our words?"

"The stories."

"Why don't you just read a book?" Brooke asked.

"Cuz books don't have any mistakes in them. They're so cleaned up but when, like, when, you know you're reading and it's something you just wrote and you're excited about it and you're reading it out loud for maybe the first time and the good parts are really good and, let's say you get to like, a dull part, something you didn't know was going to be dull, and as you're reading it you know it just don't work, and we know that it don't work and you're like embarrassed because it's happening right now and we're listening and wow, there's like all this drama going on in the room, and that…"

Lux stopped speaking so she could think for a minute.

"I need that drama," she continued. "I like it. I need that kind of contact and human stuff to live. And I don't care if you guys don't like me. It's not like you're gonna break my fingers or anything."

Brooke laughed at the absurdity of breaking Lux's fingers.

"No," Brooke agreed, "your fingers are safe with us."

"Yeah. Well. Thanks. I gotta go. If the club meets next week I'm gonna be here and fuck Aimee. And I mean that last part metaphorical, not literal."

"Metaphorical*ly*. Literal*ly*. They're adverbs, not adjectives. They describe *how* you mean, or rather how you don't mean to fuck Aimee. Respectively."

Lux opened her notebook and added a new thought about adverbs to her list of discoveries she didn't fully understand and needed to consider further. She also added the word "respectively."

"Thanks," she said, slamming her book shut. Brooke gathered up her things and wanted to ask Lux if she would come model for her. It would mean traveling and giving up several evenings or weekends to sit in the studio. Brooke decided to start out with something kind to make Lux feel good before she invited her to come out to the studio.

"Listen, don't worry, Lux," Brooke earnestly said. "You're a special girl. I'm sure Trevor really loves you very much and he does want you all for his own."

"You think?" Lux asked, fear replacing irony.

Brooke was trying to be kind and so she warmly said, "Oh yeah, honey, I'm absolutely sure of it."

The women gathered their things and walked together towards the door. Pulling the handle, Lux swung too hard and it banged against the opposite wall, leaving a deep gouge in the drywall the size of the doorknob.

15. *The Shower*

"IT WAS JUST SO damn sweet," Aimee said to Brooke as she waddled out of her apartment building into the warmth of the summer day.

"Honey, don't think about it," Brooke said, but Aimee could not stop her brain from rerunning the episode again and again. They stepped onto the street and Brooke slid her sunglasses onto her nose to escape the great, bright, golden sunshine. Aimee fumbled in her purse looking for glasses that would hide the dampness of her eyes. As they walked, Aimee retold the tale.

"I mean, he actually fainted," Aimee said. "Not right away, but after in the waiting room, and practically at my feet. He said it was because he saw the needle come so close to the baby on the monitor screen and he just panicked. Even though his wife and their baby were perfectly safe."

"Some husbands are just more, I don't know, Aimee. All husbands are different. That woman's husband probably faints a lot."

"Yes, but not all husbands take a call in the middle of

the amniocentesis," Aimee said as she shoved her sun-glasses aside and blew her nose.

"He didn't!" Brooke said and stopped in the middle of the sidewalk to turn to her friend.

"As the needle was going in," Aimee admitted.

"What did you do?"

"Well, I started to cry. And he asked me if the needle hurt me! Can you believe it?"

"Did it?"

"What?"

"Hurt?"

"Well, some. I mean it's a huge, fat needle. But not enough to make you cry."

"So what did you do?"

"I told him to get the hell off the phone."

"Did he?"

"He did. 'I gotta go, Sheila-darling,' he says. 'I'll call you back later.'"

"Who is Sheila-darling?" Brooke asked suspiciously.

"His agent. She's a tall, older lesbian. Steel gray buzz cut. Horn-rimmed glasses. Barks when she talks. Not that it matters who it was."

"I'm so sorry, Aimee."

"I called a divorce lawyer," Aimee admitted.

"Can you divorce a guy for talking too much on his cell phone?" Brooke asked. And then, "What'd he say?"

"He gave me some idea of what I can expect in terms of child support, alimony."

"No, I meant, what did your husband say," Brooke asked.

"My husband got on a plane last night for Ecuador to

shoot girls in bikinis. From there he's going on to Bucharest for a car commercial and then back to Tokyo for more rock bands."

"Did you tell him you wanted a divorce?" asked Brooke.

Brooke stopped in front of a small, charming Italian café on Cherry Lane. She opened the door and motioned Aimee inside.

"Come on, the party is in the back," Brooke said.

"I told him I was thinking about it. That I'd had enough and that he had to be here for me during the pregnancy," Aimee said as she walked to the back of the café, keeping an eye out for pastel streamers and paper cutouts of storks. "So he hands me this check for $26,000."

"That's a lot of money," Brooke said.

"That's just one paycheck for the last month he worked in Tokyo. Gives me a speech about how expensive it is to raise a kid. He says how can I chuck seven years of good times when he's trying to be responsible. He says he's inches away from being famous and that's why he has to be on it all the time. I'm glad he's doing well. I mean, $26,000 is a lot for one month. Still, the test took all of twenty minutes. He could have turned off his frigging phone."

Aimee stopped when she saw Margot waving at her from a booth in the back of the restaurant. The table was set for three. There were no pastel streamers and no paper cutouts on the table. Not that Aimee wanted streamers and decorations; she just expected something more than a back booth set for three.

"Is this it?" she said to Brooke, trying to look happy about the minute attendance at her baby shower.

"Uh-huh," Brooke grunted and sat down.

"We ordered for you already," Margot said. "We're all having pasta."

Aimee stood there, wondering where her mother was. Her mother offered constant love and support. She once drove from north Jersey to lower Manhattan in the middle of the night because Aimee's purse, along with her house keys and home address, had been stolen and Aimee was afraid to stay alone in the apartment. Certainly she would show up for Aimee's baby shower. Had Brooke forgotten to invite her? Where was Brooke's mother? Where were the friends from college whom she just assumed would be flying in from the Midwest? This was her baby shower? Where was the celebration?

"Come sit down," Brooke said, and eventually, Aimee took a seat in the booth, opposite Margot.

"My mother said she was coming," Aimee murmured as she looked about the restaurant, hoping to see a familiar face.

"She's stuck in traffic," Margot said as she slid a piece of paper across the table to Aimee.

"This is my gift," Margot said.

Aimee unfolded the thin piece of glossy paper to reveal an advertisement for an electronic baby monitor torn from a magazine.

"Top of the line," Margot assured her. "I had it delivered to your apartment. Less to carry."

"Thanks," Aimee said. She just assumed when Brooke said "baby shower" that she would spend the day as the center of attention, opening too many beautifully wrapped gifts. She would have liked to be awed by the generosity and care that her friends put into picking out things for her baby. She even wanted to wear a silly hat made of bows stuck on a paper plate.

"I was telling Margot about that photo you wanted to shoot," Brooke said, interrupting Aimee's well-deserved moment of internal self-pity.

"What photo was that?" Aimee asked.

"Yesterday on the phone. You started to tell me you wanted to shoot a pair of lovers, but we got interrupted and you didn't tell me the rest of it."

"Oh, right. Well. I mean, maybe after the baby, I guess, I had this idea to shoot a man and a woman, embraced, kissing, touching, but I want the camera to be placed somewhere almost between them, as it were," Aimee said, happy to be distracted away from everything her baby shower lacked.

"Well, how would you do that?" Margot asked. "Would you put the camera between their bodies and then I don't know, set a timer? That's how Brooke thought you might do it."

"No, no. I'd build a platform out of Lucite."

"Oh! Wow, sure. That would work. How would you build it?" Brooke asked.

"Well, um, I suppose if I had a carpenter at my disposal I would build a proper platform, except the floor of the platform would be see-through. But if it was just me, it could be just a couple of cinderblocks with a piece of clear, heavy plastic lying across it. The models would lie on the plastic, and I'd be underneath them."

"So, it would have to be at least three feet high, right Aimee?" Brooke asked. "So you could get that belly under it."

"Well, yeah. I mean, if I were going to do it now. But it's really just a fantasy," Aimee admitted.

"It would have to be good quality. Very clear, clean plastic," Margot said to Brooke.

"And what kind of camera?"

"Gee, I like my 35mm. It's fast. But, I mean, if we're talking about the fantasy shoot, I think I'd like to try out a digital camera. One of those huge mega-pixel cameras, so you could blow the image up really big."

"Nikon?" Brooke asked.

"Well, I am a Nikon girl," Aimee said, laughing, trying to make the most of her afternoon with girlfriends.

"Excuse me, I need to use the restroom," Margot announced abruptly. Aimee watched Margot head over to the toilets. She saw her whip out her cell phone and start dialing long before she got to the bathroom door.

"What's with her?" Aimee asked Brooke.

"She's got a bladder the size of a peanut, I guess," Brooke said, laughing. "Not me, I can hold it all day. I'm a camel-bladder."

"I used to be a camel, now I'm a peanut. So I know how it is," Aimee said, sympathetic to Margot's toilet-ward flight.

The waiter came with salads and Margot returned from the restroom looking very pleased with herself.

"Shouldn't we wait for my mom?" Aimee asked as her friends dug into their lunch.

"She's gonna meet us back at the…" Brooke began.

"At your apartment," Margot interrupted. "She called while I was in the washroom. Traffic's so bad she's going right to your apartment."

"Oh," said Aimee, "that's too bad."

Aimee picked at her salad, but polished off the pasta and a piece of cake. Margot took several more calls on her cell phone during their lunch. Although she was polite enough to rise up from the table and take the call privately, Aimee wished she would shut the damn thing off. Brooke tried to cover for Margot with charming conversations and gossip about old friends. It still stung though, that Toby and Ellen and Connie had not come out for her party. Even Brooke's mother could have gotten into the car and made it into the city. All too quickly Aimee's baby shower was over. Margot and Brooke split the check and then hurried her out of the restaurant.

"I'll see you guys later," Margot said as she jumped into a cab.

"Well then, see you later," Aimee said to the disappearing red taillights of Margot's taxi. It was then that Aimee realized Margot was wearing blue jeans and flat shoes. That's odd, Aimee thought as she turned and headed for home. Margot never wore blue jeans. Brooke was already hanging an arm out for her own cab.

"I'll see you, Brooke," Aimee said. "Thanks for lunch."

"No, no," Brooke insisted, "your mom called. She's in Soho. Wants us to meet her there."

"My mother doesn't know anyone in Soho."

"Really? Well, she called from a place on Wooster Street. Says she wants us to meet her there, ok?"

"My mother is on Wooster?" Aimee asked.

"Yeah."

Aimee tried to imagine her suburban mother with her A-line skirt and tucked-under hairdo standing on Wooster Street in Soho, staring at the upscale freaky people as they walked by.

"Uh, could you ask her to meet me at my apartment? I'm kind of tired," Aimee said. And then she didn't say, and I'm really disappointed in your idea of a baby shower and I want to go home and get into bed.

"Well, you can rest your eyes in the cab," Brooke told her. "We gotta get over to Wooster Street and meet your mother."

"Fine," Aimee said as she heaved her belly into the open door of the taxi. She sat there and did not move. Did not slide herself down the seat so Brooke could get in too. In the end, Brooke had to run around to the other side of the taxi to get in.

"Sixty-four Wooster," Brooke told the driver as she slammed the door shut.

They arrived in Soho and found Aimee's mother standing on the sidewalk in her denim A-line skirt and comfortable shoes. She had a big black camera bag on her shoulder and a cell phone stuck to her ear.

"This is Mama Bird, the Eagle has landed," Aimee thought she heard her mother say into the little phone before snapping it shut.

"Hi Mom," Aimee said as she threw her belly out of the cab. "Why weren't you at my lunch?"

"I needed to pick up a few things—" Aimee's mother began, and when a panicked Brooke frantically mimed turning a steering wheel behind Aimee's back, added, "and the traffic was really bad across the bridge."

"Oh," said Aimee, who had not seen Brooke's bad acting, "well, what do you want to do?"

"I need a cup of coffee."

"Ok," Aimee said, "but a quick one. I'm a little tired."

"Come this way," Brooke said and ushered Aimee into a doorway on the street. While Aimee chatted with her mother, Brooke's finger leaned towards the third floor buzzer. Before she could hit it though, a well-muscled man opened the door. He was carrying a carpenter's tool-box and he nodded to Brooke as he let them into the building.

"It's all set," the carpenter said as he left the building.

Brooke looked away and Aimee assumed the carpenter was either schizophrenic or talking into a really, really small cell phone.

"Where are we going?" Aimee asked.

"Third floor," her mother said.

"It's a private café that just opened," Brooke said as she swung open the door.

"Oh, that's interesting," Aimee said. At another time she might have been more curious, more suspicious as to what her friend was planning, but the pregnancy and the disappointing baby shower and her general fatigue combined to allow her to focus on only one thing at a time. At the moment, Aimee was looking at Brooke's shoes.

"I don't think I've ever seen you wear sneakers before, Brooke."

"Really?"

"Really."

"I wear them. Sometimes."

Aimee allowed herself to be ushered into the doorway of 64 Wooster Street. She didn't ask "What the heck are we doing?" or "Are private café's legal?" as they rode the elevator up to the third floor.

"What are those?" Aimee asked still fixating on Brooke's shoes. "Are those Tretorns?"

"Keds," Brooke said with a smile.

"Wow, Keds," Aimee said suddenly filled with misplaced emotion for Brooke's sneakers. "That's so sweet."

"You ok, baby?" her mother asked as they got off the elevator.

"Just tired," Aimee said. She planned to spill the whole story to her mother later, when they were alone in her apartment. She would tell her about his blasé attitude at the amniocentesis, about the second-rate baby shower, about how joy, like a bad boyfriend who didn't know how to return a phone call, seemed to be avoiding her lately.

"This way," Brooke instructed as she lead them to a door marked 3F. She opened the door and entered. Aimee and her mother followed.

Shuffle, whisper, shuffle and then the lights jumped on.

"Surprise," shouted a chorus of friends. Margot was there, and Ellen from college, and Toby from high school. Surrounded by a band of smiling girlfriends and her mother, Aimee, for a moment, felt the love she had been longing for.

"Oh! Oh!" Aimee gasped. "Here you are! Toby! Oh my gosh, you lost so much weight! Ellen! How *are* you?"

Aimee hugged and kissed all of them, except the two

people she didn't know, a man and a woman, sitting on stools, dressed in bathrobes. They chatted with each other near the window.

"Why didn't you all just come to the restaurant?" Aimee asked. "We could have had lunch there."

"This isn't lunch, Aimee," Brooke said.

"This is work," Margot said as she handed her a digital camera.

"These are a little dusty," Aimee's mother scolded as she swung Aimee's camera bag off her shoulder.

"I got the Nikon D70," Margot said. "I don't know if it's good, or what you want, but when you added that thing about wanting to try out a digital, we were a little unprepared so I had to take whatever they had at the rental place."

Aimee turned the beautiful camera over in her hands.

"When did I say I wanted to try out a digital camera?" Aimee said, almost whispering.

"Today at lunch. Two lovers, entwined, shot from somewhere within their tangle of bodies," Brooke rattled off as if it were a menu item and not an aesthetic description. It was then that Aimee looked around and realized she was not in just any loft on Wooster Street. It was a photo studio. One of the white walls on the far side of the room folded gently into the white floor giving the illusion of endless space. There were scrims and lighting trees all around waiting for her to call them to action. And her friends were there, all standing around in jeans and T-shirts and comfortable shoes, happy to assist her in making some pictures.

"We figured this would be more fun for you than

lunch and a bunch of pastel-wrapped presents," Brooke said when Aimee stood there, staring at them. And then the tears started.

"Oh my god! Oh my god! You guys are so great. Oh! This is wonderful! Oh wow!" Aimee gushed and cried the skin cream right off her face. Everybody had to be hugged and kissed and told how wonderful they were all over again before Aimee was ready to get to work. The sight of the Lucite platform, built to Aimee's specifications, elicited more tears and sniffles.

"There's another shoot coming in at seven," Margot warned, "so you better not start crying again."

The models at the window stopped chatting and shed their bathrobes, revealing two beautiful naked bodies.

"Ok, ok, let's go then," Aimee began and her mind began to click in that oh so pleasant way. "I want the soft box over here, and Toby, if you could get me a card to bounce some light. Margot, stand by with the digital. I'm going to start with my own camera. Ellen, will you load for me?"

"What do you want us to do?" the naked model asked Aimee.

"Onto the platform and we'll start with some kissing," Aimee instructed.

Lying underneath two naked strangers in a plastic box made Aimee feel sweaty, young, and strong. The old groove came back and she clicked and shouted instructions and encouragement. She was looking for an image that described what it was like to be inside passion. The models, who did not know each other before entering the studio, straddled and squatted and licked each other. The man had a nipple ring and the woman was pierced in an even wider variety of places. They started off being rough, and even a little cold with each other. Aimee went with it for a while, but that wasn't where she wanted to end up.

"What's your name?" Aimee asked the naked, pierced woman.

"Enid," she said.

"Ok, Enid, this is Brock. Is that your real name, Brock?"

"Uh, no. It's my professional name," he said.

"What's your real name?"

"Tom."

"Ok. Tom, this is Enid. Be kind to her."

Aimee's simple instruction relaxed the models. With an eye on the clock, Aimee found the moments she was looking for as the hands swept from 4:30 to 7 p.m.

"I gotta call it," Brooke said. "The next booking is coming up the elevator."

Aimee smiled. She wrapped her arms around Brooke and hugged her.

"Thanks," she said. "This was great."

"Ok, guys," Brooke called to their friends. "That's a wrap. Come on back to Aimee's and we'll look at what we shot today."

Back at Aimee's, Margot, with some help from Aimee' mother, plugged the digital Nikon directly into Aimee's big TV. The images of Aimee's creation flicked by, showing a hard woman growing soft.

"That one," Aimee shouted, pointing to the image on the screen. "That's the one I want. What number is it? Could someone mark it down for me, please?"

"I like the way she's kind of stretching her body to find where he's touching her," Toby said.

"And the shadow of him falling across her is terrific," Brooke commented.

Only Aimee's mother seemed disturbed about the day. She had separated herself from the black-clad mass of Aimee's friends, fixed herself a plate of food and wandered over to inspect the pile of pastel-colored baby presents.

"You alright, Mrs. C.?" Brooke asked.

"Yes, I'm fine."

"You seem upset."

"Well, it's just that. Well. I just can't understand why a woman would want that," Aimee's mother said.

"You mean a photo shoot instead of a baby shower?" Brooke asked.

"No, I mean a pierced earring on her woo-woo," Aimee's mother said with a nod to Enid, who was sitting in a quiet corner of Aimee's apartment chatting intimately with Tom.

"Well," Brooke began and then paused as if she were actually considering the full spectrum of psychological impulses that would cause a woman to pierce the lips of her vagina, "I think a clip-on would just hurt too much."

Aimee's mother laughed.

"And besides, you know, clip-ons can be so gaudy," Brooke added, causing Aimee's mother to guffaw again.

"Do you think Aimee's happy with the baby shower?" Aimee's mother asked.

"Let's go find out," Brooke said as she walked Aimee's mother across the apartment and joined the chattering on the couch.

"Are you happy with what you shot?" Brooke asked Aimee.

"Oh yes. There's one in particular that I'm going to blow up huge," Aimee said. "Thank you for the day. It was perfect."

"Come get something to eat," Brooke said.

"Oh, like I haven't been shoving it in all day long," Aimee said.

Aimee sat on the couch with her friends and ate and opened presents. They oohed and ahhed over the little clothes and toys, and one by one they left the apartment. Toby had a train to catch and Ellen was only passing through the city on her way to Europe. In the end, after kissing her mother and hugging Brooke and Margot, Aimee was left alone in her big apartment with her belly and her gifts and the fantastic photographs she created that day. It was, Aimee would tell her mother on the phone later that night, the best day ever.

16. Bugs and Mice

*L*UX'S PENCIL STOPPED DEAD on her notebook. *If I wasn't so afraid of bugs and mice, I would run through the woods with the dog in the night. I could break bones breaking chains that bind my arms to my side and...* And? The pencil tap-tapped on the word "and." She didn't know what else to write after "and." The word seemed to hang there. Sometimes she wrote "but" instead of "and." Still the next phrase would not materialize in brain or on paper. The images had been chasing her for weeks and she had come to believe that when she found the rest of the words she would know what to do about her life, at least for a little while.

Trevor entered from the bedroom in a bathrobe, half his face still showing the pillow marks. He padded sleepily around his kitchen, poured himself a glass of juice, and stared at Lux while he drank it.

"Where have you been lately, sweetheart?"

Lux kept her eyes on her notebook. *It all starts out so good until you come to "where you been, bitch?"* Trevor spoke softly, used the proper helping verb ("have"), a gentle endearment ("sweetheart") and the extra word ("lately"), which implied a more random request for information. But that didn't make it any better for Lux. In Lux's experience, any conversation that starts with "Where you been" ends with a bruise on the arm or a bite on the ass.

"I told you already, I was helping Jonella with the baby cuz she's been sick."

"Yes, but…"

"That's what happened," Lux said so firmly he knew she was hiding something.

"I understand but, um, is everything ok?"

"Yes," Lux said.

"Yes, what?"

"Yes, Trevor, everything is ok, why the fuck didn't you invite me to your son's wedding?"

Trevor stopped as guilt hit him square in the face. I didn't invite her to the wedding and now the little bunny is angry with me, he thought as he misunderstood what she was saying. Trevor believed that because Lux was shouting at him about being left out of the party that she was angry at him about being left out of the party. It was not true. Lux couldn't give a rat's ass about Teddy's wedding. Lux was afraid and she was doing her best to avoid getting hit, or even worse, bitten.

"Parry" was one of the vocabulary words on Lux's list of concepts and phrases that she wished to own and operate. Once she got the right spelling and found a dictionary, she learned that it means 1) to ward off weapon or attack; 2) to avoid answering a question directly. Every fight Lux ever had, even the battles she won, ended with a new bruise on her body because she had never heard the word "to parry" and therefore did not understand that she could also defend herself by moving away. She liked the concept and was working on perfecting it. Her inquiry as to the location of her wayward wedding invitation was a defense disguised as an attack. This was far too complicated for Trevor to understand. Nor should he be expected to.

"The wedding. Yes. Damn, Lux, I'm sorry. That was a horrible mistake. Is that why you're angry? The invitations went out weeks and weeks ago and my wife wrote up the guest list and, oh bunny, it was an awful night. You would have had a terrible time. I had a terrible time. But I should have brought you."

"I wouldn't have come, Trevor. I don't want to meet your ex-wife or your kids or any of those kinda of people in your life. Do you understand? I don't want to meet them."

"Oh. I see."

He didn't see. All he saw was Lux pushing away from him. He assumed she was disappointed with the realization of his limitations. She'd obviously seen the reality of his age and the smallness of his status in the world.

She appeared at his door last night looking tired and sweaty. Her hands were chapped and raw, as if she'd been swimming for too long or washing something in harsh detergents. He'd rubbed cream on her palms and fingers before he took her out to dinner. Over burgers and beer she quizzed him, first about compound interest, then Mozart, then how the stock market worked. What did the word "respectively" mean and how did you spell it. He knew all the answers and delighted in telling her how smart he was. Then they came home and made love in his bed. He fell asleep blissful.

At 9 a.m., she had jumped up out of his bed and made several calls to Carlos. They discussed paint and the location of keys. Trevor burned, knowing that Carlos was an old lover, an old, younger lover. He rolled over and tried to forget it. He closed his eyes and searched for her in his bed, but she was already gone. Up and about and getting ready for the day.

When he finally dragged himself out of bed, Trevor found his little bunny sitting at the table in the dining room, in love with her notebook, rereading the same page. She sat, comfortable in a panties and T-shirt as only a young woman could be, scratching her pencil around the page, half-naked and not paying any attention to him. And now this fight about the wedding. He wished he'd just invited her.

Trevor put down his glass of orange juice and crossed the apartment in three steps. He kneeled down on the floor next to Lux and grabbed her hand a little too hard. She pulled it away.

"What did you say to Carlos today?"

"Nothing much."

"Why did you have to call him so early."

"He's, ah, painting something for…my mom. I was supposed to let him into the…her house so he needs to know where keys are."

"Why don't I take you shopping today," Trevor said, employing his own awkward parry in response to her hesitant answer.

"No. I don't wanna," she said, not really looking at him. "I got stuff to do. And I still gotta get there and make sure Carlos doesn't fuck it up."

Lux went back to her notebook, reading the first two lines of her thoughts again, willing herself to find the third line that would certainly set her free. Trevor stood up, slowly as the floor had been hard on his knee. He had to have her, had to keep her. He wanted to remind her of how good it had been between them. He lifted up her hair, still wet from the shower and kissed her neck.

"Trev…"

"What?"

"Don't."

"Why not?"

"Cuz."

He slid his fingers down her hand and pulled the pencil out of her fingers. He stood her up, turned her around to face him and kissed her lips. He slid his hand into the waistband of the panties as he licked her neck and breasts, then her navel. He pulled off the lacy little thong.

The possibility of finding the third, perfect line evaporated. Lux stared at the top of his head, knowing she was meat. She didn't have enough words yet to express the nuances of what she was feeling at the moment so instead she just mooed like a cow.

"Moo," she said again as if the word meant something.

Trevor laughed, wondered if she was crazy. He took her moo as a signal to proceed because that's what he wanted to do.

Without the right words she could not hold or share the feelings that were raging around in her head. Without the right words the feelings couldn't even become thoughts that she could turn over and examine from any angle other than desperation. Brooke had said that Trevor loved her and wanted her for his own. But Carlos had once owned her and it took a beat down from her brother to get her freedom back. She did not want to be owned by Trevor, did not want to be owned by anyone ever again. Lux did not understand that the word "own" could be used to both to describe a possession and to imply a singular love and so she could only assume they were both equal to her experience of the word "own" when applied to her understanding of "love." That was a dark and ugly place to be, something to be avoided at all costs. She stood quietly and waited for Trevor's love to end.

Trevor was the king of cunnilingus. He was sure his wife had stayed with him several years longer than she wanted to because of it. She hated him but wanted custody of his tongue. No judge was going to order him to give it to his ex-wife every other weekend and so she had hung on as long as she could. He would make desperate, panicked love to her, hoping she would love his tongue enough to overlook the rest of his faults. It was happening all over again as Trevor used everything he had in an attempt to bind Lux to him to no avail.

She'd been here before. Not really in the mood. Other things on her mind. Sometimes Carlos could get her going, even when she didn't want to be revved up and turned over like a motor in his wrench. She stood there, waiting. Maybe Trevor had that magic too. Maybe when it was over she'd be glad he had insisted, but for now she was just mad. The thoughts and feeling were stuck in her chest like food that goes down the wrong pipe. She stood there letting him put his mouth in her crotch, waiting for Trevor to do something interesting.

She's a fucking mannequin, Trevor thought. When is she going to touch me, even lightly? He ran his tongue around the lips of her vagina and reaching the clitoris, believed he felt a spark of interest lighting up in Lux. She put her hands on his head at least and he took it as a sign to go further and deeper. When she finally started making some noise he pushed her back and entered her quickly. She rocked and moaned but when he looked in her eye the image reflecting back to Trevor was that of a thief, a bore, a brute, and Trevor lost his erection immediately.

Well, Lux thought, Mom said that happens a lot with older guys.

"Sorry," Lux said cautiously. She'd seen this part in a couple of different movies, the part where the guy can't get it up and so the girl gets killed. Trevor didn't seem the type, but wasn't Diane Keaton surprised when Mr. Goodbar started to beat her. Carlos could be really sweet too when he wasn't being a fucking asshole. You never could tell with guys. Best to play it safe.

Lux slid out from under Trevor.

"That was great, really," she said trying to sound upbeat and satisfied. Trevor sat down hard on one of his kitchen chairs. His naked body seemed to gray and lose animation as it sank into the vivid blue vinyl of the seat. Lux grabbed a quick shower, and then her keys.

"I'll call you later, Trevor," she promised and bolted for the door, heading out to meet Carlos and talk about paint.

17. Lord of the Rings

"ARE YOU OK?" MARGOT hissed at Aimee in the darkness.

"Fine, yeah, fine," Aimee whispered back as she found her seat in the theater again. She was puking about every four hours now, well up from last month's record of once or twice a day. The nausea was usually followed by thirst and an irrational hunger for protein that gave Aimee deep insight to all those vampire movies. She glared at hot dogs with the lust of Dracula's newly raised bride. She finished chewing the slice of sugared ginger that had been recommended by the health food store to settle her stomach and then started on the strips of roast beef she had smuggled with her into the movie theater.

"This is the best part," she whispered to Margot as Merry and Pippin set off a burst of stolen fireworks and Frodo, fearing the dragon had come to the shire to claim his beloved uncle, sheltered the older hobbit as best he could.

"But, didn't we just see these same characters come back here from a long journey? And didn't that short, white-haired man…"

"Hobbit."

"What?"

"Bilbo is a hobbit."

"Right. I knew that," Margot said. "The Bilbo hob-bitman, didn't he just sail away with all those elves and Frodo and the Gandalf guy? Why is he back?"

"Because," Aimee whispered, "that was part three. This is part one."

Brooke's head rolled too far forward and she woke with a startled snort.

"Huh? Oh. Hey, remember I wanna party with every-one on the island," Brooke said and then fell right back to sleep wedged between Aimee and Margot like the Dormouse between the Mad Hatter and the March Hare. Margot laughed and pushed Brooke's mouth closed so she would not snore.

"See, we came in at the tail end of part three and now we're back to part one," explained Aimee. "Now we get to watch the whole thing from the beginning."

"And that's a good thing?" Margot asked, unsure of the cost/benefit of such a time commitment.

Aimee nodded merrily and turned back to the screen.

Oh, why not, thought Margot as she dug into the goodie bag she had smuggled into the theater.

Earlier that morning, Margot had been sitting at home alone, feeling trapped, when she decided to call Aimee.

"Help me!" she giggled when Aimee answered the phone.

"What's up girl?" Aimee asked, glad to be of service

to Margot.

"I'm trapped in a circle, and I've got to get out before I bankrupt myself!" Margot wailed, laughing at the same time so Aimee wouldn't be too freaked out by her need.

"What happened?" Aimee asked.

"Well, usually it's not a problem but this month I just could not pay off my entire credit card bill and so I thought I would try to distance myself from my one true love," Margot began.

"And your one true love is who?" Aimee asked.

"Henri Bendel," Margot said as if it were obvious. "And so I made, not a spiritual choice, but an economic one and decided to spend the morning in my own kitchen, working on a new adventure for Atlanta Jane."

"Excellent choice."

"You'd think. So I start to make a very un-Margot-like list of all the possible things my Atlanta Jane could do. I start to type stuff like ride horses, save the town, make love to Peter, confront a crooked sheriff, go shopping."

"Go shopping?" Aimee asked.

"Exactly. I'm sitting there, staring at the blinking curser at the end of that delicious word 'shopping.' Atlanta Jane doesn't go shopping. I go shopping. And the thought whirled around in my brain in such a confusing way that I got right up from my desk, put on my sandals and went shopping."

"What'd you get?" Aimee laughed.

"Something good, but something kind of disturbing happened when I got to the store."

"What?"

"Ok, please don't think I'm silly but it was like this peace settled upon me as soon as I got out into the shops. I was making good decisions, narrowing the field, creating a terrific outfit and the annoying work of being a full human being kind of fell away."

"That's a problem?"

"Well, I'm not sure if I want shopping to be my best and only friend. It was like the pleasure centers of my brain were all ignited over a new pair of earrings. I bought a fabulous gray-green suit with this green-gray blouse to match."

"That'll go great with that string of peacock Tahitian pearls you got last week."

"Exactly. And then the sales girl scurried off to find some shoe/purse ensembles that they had not even unpacked yet."

"I love when they scurry," Aimee admitted.

"Oh god, yes! It makes me feel important, if only for a moment or two. So I buy the whole outfit and race home to try it on with the pearls. And here I am prancing around my apartment, and these thin elegant fabrics feel like protective armor, like a new, better skin. And I'm so happy and the problem of the day has been solved and then guess what happens."

"What?" Aimee asked and she really wanted to know.

"Atlanta Jane suddenly appears in my living room."

"You're kidding."

"No!"

"What was she wearing?"

"Her dusty buckskins and she was carrying a rifle. She looked good. She immediately began telling me off."

"Margot, you tell the best stories!" Aimee laughed. "So what'd the fictitious Miss Atlanta Jane have to say to you?"

"'What did you do today? What did you make today? Who did you talk to? Where are your friends? What about me?' She's scolding me in this flat twang. 'What are you doing with your life? That mismatched girl, Lux, she needs to be taken shopping. *You* need to have a human experience.'"

"She said that?"

"She did."

"So how are you going to make that happen?"

"I'm doing it right now, Aims. I'm calling you! Let's go do something today."

"Great!" Aimee sang, happy to be included in Margot's personal epiphany. "I was planning to spend the afternoon looking at paintings. Why don't you come with me?"

Aimee's Sundays used to be shared with her husband, wandering the halls of a museum or gallery looking at photographs. They never looked at paintings because they didn't interest him.

"I bet we can get Brooke to give us a tour of the Met," Aimee told Margot on the phone. "She was a docent there for a while, when her parents still lived on Fifth Avenue. You'll love it. She knows everything about the stuff in there."

"That's great. You want to call Brooke, or should I."

"Well, it's before 1:30, so you call her."

"What," Brooke groaned when her cell phone rang.

Margot quickly explained her need.

"Well, I usually sleep all day Sunday, but hey why not. I spent the night at Bill's house so I'm already in the city."

They met on the steps of the Metropolitan Museum to find it unpleasantly crowded. They stood in line for twenty sweaty minutes and Aimee's feet swelled until they looked like sausages.

"I'm sorry, I have to sit down," Aimee said. "It's ok if you want to go in without me."

"We're not going to abandon you and your chubby ankles," Brooke declared. "We just have to form a new plan."

Lunch was an option, and lunch plus *Lord of the Rings*, Aimee promised, would be even better. Aimee led her friends downtown.

They made individualized snack decisions at the deli before coming into the movies. Margot had carrots and sliced apples, Brooke got crackers, and Aimee bought beef. When Brooke stopped at the door of the building and eyed the movie poster with some concern, Aimee found the perfect words to reassure her.

"The theater is air-conditioned," Aimee promised.

Brooke fell asleep immediately, overwhelmed by the cool darkness and the previous evening's revelries. They'd quietly entered the theater close to the end of the third installment. The snacks were perfect and the movies lush and beautiful to look at. The characters were so very serious and Margot so very disinterested in do-or-die heroism that she laughed inappropriately at several moments.

Controlling herself, Margot struggled to understand why the salvation of Middle Earth was so important to her new friend.

She lasted through the final twenty minutes of the third movie and all of the first. When the second film started up again, when the half-naked Smeagol was captured by Sam and Frodo, Margot felt she had enough of this fantasy. The gray, starving, sexless skin and bones of the computer-generated character was too much for Margot. She was looking for a way to escape when Brooke woke up, declared herself hungry, and got up to pee.

"Come on, Aimee, let's go," Margot whispered to her friend and for good measure got up out of the chair and followed Brooke into the lobby. Aimee came lumbering after. Alone, she would have spent the whole day there. Still, she was surprised and pleased that the other women lasted as long as they did.

They picked a café and sat close to the restroom to accommodate Aimee's frequent need to pee and puke. Margot ordered a salad, Brooke a coffee, and Aimee a steak with potatoes, broccoli, and a chocolate milkshake.

"Why not," she laughed. "It all comes up anyway."

"How many times have you seen those movies?" Margot asked when the food came.

Aimee held up two fingers.

"Two times?"

"No, too many times."

More laughter and then Brooke, who was only just starting to wake up, spoke with some concern in her voice. Hiding was not something she imagined her old friend Aimee would happily indulge in.

"Why?" Brooke said incredulously.

"Why keep seeing a movie I like?" Aimee asked, already in defense mode. "Why not? I like that the men are so heroic and the women are so beautiful and the bad guys are really evil."

"They're probably not really evil," Margot said.

Brooke was staring at Aimee, trying to figure out the right way to begin her intervention against her friend's growing movie addiction. Margot filled the space by thinking out loud.

"It's bad press. The losers always get bad press. The story is written by a hobbit and he had obvious prejudices against Orts."

"Orcs."

"Whatever. I just mean that if you told the story from the other side you would see different issues."

"No," Aimee said. "The Orcs are evil."

"How do you know?"

"They're born evil."

"That's very un-American of you. Very undemocratic," Margot said, enjoying the hypothetical argument. "What if they change, grow beyond the limitations of their status? What if some little Orc-girl is born in the mud and shit and wants to raise herself up higher than what is expected of her?"

"It's not possible," Aimee said.

"There are no Orc girls," Brooke added helpfully. "The Orcs are an all-male race of beings."

"Oh, well, then they're totally fucked," Margot

laughed and speared a tomato with her fork. "Still, you have to agree that regarding the character of the Orcs, it is a rather one sided story."

"I like the guy with no eyebrows," Brooke said.

"What guy with no eyebrows?" Aimee asked, as her stomach began to turn sour.

"The guy who becomes the king," Brooke said, as if it were obvious which character in the movie had the least eyebrows.

"Aragorn?"

"Yeah, that's the one."

"He has eyebrows."

"Well, just barely and they're so close to his eyes you can't really see them, but, other than the eyebrows, a good man, I think. I mean from the parts I saw. Now that elf, he had serious eyebrows. Aimee, are you ok?"

Aimee jumped up from her chair and rushed to the bathroom.

"Is that normal?" Brooke asked.

"I think so. Being pregnant makes you sick, right."

"Yeah. That's true."

In the cramped space of the bathroom, Aimee held onto the sides of the toilet and threw up more than she thought she'd eaten. She felt hot and dizzy and nasty. She wanted to die or at least be in her own bed so she could lie down. And then there were tears that felt like a physical force in her head drilling through the front of her face to get out. She swallowed them down and up came more vomit. Aimee was on her knees, begging, "no, please no" as more came up, and then again. All the food was out of her stomach and only liquid came now, a smelly yellowish fluid.

At the table, Margot and Brooke were still analyzing their friend's obsession with the movie. Brooke kept looking from the door to the ladies' room and then back at her watch.

"She's been in there too long?" Margot asked.

"Yeah, I think so," Brooke said.

Margot got up from the table, followed by Brooke.

Aimee was still on her knees in front of the toilet, her feet thrust out the front of the tiny stall. One of her sandals had fallen off and she was crying.

"Hey, Aimee, you ok?" Brooke asked gently as she picked up the sandal.

"No. I ruined my dress."

"Is it ok if I open the bathroom door?"

"Ok," Aimee said in a small voice.

Brook opened the door, reached in and quickly flushed the toilet. She slapped the lid down and helped Aimee to her feet. Aimee sat down on the toilet seat and Brooke wiped the tears off her face. Margot peeked in.

"You ok, honey?"

"Yeah. I just wanna go home, though."

Margot grabbed a paper towel from near the sink and Brooke wiped away the thick yellow fluid from the front of Aimee's blue jumper.

"Is it because of what I said about the Orts?"

Aimee laughed a little, but the action was so close to crying that more tears came out.

"I'm gonna pay the check and get us a cab. We'll take you home," Margot said.

"I'm sorry I ruined the day."

"Oh honey, don't worry. The day was ruined for me the minute you suggested those stupid movies."

Aimee whimpered a little, afraid laugher would hurt and start her puking again.

"I think you should see a doctor."

"I will."

"I think you should see a doctor today."

"I have my regular appointment next week."

Margot stuck her head into the bathroom.

"I got a cab. You need help to the door?"

Aimee leaned on her friends and waddled to the door. Margot grabbed the several bags of extra food she had bought at the takeout counter and then the three of them got into the cab and zoomed Aimee back to her apartment.

Margot remade the bed with fresh sheets and Brooke helped settle Aimee into them. Before Aimee could say "I'm starving," Margot whipped out her shopping bags filled with the rest of their lunches, a whole chocolate cake, and dinner for Aimee to eat later, when she was alone. She also had several bottles of seltzer, not club soda.

"Thanks," Aimee said. "Thank you both so much."

They talked well into the night, hitting on hundreds of subjects. When they came back again to Aimee's favorite topic "What a Freak Show That Girl Lux Is," Brooke broke out from Aimee's domination of the subject.

"I think she's nice," Brooke announced.

"Ew, you're gross," Aimee laughed, licking the back of

a fork full of chocolate cake. "How can you be a friend of mine and her friend too?"

She would have said more but a deep cramp told her that another round of puke was coming. She didn't want to end the pleasant comfort of her friends in her room and cake in the bed by jumping up and running to the bathroom so she sat quietly hoping it would pass and miraculously, it did.

"I don't like her with Trevor," Brooke said.

"She's so wrong for him," Margot said too quickly and Aimee laughed.

"Margot!" Aimee teased. "You and Trevor?"

"We're friends. There was one kiss and then nothing."

"A kiss? When?"

"A couple of months after his wife left."

"Does he kiss good?"

"I thought so."

"And then what happened?"

"Nothing."

"Nothing?"

"I guess then he met Lux."

"That little bitch! She stole him from you."

"Hey!" Brooke said. "She didn't know our Margot had staked a claim on him."

Our Margot, Margot thought. I like that.

"I didn't stake any claim to him, Aims. I just kissed him."

Aimee didn't answer. When her friends looked over at her, both thought she had turned rather pale. Aimee was fully focused on herself and the burning sensation inside her body. Something was breaking inside, literally, not figuratively. Aimee froze in pain and when it abated for a moment, she kicked her legs, pushing friends and cake and covers off the bed. Aimee was bleeding.

A cab was too risky, the ambulance would take twenty minutes. Margot called the firm's car service; they could be there in five minutes. Margot and Brooke carried Aimee to the elevator in her nightgown. The car arrived a minute later.

"Lay down, lay down in back," Brooke shouted. "Margot, you ride shotgun and I'll hold her head back here.

"No, no, no, not shot, no gun. She's just bleeding," Margot was telling the hospital. "Yes, about six months. We're about fifteen blocks away. Right. Ok."

Margot snapped her phone shut and told the driver.

"The emergency entrance is on Seventh Ave."

The driver nodded and handed her the chit for her signature. Margot signed and entered the firm's billing code for client development.

"It's gonna be fine," Margot told Aimee as she signed for the car. Brooke was stroking the tears out of Aimee's eyes and telling her the same thing as they helped her into the ER.

"It's just way too early," the young doctor said as he examined Aimee. "She needs at least another six to eight weeks before she can breathe on her own."

"She?" Aimee asked. Margot and Brooke, both crowded into the examining room, looked up in surprise. Brooke clapped her hands with joy.

"Oh, sorry. Did you and your partner not want to

know? I'm sorry. I didn't read through the whole chart. Jeez, I'm sorry."

"It's all right," Margot said.

"I'm sorry, I ruined it for you both," the doctor said to Margot.

"I'm not the partner," Margot laughed. "I'm just the friend and transportation."

"Don't look at me!" Brooke said because he had looked at her in that way that needed such an exclamation.

"My husband's out of town for a while," Aimee said smiling at the thought of a daughter.

"Well, he should come back in town because as soon as we stabilize you, you're going to have to be on bed rest till the end."

"And what exactly does bed rest entail?" Brooke asked.

"Nothing," said the doctor as if nothing was really something very big indeed.

"Nothing?"

"You can't move or get up at all. We'll start you in here with a catheter. Next week you can start getting up to go to the bathroom, but then right back to bed."

"And she gets up for eating of course," Margot said.

"No. She can sit up in bed for the meal but then she lies back down."

"But I can't," Aimee started. "I have to go to work tomorrow. I have cases open all over my desk. I have attorneys waiting for my paperwork. I can't do nothing! I'll lose my job!"

"Your desk will still be there when you get back to it,"

Margot said. "And the firm covers a hundred percent salary for this kind of short-term disability. It's in the newest benefits package. This won't even eat into your sick days."

"But how am I supposed to do nothing!" Aimee wailed at the very thought of it.

"You can't take any pressure on your cervix or it will open up again," the doctor told her. "Your baby's only three pounds. Her lungs don't work yet. She needs to gain at least another two or you're gonna have trouble. Call your husband. You're spending the night here. Tomorrow night as well."

Aimee slept while Margot called. Then Brooke called, trying to track him down.

"He just stepped out," said the receptionist.

"You can try him at this number," said his agent.

"You is got the número incorrecto, idiota," stuttered an exasperated man the third time she called the number in Tokyo that was supposed to be his cell phone.

Everyone knew where he was but no one could actually get him to come to the phone in person. For two days they left messages and waited for him to call. At the end of the second day, Margot and Brooke came back to the hospital and took Aimee home.

"He'll call," Aimee promised as Margot tucked her into bed. Brooke had gone home and Margot was planning to spend the night.

"You don't have to," Aimee said.

"I want to," Margot smiled at her friend. She brought the TV and DVD player into Aimee's room and almost choked when Aimee asked for all of the *Lord of the Rings* DVDs to be stacked into the player.

"Don't tell Brooke, though," Aimee laughed. "She thinks I've got an addiction."

"Right now you do what makes you happy," Margot said, kissing Aimee's forehead. "But if that movie plays again I'm going in the other room and reading the paper."

"Go home. I'll be fine."

"Guess what, I don't have anything else to do," Margot confessed. "It's nice to be here with you. It's nice for me, I mean. I'm going to sit here and read over some things I need to look at for work. In a couple of hours I'll make us dinner. If you need anything give a shout."

Margot turned on the machines and handed the remote control to Aimee. As she left the room, she heard the low flute playing, signaling the beginning of another trip into Middle Earth. After about a minute Aimee switched off the TV and called to Margot.

"Hey, Margot, you wanna just come in here and talk?"

18. She Busy...

CARLOS SAT IN LUX'S apartment, surrounded by cans of bright white satin paint, masturbating. He had a full technique for whacking off that involved the gel his sister used for her hair. Corn oil was cheaper and much better for him and for the skin on his dick, but it was harder to transport. The sticky hair stuff got hotter in the friction of his hand, but if used too often, it gave him a rash. However, packaged in its handy tube, it was the fluid of choice for masturbating away from home.

Lying down on the drop cloth, Carlos had one hand stroking the long shaft of his penis and the other tucked up his shirt and curled around his own nipple. As his balls started to contract, his sphincter tightened and his breath came harder and harder. Just as it got so good, he slowed down the stroking of his hand and willed himself to stop. Carlos never came when he masturbated.

"Ooooooh!" Carlos groaned and crumbled into a fetal position on the floor of Lux's new apartment. He had been thinking about her and so it was particularly hard to control his desire to shoot sperm all over the floor. Lux, his first girl, the first one whose shoulders he had pushed down on until her knees bent and her mouth was level with his crotch, had been off-limits for four years. Joseph would cut him or cut him out if he ever messed with her again. Carlos assumed it had everything to do with Joseph's weird quasi-Catholic disapproval of his only sister's sexuality and nothing to do with the fact that he had twisted her pinky finger so far that it had fractured, the bone breaking through the skin.

He lay curled up on the hardwood floor of an apartment he didn't know she owned, trying to gain control of himself and the memory of her skin. He wanted to finish painting the trim before it got too hot. Maybe he'd take her to a movie if "Old Cock," as he liked to call Trevor, would let her out for a night.

The key in the lock made a clicking sound and Carlos jumped to his feet.

"Hey! What's with the chain?" Lux called from the hallway.

"I'm coming," Carlos called, even though he wasn't in any sense of the word. Carlos gently slid his still-rigid penis into his underwear and threw on his coveralls. He carefully opened up three cans of paint and set them out on the table before sauntering to the door.

"Who do you think's coming to get you?" Lux asked, indicating the safety chain with her cup of coffee.

"Just a habit," Carlos said, flipping it off its hook and opening the door.

"Fuck, you look beautiful," he said as she entered.

"Out of the frying pan and into the shit-eating fire," Lux said to him, knowing he would have no idea what she meant. He didn't care what she said and rarely listened to her, which had always given her the freedom to speak as she pleased.

"Do you think I swear too much?" was the next non sequitur to fall out of her mouth. She followed him down the small hallway that lead to the living room. Carlos didn't answer. He listened to her babble waiting for the odd phrase that made sense to him. Only then he would answer.

"Fuck you, Carlos!" she said as she entered the living room.

"What?" he answered.

"It's eleven o'clock! What did you do all morning?"

"First I got the paint. Then I had to find the keys and then when I opened the first can it didn't look right so I opened a few more and they didn't look right either so I was about to call you when you walked in the door."

Lux looked at the paint.

"What's wrong with it?"

"It's white."

"Yeah."

"I thought it was supposed to be…red."

Being the boss is weird, thought Lux. He's lying through his ass, but what am I gonna do?

"No," Lux said. "White is right."

"Good. All right so, unless you want to stretch out on the drop cloth and I'll go down on you, and you don't have to touch me at all, baby, it'll be all about you this time. Oh yeah, I can feel you in my mouth right now."

Carlos showed her his tongue whipping in and out of his mouth, shaking like a rattlesnake's tail, the very tip of his tongue accentuated and attenuated to a stiletto tip promising a dance of precision and intensity that, in Lux's experience, could only be matched by the Shower Massage by WaterPik.

Lux watched as Carlos kept working the muscles of his tongue. Trevor had lent Lux a weird, old book called *The Inferno* and showed her how to understand the words. She devoured the thing, laughing through the night as she read.

"What's so funny?" Trevor asked her. He lay beside her in his bed, reading a biography of a dead sports legend, answering her frequent vocabulary questions and marveling at the pleasure she took in reading.

"It's written funny," she'd told him. "But it actually makes sense once you know the code."

Limbo seemed stupid and unfair, Lux had declared, but she got a big kick out of the descriptions of wicked people in hell, suffering punishments appropriate to their sins: liars stuffed in shit up to their noses, lovers pounded by incessant winds because they subjected reason to desire. She thought it was good in a comic-book way. And yet, here in the living room of her new apartment, staring at her ex-boyfriend's flicking tongue, Lux discovered the pit of hell beckoning her down.

Carlos, she thought, Caaah-ah-ah-ah-arlos. Carlos and that sweet peach kiss could be all over my body and wipe out that total-failure thing that just happened with Trevor. All that could disappear in the intoxication of Carlos and his snake tongue. I could be arching my back and braying like a mule for twenty minutes or more, all the kinks in my muscles and my mind will wash away with the flow of spit and come down my thigh. Trevor doesn't own me, she bargained with herself. I just want to live in his house until I can buy a second apartment. I need at least twelve months of rent on this address before I got the down payment for another. And President Clinton said it wasn't sexual intercourse if you just use your mouth.

"No," Lux told Carlos, "you're gross."

"What?"

"Put that thing back in your mouth before you curdle the paint."

"Paint don't curdle."

"It would if you stuck that long, nasty thing in it. Now I got a tenant moving in here tomorrow and we ain't done none of the trim. So let's get going."

"Bossy bitch," Carlos said and then showed her the snake tongue again.

"You gonna put someone's eye out with that thing and then where'll you be?"

"Old Cock musta forgot where the cootchie lives and put his tongue in your eye. You poor, poor pussy."

Lux laughed.

"Yeah, just paint. I gotta hand over the keys at nine tomorrow, and I don't want the place smelling of paint."

"What do you care if it smells of paint?"

"Cuz. I. Want. To do a good job so they'll hire me again. It was good money, and it wasn't so hard."

"Cuz I did all the work."

He had done most of the work. He knew how to lay down tape so the off-white paint on the walls made good clean lines when it met the brighter white of the ceiling and trim. He'd found the guy to redo the hardwood floors on the weekend for cheap. For fifteen dollars per hour plus lunch Carlos had been her mule for six weeks.

"You did a good job, Carlos. If I get another one, we'll do it again."

"Ok. Yeah. You think you'll get another one?"

"I hope so."

"You pay under the table again?"

"Yeah."

"Ok, but you gotta do it and not tell Jonella cuz she and the city is all over my money with that child support bullshit."

"Your teeth are falling out," Lux said, and she meant it metaphorically.

"Uh huh," Carlos said as he tuned out and reset the filter that would alert him when she said something that had to do with him. Carlos dipped a clean brush in the bright white can of paint. She was one whacked-out girl. All the time he'd spent with her he could fill a book with the weird shit she said, if he had, you know, actually listened.

Lux watched him work. Tenants were moving in on Monday. Within a year she'd have her cash reserves back up to $30,000 at least. Her attorney told her she could buy another property right now using the equity of this apartment as down payment, but it seemed too crazy to her. She didn't really understand what he meant. And, because the attorney charged by the hour, Lux had intended to ask Trevor to explain the details about home equity this morning. And she would have if he hadn't been so obnoxious and possessive.

He'd called her cell phone four times in the half hour it took her to cross the park that stood between his apartment and hers. First to apologize, then to beg, then to cry. The fourth time she didn't take the call.

When Aimee said Trevor loved her and wanted her for his own it had seemed like nonsense. But then Brooke confirmed it. Lux thought Trevor liked her and wanted to have sex with her but that was all. He didn't want to keep her forever no more than she wanted to be his wife. She had planned to live at his apartment, having fun, sex, dinner, and conversation until he got tired of her and asked her to leave. Brooke had warned her that it was all a trap. And his behavior today proved it. Lux felt she had to act and act fast if she was going to save her life. She believed she had to get out before it was too late.

"Oh sweet, sweet pussy that my Lux has," Carlos was singing loudly and tunelessly in the other room. "And I'm gonna wrap my mouth around it as soon as I finish up this trim painting. Which should be in less than ten minutes."

Why not, thought Lux. I don't belong to no one but me. She waited until he was almost done with his work. Then she took her shoes off.

"I'm gonna try out the shower. Make sure it works," she called to Carlos knowing he would jump at the thought.

She poked her head into the room where Carlos was painting to see whether he'd heard her. He was just pulling the tape and wrapping up the canvas.

"I left a check for you on the kitchen table, Carlos. Made out to cash like you asked. I'm just gonna try out the shower now. See you later."

She closed the door, slipped out of her pants and left them in a small pile in front of the door. Then her socks made a second pile. Underwear sat on its own. Then came a shirt, a jacket and finally, she hung her bra on the door-knob of the bathroom before she ducked into the shower and turned it on.

Carlos shoved the check in his pocket and then stepped over Lux's shoes, her socks, pants, and underwear. He was thinking about what he was going to do to her in the shower, how he was gonna grab both her small hands into one of his and hold them up over her head, let the water run down all over her body while he sucked on her nipple and fingered her pussy. How he was gonna tease her and lick her and make her wait until she was begging him to stick himself deep into her.

He was stepping over her shirt and her jacket when he saw her cell phone sticking out of the pocket. He picked it up and thought about calling Jonella. He'd get Jonella over here so he could tickle Lux's clit with his tongue while Jonella slapped her breasts to make them bounce in that way that made him crazy. Maybe he'd even do Jonella first while Lux waited and watched. Maybe he'd do them both together, just for old times' sake. While he was considering the permutations and trying to remember where Jonella said she'd be today, Lux's little cell phone rang.

"Who dat?" Carlos answered the phone on the first ring.

"Ah, well this is Trevor. Is Lux available?"

"No, Old Cock," Carlos crowed into the tiny phone. "She busy."

19. *The Punch*

*I*T WAS THE BLOOD that did him in. Just a tiny spot of blood that spurted from Trevor's nose on to the wrong person's blouse. If it weren't for the blood, everything might have been ok.

In all his life, Trevor had only been punched once, by his son, accidentally during a game of flag football. Teddy's fist had wrapped around his opponent's flag and then would have shot up into the air in triumph, except that it connected with his dad's chin on the way. Trevor's head snapped back and he wore a substantial bruise as well as a neck brace for several weeks.

When Lux punched Trevor, standing in the lobby of Warwick & Warwick, LLP, her right fist connected with the side of his head, right at the temple. The broken vessels would leak blood into the whites of his eye and turn the area directly underneath the eye first to black, then purple, then green, until it faded away altogether.

Lux was strong, but she was not particularly fast, and she gave him plenty of warning, albeit in a language he could not understand.

"If you don't back off, Trevor, so help me I'm gonna smack you."

In the language Trevor spoke, the word "smack," like its synonyms "punch," "beat," and "hit" translated to an empty threat, whereas Lux knew it to be fair warning of the consequences of a foolish action repeated.

After several delightful damp hours with Carlos she had struggled back into her clothes and found seventeen messages from Trevor on her cell phone. He also called her mother, as well as Jonella. It was not so much the number of calls but the fact that she had never given him either of the other telephone numbers that made the noose feel so tight around her neck. He didn't even know Jonella's last name, and yet he had tracked her down. Lux knew the relationship was on a bad path and she couldn't keep running to her brother Joseph to save her every time things got sticky. So she jumped off the train before it crashed. Monday after work, she packed her bags and moved back into her mother's house.

All that week, Trevor did everything he knew to get her to come back. Flowers. Emails. Theater tickets. She had been warning him to "back the fuck off" for several days but even in their simplicity, Trevor misunderstood her words and her actions.

Even at the last minute he did not see it coming. If he could have slowed it down and watched it after the fact, Trevor would have clearly understood that when he cornered her in the lobby at work and Lux said, "If you don't back off, I'm going to smack you," she was already balling her hands into fists. She gave him ample time to move away from her. Instead he moved in closer, begging,

"Bunny, can't we just discuss this?" At that point, Lux set her legs in a wide stance. She brought both hands up into fists in front of her face.

Jonella would have known what was coming next. Carlos, Joseph, and any kid on the playground who had ever been hit would have recognized that Lux, with her fists curled and at eye level, was preparing to punch. She waited, giving him yet another chance to back away, but Trevor was a foreigner, a tourist stumbling into an insurrection. He moved forward, reaching out to touch her and then—wham.

The left stayed at her face to block the blow she reflexively assumed he would return to her. The right pulled back at the elbow and flashed across to connect with the side of his head. Smack.

The blood and the damage to his nose was not entirely Lux's fault. Trevor rebounded off the wall behind him and then fell forward, hitting his face on a table full of magazines. After he hit the floor, Lux stepped over him and walked slowly past the stunned receptionist, through the maze that was the law firm and over to her own desk. The muscles in her stomach were so tight she could not breath properly. Her soon-to-be-former boss would later describe her to friends as "panting like a dog," which she was. Lux grabbed her purse, her lunch, and her notebook and then walked back past the receptionist.

When she got back to the lobby, Mr. Warwick himself, as well as Margot and some of the other senior attorneys, had already gathered around Trevor and were pressing well-ironed handkerchiefs to his bleeding nose. Trevor stared at Lux as she passed him. He noted that she was carrying her purse and a paper bag. She walked out of the office and headed for the elevators.

"There she goes! There she goes!" the receptionist shouted as Lux punched the elevator button down arrow.

"Leave it, Mrs. Deecher, leave it," Trevor shouted. The receptionist was named Beecher, but Trevor had broken his nose.

"I'm calling the police," Mrs. Beecher announced.

"Doe! Doe! Don't!" shouted Trevor and all the others agreed.

"No police!" Margot said too loudly.

"It's best that we deal with this ourselves," Mr. Warwick said. He turned to Trevor.

"What the fuck happened?"

"I don't doe, sir. I fell and hit the coffee table."

Mrs. Beecher listened closely. If Trevor was planning to lie, she would have to hear the story now if she was to corroborate it later.

"It wad just an accident," Trevor said with weight and finality. The matter was closed. Margot sighed, relieved that the whole incident was about to become just a moment of clumsiness that could be forgotten when the bones healed and the bruise faded.

"It wasn't," said Crescentia Peabody, scratching at the little red circle of Trevor's blood that had ruined her ivory silk blouse. It was the one with the ruffled collar, the one she liked. That woman, Margot, the attorney who had presented the contract for the Christmas clitoris instead of the Christmas catalogue, was fussing over the man with the bloody nose. What had happened between the thin, badly dressed red-haired girl and this middle-aged man was none of her business, except for the spot on her blouse. That little red circle made her more than a spectator of their lives and so she reported what she had seen.

"The girl with the red hair, they were fighting and she kept telling him to back off, to leave her alone but he kept touching her and asking her to just please to come into his office so they could discuss it quietly between them. She started to cry but he wouldn't leave her alone and when he grabbed her by the arm she hit him. Rather hard, too."

Crescentia was quite correct in her assessment of the events. Mrs. Beecher had witnessed the same slim slice of Lux and Trevor's life together and would have described it in a similar fashion, albeit a bit more generously tilted towards Trevor because he had always been pleasant to her.

"Find that woman," Warwick instructed. Then he pointed at Trevor, "You. In my office."

Margot desperately wanted to follow Trevor into Warwick's office. He was such an honorable idiot. He would probably tell Warwick everything, including the things Warwick didn't need to know. Mano à mano, he would provide the old man enough gunpowder to fire Trevor for his indiscretion. Oh, they would laugh about it for sure, and Warwick might slap him on the back for landing a live one, but sooner or later he would also kick him in the ass for being an idiot and eventually fire him for fucking a secretary.

"Find that girl," Warwick ordered Margot as she tried to enter the office.

"But I think I can be of greater assistance here in your office."

"I still know how to write a contract, Ms. Hillsboro. What I need from you is damage control. I don't know how to talk to women. Trevor is obviously a total idiot. I need you to do that talking thing you women do, that sisterhood thing that you do. Go, not as an attorney, go as a woman, track her down, chat her up, and get her to sign the release that Trevor and I are about to write up. I want you to go down to human resources and pull her file. Now move."

Margot looked past Mr. Warwick and saw Trevor sink down into the burgundy leather couch and rest his head in his hand. She prayed he would value self-preservation over the need to confess.

"And don't come back until you have a signed agreement, Hillsboro."

On the trip out to Queens, Margot began to feel a little queasy about her assignment. Warwick wrote out a release indemnifying Warwick & Warwick, LLP, from any liability in whatever case Lux might have against Trevor. In her briefcase, Margot had two cashier's checks for $5,000 and $10,000 respectively. If Lux wanted more than $15,000 she would have to make a phone call. Warwick was standing by, waiting for the call.

Lux was sitting on the front porch of her mother's house when Margot arrived.

"Why don't we go inside?" Margot said.

"Mmmm, no, I don't think so."

"I've never conducted business on the stoop, and I'm not prepared to start now."

"There's a coffee shop down the road if you don't

mind the walk," Lux offered.

"No, we have some personal things to discuss. I think a coffee shop would be too public."

Lux stepped protectively in front of the door to her mother's house. Inside, her mother and her brother were stoned on the couch. The kitchen was dirty. The linoleum was yellow, except for the blotchy white bits where the ammonia of the cat's piss had burned a clean spot.

"You can't come in my house."

Ah shit, she's gonna sue, Margot thought. She's gonna sue big. This is clearly hostile. How am I gonna get her to sign this?

"What can I do to get you to invite me into your house?"

Lux's eyes lit up. She licked her lips. She took a deep breath and made her request.

"Ok, explain to me why you can borrow money against the equity in your house."

"Huh?" Margot asked.

"Are you deaf?"

"No, I'm just, eh, well, ok, you're allowed to borrow against the equity in your house because it's your money and you can do anything you want to do with it."

"Anything?"

"Yeah."

"Can you buy something else with it?"

"Of course. It's yours."

Lux stood quietly and thought about this until Margot interrupted her.

"Shall we go inside now?"

Lux pushed open the front door and allowed Margot

to enter her mother's home. The smell of cat pee was overwhelming.

Through the doorway of the kitchen Margot could see an older woman and a younger man laughing at an afternoon TV show. The kitchen was painted orange with pink trim and there was a collection of glow-in-the-dark Madonnas crowding the cracked Formica of the kitchen table. It was, in Margot's estimation, a social landscape by Federico Fellini.

"So? What do you want?" Lux asked as she sat down opposite Margot and fiddled with one of the many green- ish Madonnas. Margot hesitated, momentarily transfixed by the velvet clown paintings she suddenly noticed behind Lux's head. Lux turned to look where Margot was staring.

"Yeah, my father got one of the best collections of acrylic-on-velvet clown paintings in the nation. You mighta heard about it if, you know, you read the right magazines."

Margot's eyes began to water from the animal smells inside Lux's mother's kitchen.

"Could you open a window?"

Lux got up and opened the window over the sink. She stood there and did not return to the Formica table.

"So? What do you want?" Lux asked Margot.

"Uh, well, the law firm of Warwick & Warwick wants to apologize for what happened to you today."

Lux's eyebrows shot up nearly to her hairline and a small smile played around her mouth.

"Yes," Lux said dryly. "It was awful."

"I'm sure it was. Along with the apology we'd like to

offer you $5,000 for your suffering provided you sign this release of liability for the firm."

"Gimme," Lux said reaching out for the papers Margot was pulling out of her briefcase. "Can I get a day to clean out my desk and take anything personal off of my computer?"

"You're not fired," Margot said.

Lux looked up from the contract, her pen poised to scribble her name.

"What? Is it my birthday? Or April Fool's Day?"

"You waive your right to sue, come back to work tomorrow, and we'll give you $5,000."

"I don't think I want to see Trevor again so soon."

"Trevor has been let go."

"Like fired?"

"No, not like fired, actually fired," Margot quietly confirmed.

Lux pushed the papers away from her.

"Ten thousand then," Margot said.

"You're a fucking vampire, aren't you?" Lux said.

"Fifteen thousand is my final offer. I'll give you five minutes to think it over. After that, it's gone," Margot said.

Lux regarded Margot as if she were some strange new species of human being.

"I'm gonna take a guess here, right, and say you escaped from like some Midwestern town full of fat-assed, goofy white people who all clap on one and five. You know what I'm saying here?"

Margot looked at her blankly. She had no idea what Lux was saying.

"I'm talking about, like, people who go on vacation

wearing identical tie-dyed shirts so they don't lose each other, right? So, you like, come here to escape but a person can't escape, right. You can never, you know, escape from where you went to high school. What I'm trying to say is that a person can leave it and a person can say they don't like it but even the leaving of it, it still stains you. Like, take me for example, wherever I run, I'm always gonna be slightly dented, and broken. I live with that. But you know, Trevor, he's a clean guy. You follow me? Yeah, he thinks he suffered on account of he got dumped and had to give up his summer cottage, oh boo hoo hoo, but he don't know broken. If I do this to him, he's gonna know broken."

"It's not our intention to punish anyone, only to protect the firm from untoward publicity and expensive lawsuits."

"I want the money," Lux began, "but Trevor stays. I'll quit. He keeps his stupid job and I get two and four."

"No, the deal is $15,000." Margot informed her in haughty tones

"Yeah, $15,000. Two and four means I always know where the downbeat is, Margot."

Margot found it curious to sit in an orange and pink kitchen surrounded by a collection of supreme kitsch and be corrected by Lux Fitzpatrick. Maybe it was just the growing contact high floating in from the next room.

"We're talking about music?"

"Yeah, people with, let's call 'em, bland souls, alright? These people tend to clap on the first and third beat because they can't feel the rhythm that snaps on like, the second and fourth. You know, beat, because we're talking music, all right?"

"I didn't know that."

"Now you do."

"Thank you."

Lux nodded.

"Return the favor and explain to me why it's, you know, good to borrow against the equity of your house," Lux ordered.

"Oh, ah, well, ok. Money is good and it's a tool and it's your money and you should use it. Don't let it just sit there, make it work. If you have a hammer and you lock it away and don't use it, it's not very useful."

"How do you get to it? How do you make it, you know, available?"

"You take a second on your home."

"A second what?"

"Mortgage."

"What if you don't have a first mortgage?"

"Well, then you're in very good shape. Any bank will, most likely, give you a line of credit if you own property outright."

"So you get this line of credit thing at a bank. When you go to the bank, what do they want to know about you? You know I mean like the person who's getting the money."

"Everything."

"Oh," Lux said, deflating.

"I mean, every financial thing. Not your personal issues."

"Do you need a job?"

"It helps. But if there's enough equity you can get a loan without disclosing income."

"I see."

Lux stood up, effectively ending the meeting.

"Thanks for coming by."

Margot's hands fluttered over her briefcase and her papers as she rose from the Formica table. She was just getting used to the stink and had a sudden urge to examine each one of the glow-in-the-dark Madonnas, but Lux was already standing at the front door, opening it.

Margot rose from her seat and followed Lux into the foyer. She didn't want to leave. She wanted to peek around the wall into the living room and see what blobs lay in front of the TV. She wanted to crawl into Lux's childhood bedroom and see if there were cheerleader pom poms still stuck to the walls. Lux opened the door and ushered Margot out of her mom's house.

"What are you going to do about a job?"

"I'll find one."

"Doing what?"

"Dunno."

"I'll see that Mr. Warwick writes you a good recommendation."

"Whatever. I'll call your voice mail and leave my attorney's telephone number. You can fax him the release and messenger over the check. Fifteen thousand; Trevor stays. I go. Aimee will be thrilled, I'm sure," Lux said standing on the front stoop.

Margot nodded, said nothing. When did Lux become a woman, and a businesswoman at that? When did she get an attorney? Margot looked at Lux standing in the doorway. Same bad hair. Same bad clothes. Lux turned and walked back into the house.

"Have lunch with me," Margot shouted through the screen door. Lux turned and looked at her like she was crazy. Margot upped the offer.

"If you have lunch with me I'll tell you all about compound interest."

"Trevor already explained it to me," Lux laughed as she shut the door. A moment later she came out again.

"And if you love Trevor so damn much, how come you're not saving his ass on this?" Lux demanded.

"I don't," Margot started to lie but then changed directions. "How do you know how I feel about Trevor?"

"What am I? A stone? I sat in that conference room and I heard your whole stories about Atlanta Jane and her man who sounds so much like Trevor. I know you because I know how you want to have sex. And you want to do him up against the furniture in his house. But you can't now, cuz I beat you to it. So if you love him so much how come I'm the one who's gotta protect him?"

"It's, um, it's, you know, it's not my firm. I'm not even a partner. I just work there. And I have to be careful of my own job."

Lux stared at Margot and then shook her head in disgust. She went into her mother's house and, although Margot stood there, waiting, expecting something else to happen, Lux did not return.

20. *Whores*

"I GAVE IT MY ALL, Trevor. I wheeled and I dealed and I talked Lux into giving up her job so you could keep yours. It was hard. I mean, she really liked working with us, but I managed to convince her that it would be easier for her to get a new job than for you to start over again. In the end, I had to up it to $15,000 but she finally signed and now it's behind us. So drop your pants and make love to me quick."

"I can't tell him that," Margot gasped.

"It's close to the truth," Brooke countered. "You rode out to Queens, saved his ass, got him out of trouble, and it cost the company $15,000."

"She signed willingly and she gave up her job before I even suggested it. It was all really very, what's a good word?"

"Weird?" suggested Aimee, lying flat on her back.

"Honorable. But some of it was weird, considering the house and the zombies on the couch. Boy, Lux lives in the Fun House."

"You think she's gay?" Brooke asked hopefully.

"No," said Margot. "She was definitely having sex with Trevor and seemed to enjoy it. A lot."

"Maybe she swings that way sometimes, though?" Brooke asked again.

"She didn't give any indication of it, although we weren't talking about sex. Well, we weren't talking about more sex, just the sex she's already had with Trevor and how it reflects on her work situation."

"What's she going to do for money?" Aimee asked from the warmth of her cozy bed. She had been stuck in bed for weeks and had missed the whole "Lux Slugs Trevor" headline at work.

"Live at home, I guess, and oh my god, you would not believe what her mother's house looks like. It was decorated in what I would call the Crazy Toddler School of Design. Every wall is a different color and there are these collections of old toys and kitsch all over the place. It explains so much! Of course she dresses the way she dresses. She grew up inside some wacky children's show. Well, a drunk and stoned children's show. My god! The smell of cat pee and marijuana from her mother's kitchen was overwhelming! I'm amazed and impressed that she got this far in life."

Margot and Brooke both looked involuntarily at Aimee.

"What?" Aimee asked.

"You don't mind us talking about Lux?"

"Why should I mind?"

Whether she realized it or not, Aimee had Queen Bee'd them into avoiding Lux, or at least, pretending to avoid Lux. And though they were too old to fully bend to her will, neither Margot nor Brooke spoke about Lux to Aimee.

And yet they were in contact with her. Margot had a professional need to call on Lux again and was looking forward to it for personal reasons. Brooke invited Lux to Croton-on-Hudson, her parents' pool house to begin a portrait. The portrait would require several sittings and Brooke hoped they would stay friends. The women were grown up enough to do as they pleased, but could not bring themselves to suggest including Lux in their witty, congenial salons at Aimee's bedside.

They tried to check in on Aimee at least once every day. Brooke and Margot stopped by Aimee's apartment bringing groceries, DVDs, and good cheer. On Tuesday afternoon, they brought The Tuesday Erotica Club.

"Who wants to go first?" Margot asked.

"I do," Brooke and Aimee said at the same time.

"No, no, you go ahead," Brooke said. "Mine's just a little ditty I zipped off last Friday on the A train."

Aimee opened her manuscript. The computer was impossible to use while lying flat in her bed and so she had handwritten her piece. She keenly felt the lack of instant computerized "spell check." After so many years of typing she found she could not remember how to write cursive. Printing made her hand cramp and, of course, erasing was a bitch. In the end, she scribbled out the bits she didn't want and, rereading her manuscript, she realized her efforts did not look so different from the papers Lux produced.

"*I'm standing at the door,*" Aimee read. Lying flat on her back, she held the paper above her head. "*He puts the* cash on the table and I start to do all those things that look like love, but they're really all about money and survival. I'm wearing a dress that barely covers me. It's easy to get out of and hides the stains. He's been here before so I kind of know what he likes. I wait until he tells me to take my dress off.

"He tells me to show him my tits so I slip the top of the dress down my body, revealing my breasts one at a time. He likes to look at my individual parts. Me, whole, doesn't do anything for him. He likes my breasts pushed into each other creating a luxurious cleavage, so I push them into each other, taking care not to cover the nipples. He likes to see the pink nipples poking through my fingers. My breasts are supple. It doesn't hurt.

"He gets up from his chair. It's a sudden, compulsive move as if he too has urgent needs to fill. He grabs my breasts in his own hands, and I'm caught off balance as he pulls a nipple into his mouth. He pushes me up against the wall, pulling the rest of the dress off my body.

"'It's fifty extra for the bottom,' I remind him. He nods and grunts, agreeing to the price, promising to pay when he's done with me.

"'Cash on the table,' I whisper, pushing his hand away, lest he forget who we are and what we're doing. He digs out the cash and counts it out on the table where I can see it. Is he relieved? Or angry? It doesn't matter. He comes back to me. He pushes my body down to the floor and spreads my legs apart. He's paid for the bottom, and he's going to use it."

Aimee stopped reading. She let the manuscript fall to her chest.

"Then what happens?" Brooke asked.

"Well," Aimee said, "after writing that last sentence, I

sat here in bed watching the sun move this little square of light across the covers. I didn't move or do anything for a really long time. When the light got to my chest I called the bank and transferred all the money he's sent me from our joint savings into my private checking. Then I called his agent and got the hotel phone number where he's staying in Tokyo. Then I called my lawyer and had him fax the initial divorce papers to Tokyo."

Margot and Brooke sat quietly, unsure of what to say.

"By then it was after six. And I just lay here in bed until suddenly it was ten. I think I was waiting for tears. Didn't come. I couldn't move. I think if I had to get up and go to the office I wouldn't be able to. I felt like I couldn't do anything but lie here and look at the ceiling, which works really well considering I'm not supposed to do anything but lie here and look at the ceiling. Eventually, I'll probably have to move," Aimee said finally. "Out of the apartment, I mean. I can't afford this big place myself."

"Wow," Brooke said.

"It's because of this," Aimee declared, waving her manuscript in the air. "I thought I'd play and explore what it might be like to be a prostitute and guess what, all the feelings were already here in my chest. I mean, I'm not the sex whore, but I'm the love and affection whore. He sends me money so he can treat me like shit. So he can be loved when he feels the need to dip into a family. Fuck him. That's not me."

"Geez," Brooke said, "from now on I'm going to be very careful what I write about."

Margot and Aimee laughed.

"How do you feel now?" Margot asked.

"Triumphant then terrified. Relieved and then frightened. Like, right now, everything's fine, but I really didn't want to be a single mother. When I told my mother I dumped him and that I was afraid of being a single parent she told me, 'Lesser women have survived it.'"

"She's right," Margot said.

"Yeah, but I was expecting her to say something like 'you're not alone darling, Daddy and I are here for you.'"

"I'll help," Margot blurted out.

"Of course, we'll both help you, Aims," Brooke said softly.

Aimee knew that a baby started out in life as a well of need so deep it cut almost to the center of the earth. She was afraid if she and her baby started asking for help they would never stop. Brooke and Margot, at the same moment, were thinking that if they shared the load they could share the love.

"Thanks," Aimee said. "I think I'll be ok."

"No, really," Margot said, "I want to help."

"Ok, but it might be more than just navigating a toy store," Aimee warned.

"We're here for you," Brooke said.

Aimee smiled and was surprised to find her cheeks growing red and her eyes getting wet. The bold act of filing for divorce had made her feel so strong until the moment after she had done it.

"So, anyone have anything else to read?" she asked, brushing her hand over her face. She didn't want to wallow in anything, be it sorrow or love. She wanted to break away from the pain he had caused her and push on with life.

"Nothing to compare to your great personal insight," Brooke said, "but I did try my hand at a little poem about masturbation."

"Knock us out with it," Aimee said.

"Ok, here we go," Brooke said. She recited her new poem from memory.

"While resting my hips on a pillow,
I indulged in my own peccadillo.
And tried not to think
How my mother would drink
If I up and married my dildo."

"Oh! Bravo! Bravo!" Margot cheered.

"Not a perfect rhyme," Brooke confessed, "but then what rhymes perfectly with 'dildo.'"

"Well, 'Bilbo,'" Aimee offered, "but I can't see that fitting in your poem." As they tried to find the perfect rhyme for Brooke's limerick, Margot's thoughts drifted from 'vibrator' to 'sex' to 'love' and then settled firmly on 'money.'

"Do you think that's what it's really like?" Margot asked. "I mean, to be a prostitute."

"I have no idea," Aimee said. "Ask Lux."

"That is unkind," Brooke said.

"I didn't mean it nasty," Aimee said. "I meant she blew up big time, and I only intimated that she was selling it. And I'm thinking that maybe it cut closer to home than I could ever understand. I mean, if it's not a possibility, then you're not afraid of it and—oh my god, do you think Lux was really a prostitute?"

"She does have some money stashed somewhere," said Margot. "She's not asking for references and she doesn't seem to have any intention of getting a job. She's got an attorney on retainer, a really old guy. One of those guys who has been dead for three years but keeps coming into the office anyway. I looked him up and sure enough, vice was his main cash flow. He's only got Lux and this one other old lady as clients."

"You don't think he's her pimp?" Aimee asked. "We should report him. I mean, shouldn't we protect her in some way?"

"No, no. Can't be. Can it? Pimps have to be tough bastards, right?" Margot asked Brooke.

"What are you asking me for? I grew up on Fifth Avenue. The closest thing to a prostitute was my nanny. She loved me on salary."

"Well, this old guy is not her pimp. He can barely hold a pencil. Although, he marked up my release form pretty good."

For a moment there was silence, all three women considering their own thoughts.

"I've been a bitch haven't I?" Aimee asked.

"Of course you've been a bitch," Brooke laughed. "About what?"

"About Lux. She dresses horribly. And she's rude and vulgar. And she's way too young and way too pretty. Too many opportunities in front of her. But here we are talking about whether or not this poor kid is a hooker, and I realize how much I have that I take for granted. I gotta be nicer to her. I've been Grima Wormtongue when I should have been Aragorn."

"You lost me on that last sentence but the first thought was dead on. Yeah, you've been a right bitch to her," Brooke agreed.

"I'm going to be better. I'm going to be nicer to her. Why don't you guys invite her over with you the next time you come?"

"Yeah," Margot said. "As soon as she signs the release I can talk with her again."

"Should we redo her?" Aimee asked. "Take her shopping and get her a proper haircut?

"I like her the way she is, and anyway, you can't get out of bed," Brooke reminded her.

"I'll invite her to join us for lunch when I deliver the final papers and her check. But remember, Aimee, she's not a puppy or an orphan," Margot interjected and would have said more, except that the doorbell was ringing.

"You expecting anyone?" Margot asked.

"Yes, I am," Aimee said. "I'm selling the vagina."

"Does anyone want it?" Brooke asked politely.

"You'd be surprised how popular that vagina is," Aimee said.

Margot stared at her friends in horror.

"What," Margot asked, "are you talking about?"

"The huge blond vagina he keeps in the living room."

Margot still could not imagine what Aimee was talking about.

"I sold it to a club in the meat-packing district for twelve grand," Aimee said. "Framed, of course."

"A photograph!" Margot said triumphantly. "You're talking about a photograph."

"Of course," Aimee giggled from the bed. "I'm starting a new life. And that beautiful new life does not have room for a blond vagina, seven feet tall and five feet wide."

21. Viagra

"YOU DIDN'T LIKE THE dress I bought you," Bill said instead of hello when Brooke turned her key and walked into his apartment. In the cool darkness, Brooke leaned against a carved panel of exotic wood and regarded him over the tops of her sunglasses. The twelve-room apartment, though sumptuously decorated, was overstuffed with expensive furniture done up in too-delicate fabrics that made Brooke feel there was no place to rest her butt. Brooke inherited a similar property from her maternal grandmother and lived in it briefly before moving to a livelier part of town.

"Honey, you're an old line, prep school fashion retard who still thinks Bean, Bass, and Brooks Brothers make up the triumvirate of the fashion universe."

"But it was better, right?"

"Better?"

"Than the last dress I bought."

"Oh god, yes. That peachy colored prom dress! This one was much better."

"Well, at least that's something. You don't mind if I

keep trying, do you?"

"I'm your doll. Dress me as you like."

"Really?"

"Well, no. I mean, yes. You can buy me clothes but really Bill, I can't promise to wear them. I mean, out of the house, that is."

Brooke stood on her toes to kiss him. She lost her balance and leaned in a little against him. The feel of his exquisite, toned body flicked a little switch in her that she immediately turned back off. They had a beautiful evening planned, and she didn't want to pressure him. Maybe later, or tomorrow morning, she would raise a difficult subject. She had no proof he was sleeping with someone else, only a suspicion. When he was ready, he would tell her what was wrong.

The ruby pumps would make her just about as tall as Bill. Like Brooke, Bill was long and thin and blond. Like a matched pair of patrician gods, they would look amazing together tonight.

"Do you think I should wear the roll collar or the one with the sharp points?" Bill asked her.

"Points are in, I think."

"Mother said the roll collar."

Brooke heard, but didn't answer. Bill had a large selection of tuxedos and one was as beautiful as the next.

Her ruby Lanvin had arrived and Bill's housekeeper hung it on the back of the door in Bill's bedroom. Brooke slipped out of her clothes and into the shower. Wrapped in a towel, she splashed cream on her body and flicked makeup onto her face. She flipped the dress over her head and let it settle onto her body. Brooke was an old hat at the process of becoming stunning.

He was waiting in the foyer when she skipped down the stairs, the red gown dancing around her ankles. The purse had a little golden strap that she placed on her wrist so she could slide her hand into his when they danced. She let the purse dangle for a moment when he turned and she did her "ta da" pose so he could admire her dress.

The way he looked at her, she knew he loved her. He loved her jokes, and he loved her style. He had come to love the tattoos that once horrified him. He loved her paintings and that, for her, was like loving her soul. He loved her feet and he loved her legs, her fingers and her eyes. With all that love pouring out of him, surely they would find a way to get their sex life back on track.

"My cell phone fits in my purse but if I take it, nothing else will fit in. So, it's either cell phone and lipstick; or cash, hairbrush, and lipstick? What do you think?"

Bill smiled blankly at her.

"Let's go," he said, and a mischievous little smile played across his lips.

The evening's benefit for muscular dystrophy was to take place at the Guggenheim, one of Brooke's favorite places in the city. Now that he was a judge, all his old lawyer pals courted his presence with determined intensity. Bill and Brooke would be the center of a fierce social storm that was both flattering and annoying. Yet Bill walked into the museum with Brooke on his arm like a tall ship sailing through friendly waters. His smooth, placid face belied the trouble he started to feel in his legs.

"You look lovely tonight, Mrs. Simpson," crowed a

young lawyer who would have loved to lick the Lanvin right off her. "Hey Your Honor, mind if I dance with your girl?"

"Actually, I do," Bill said as he swept Brooke onto the dance floor.

"My goodness, you're very possessive tonight, Bill," Brooke said.

Having attended the same coming out parties and the same prep school balls, Bill and Brooke knew all the same waltzes the way a dog knows its own flannel plaid cedar bed. His hand found the bare small of her back and she rested hers on the soft smoothness of his neck. She put her cheek against his, and her chest against the front of his tuxedo. When she pressed against his lower body, she felt he had an erection.

Brooke stumbled a bit in her ruby red pumps.

"Is that for me?" she asked him, and when he did not answer she looked around for whatever had recently passed through Bill's eye line. Was it a desire to triumph over the young lawyer that got Bill revved up?

"Is it the paintings?"

"No."

"The mobiles?" she asked and pressed against him again as they danced, just to make sure it was really there. Sure enough, something big and hot was ruining the smooth line of Bill's tuxedo pants.

"Is it my dress maybe?" Brooke guessed.

"Shush. Just dance with me."

They slithered across the dance floor, pressed tightly together and Brooke could not help the way her blood moved to the center of her legs and started creating a warm, damp hopefulness.

"Is it me?" she asked finally.

"No," he said. "I mean, yes. It's for you. My doctor prescribed something. He said it would take about four hours to kick in, but he was off by about three and a half."

"You're kidding," Brooke said and stopped dancing.

"No, I am not kidding, and don't you dare walk away from me," Bill said and pulled her closer into himself.

"You can't hold me all night in front of your chemically enhanced problem."

"Yes, I can."

Brooke pulled away and headed straight for the bar, leaving Bill feeling exposed and foolish on the dance floor. He walked calmly towards their assigned table. He moved slowly, as if he didn't have a care in the world. Anyone who noticed the untoward bulge in Bill's tuxedo would certainly believe it to be a shadow crossing his crotch and not the largest, most uncontrollable erection Bill Simpson had ever experienced. Bill sat down carefully at the table and took out his cell phone.

"Brrrrrrrrrrrring ba ba doo dah!" Brooke's cell phone sang from inside her tiny evening bag. She knew it was him. He was sitting just a few yards away, and she saw him dial.

"I did it for you," he said when she answered. "I did it to make you happy."

"I AM HAPPY!" Brooke shouted into her cell phone. She slapped it shut and in an instant crossed the few feet to where Bill sat. "WHY CAN'T ANYONE BELIEVE THAT I AM HAPPY?"

"Don't shout," he begged her as he waved to a familiar face and the face's pregnant wife.

Brooke slid into the chair next to him. She wrapped her arm around his shoulders and whispered in his ear.

"I am very happy. And I love you."

"I love you too, Brooke. It's just that I'm…"

"What?" she asked. He looked at the perfect red of her mouth. He considered the way the ruby of her lipstick made her mouth look wet and promising.

"You're what?" Brooke asked.

"I've come to realize that, um, I'm, um, I'm not enough for a vibrant, exciting woman like you," he said finally.

Brooke dropped her hand into his lap and wrapped it around his protruding erection.

"What part isn't enough?" She slid down his zipper and pushed aside his underwear. Bill gasped as she took hold of his penis. He put both hands on the table and grabbed the white linen cloth.

"Is it enough that you love me? That you have loved me for more than twenty years?"

Bill wanted to answer, but he couldn't think of any words.

"I think it's time for us to settle down and get married," she said honestly as she stroked his erection.

He knew Brooke deserved more than he could give her. He thought she deserved a better man but at the same time dreaded the idea that she might someday find one. He thought someday they would get over this whole sex-thing and grow old together, just holding hands. At the present moment, however, he thought it best to hold onto the table as the blood rushed away from his head.

"Brooke," Bill gasped, "stop for a minute."

"Nope," said Brooke as she pulled and released, pulled and released.

"Let's go, let's g-g-g-go out onto the patio," he begged. "I have to tell you something."

"Oh, hello Mr. Adelman. Mrs. Adelman." Brooke called to an elderly couple who stopped by their table to pay respects to Bill.

"I thought your ruling in the Baldwin vs. Sterling case was dead on," said Mr. Adelman.

"Thank you, Mark," squeaked Bill. The Adelmans looked concerned.

"Laryngitis," Brooke quickly offered. "Fever went away and the doctors says he's fine, but the voice just hasn't come back yet."

"Hot tea with honey's the best for what you've got," Mr. Adelman offered.

"Oooo! Bill, honey would be fun," Brooke said.

Bill could only nod to the Adelmans as his testicles contracted and released, contracted and released in time to the more urgent pulls by Brooke's hand.

"It really soothes the throat," Mrs. Adelman agreed.

"Would you like me to get you some honey, Bill?" Brooke asked as she moved her hand from the elbow only, taking care not to alter the straight line of her shoulder.

"I think I'll be fine if we just sit here like this, dear," Bill said.

The Adelmans smiled and continued on to greet other friends, totally unaware of what was happening underneath the white linen cloth of table five. Brooke was, after all, a debutante and she had learned a skill or two at all those interminable balls.

"Let's go home," Bill said as soon as the Adelmans had cleared.

"Let's stay," Brooke said, smiling, tugging, rubbing.

"I think we should go."

"Ooo! Look! Is this butter on the table?"

Their eyes met and in an instant Bill saw all he would lose if he opted for honesty. He suddenly pulled his erection out of her hands and tucked it into his pants.

"Butter would ruin my tux," he told her as in one continuous action he pushed himself away from the table and flipped open his phone to call for his car. He grabbed Brooke by the arm and dragged her through the party towards the door.

"Good evening Mrs. Crane. Great to see you, Ed. Hey Sal, how's your tennis?" Bill said, returning smile for smile, wave for wave, droll, empty banter that belied the fierce grip he had on Brooke's hand. Her dress fluttered behind her and her shoes clicked over the marble as she danced after him.

"Good night, Tomas. Sorry we have to cut out so soon. Bill has a terrible headache. Yes, yes, call me and we'll catch up."

He paused only to wait for the revolving door to empty.

"Brilliant party," Brooke called to their host as Bill pushed her through the glass door and onto the street. His car was pulling up as he kissed her hard on the mouth and pulled her into the back.

"Drive slowly," Bill ordered his driver as he zipped the partition between them closed. Brooke would have been happy to wait until they got home, but Bill was pushing up the ruby folds of her gown. He would have pulled off her underwear, had she been wearing any. He undid the closures of his pants and, grabbing Brooke by her dragon, he lay back on the leather seats of his car and entered her with a full, thick erection.

"I love you, Bill," she said to him, but a moment later she didn't care what he answered. There were things to discuss, but intelligent thoughts were fading now in favor of sensations. It was like old times, back when Bill was first discovering her and could still be excited by sex in any format. He reached up to touch her mouth as she moved back and forth across his rigid penis. By 34th Street she had started to come. It started at the back of her neck and rolled in waves down her spine. As she started to say "o, o, o," Bill sat up and kissed her mouth, her neck, and her breasts.

As she was ending, as she was feeling like she could never have sex again, she began to realize that he had not come. Not even close. His erection was carved out of cement.

The driver pulled up in front of Bill's apartment building and waited for more instructions.

"Once around the block," Bill shouted hoarsely from the backseat. Even with the traffic, it was not long enough. Brooke found her shoes and Bill reordered his clothes before they raced each other into the lobby and up to the apartment.

He lay naked on his back in his bed with an erection running directly perpendicular to the ceiling. A perfect ninety-degree angle. Brooke entered from the bathroom and he sat up. She slipped off her gown and stepped out of it. Bill stood up (his erection now exactly parallel to the floor) and kissed her face and her eyes and her lips.

"Can you continue?" he asked.

She nodded, surprised and pleased that he wanted to.

Grunt for grunt, the second time was not as good as the first. In his car it was still such a surprise to be making love to him that she had not been able to think about anything at all. In his bed, she knew that he was no longer the best sex partner in her life. She could feel that he did not glory in her body the way she did in his. It dragged down her passion. She knew as he reached for the jelly and entered her from behind, even as her body held tight to his, that he was not with her the way she was with him. And in the end, after giving her several more satisfying orgasms, he still could not come himself. In fact, no matter what they did they could not get the erection to go away, and in the end they decided to jump into a warm bath and try to relax.

"Don't touch it!" he warned when she slipped into the wide marble bathtub.

"I wasn't going to," she promised. "You want me to wash your back?"

"Yes, please," he said weakly.

When it finally shrank back to human size, Bill got out of the tub, dried off, and slid naked into his bed next to Brooke.

"I love you," he said to her. She reached out across the sheets and said, "I know you do."

A quiet, joyful exhaustion settled in on both of them. Brooke thought she knew his limitations. He had bad taste in dresses, good taste in art. Maybe with a better urologist they would overcome this little hump, or lack of hump, in their relationship. Regardless, she believed they were stuck to each other. And we have a lot to be happy about, thought Brooke, even given the blatant imperfections in our glue.

22. *Bad Sex*

*S*HE TRIED NOT TO look at the bruise on his face and the blood in his eye where she had slugged him. Lux was working too hard to bother thinking about past failures.

He had not, as was his habit, gotten an immediate erection upon seeing the fabric slip off her nipples and fall to the floor. She gyrated over the bed clothes and pulled the sheet off Trevor and pressed her beautiful body onto his, but still he lay there with a look of pained confusion across his face and no delightful engorgement to help him through his discomfort. She bumped and ground down and licked and teased but still nothing, until she tickled the inch of skin between his testicles and rectum. Only then did he moan and suddenly fill with passion. Lux thought about the way a pot can suddenly boil over and splatter all across the stove.

The papers had been signed and the money was in her bank. Lux was ready to go back to life as normal, except she would live at home and have a different job. It would be better this way, she knew. They wouldn't see each other every day and so she wouldn't feel so threatened and trapped by his love. Late at night, as she slid her key into his door she thought for a moment that she should have called first. But that would have ruined the surprise. He probably thought she needed more time, but in truth, she missed him. Lux entered the apartment and went straight for his bed.

He was still awake, just out of the shower, lying on his back, staring at the ceiling and thinking about loss and his recent near-death experience. He kept telling himself it was not death. She had only threatened his job, his reputation, but not his life. The bruises would heal. He turned sharply to the door when he heard the key in the lock, panic raising his shoulders almost to his ears. He looked for a weapon or a hiding place or the telephone. He was dialing 911 when the door slid open and he saw it was her. She who could destroy his whole life.

And yet, when she stood there naked in front of him he could not find the words to tell her to get out. "Get out," his brain had screamed, but he could not form the words on his lips. The fear that inhibited his initial erection went numb when her hands traveled around his body. Numb but not gone. As he looked down at the top of her too-red head bent low over his crotch he felt like a very large, very old animal stretched too far between the branches of a too-high tree trying to grab a sweet fruit that was just out of reach. He felt like he was going to fall; and in the height of painful pleasure, Trevor actually groped the bedclothes with his hands looking for some branch to pull himself up and away from her. She was going to destroy him, he just knew it.

Lux was working to pleasure her man. Margot had been correct in her assumption, Trevor had a lot of dick to work with; and suddenly Lux was thinking about all Brooke had said about how too big could be a problem. Trevor had always been the perfect fit but tonight her jaw was aching and her back was tired. And he didn't seem any closer to loving her.

She put her hands on his thighs and rubbed him all the way up to his chest. She let his penis fall out of her mouth and pushed a little on his chest to indicate that she wanted him to lie back down on the bed. Trevor didn't move. She rose up and pulled him down onto the bed. He lay there as she climbed on top of him, shoved it in and started to rock. Since he wasn't helping, she fondled her own breasts. It took her three or four cycles of rubbing and rocking before he broke.

Lux thought about the moment an amusement park ride kicks in, the fast, hard jolt and then suddenly you're off on your adventure. When Trevor finally bucked and started to make love to her in earnest Lux thought, at last, I've won.

Their lovemaking lasted exactly fifteen minutes. Trevor came and Lux didn't. Then he rolled off of her and excused himself to the bathroom. A moment later he returned, his face red and damp from a quick, if too aggressive, scrub. Lux, a little tired and a little confused, smiled at him, hoping for the same in return.

"Lux," Trevor said, "I'll need my key back."

"Oh!" Lux said. "But…"

But before she could protest he was in her purse, winding the two keys that allowed her entrance to his home off her key chain.

"Please, get dressed."

Lux sat there in his bed, wrapped in the good quality all-cotton sheets his ex-wife had bought on sale at Macy's. She had assumed when she walked in the door that she would be staying the night, if not the weekend. It was one o'clock in the morning, and she did not know where she would go. It seemed too late to take the subway back to Queens, and she did not have enough cash for a cab. Moreover, why would he want her to leave? She had gotten him his job back. The mess at work was over. Just by coming to his apartment, she had said he could have her again. What part of that didn't he understand?

"Get dressed, Lux," he said again and still she sat there, not understanding at all.

"You have to go. Get out. You can't come here ever again."

"Yes, I can. I can do whatever I want to now. I don't work there anymore. You don't have to worry. I have some money, Trevor. I don't need anything from you. I never asked you for money and you know what, I don't need it, so fuck you on that. I just want to be with you."

"I packed your things and had them sent to your attorney's address."

"Why?"

"Just go," Trevor said, starting to get angry. Nothing had been said to him, but he believed he was on probation at work. He believed he had lost all seniority and would be the first to be laid off when times were bad. At the end of his career he was back to the beginning when he had to be on his best, boot-licking behavior at all times. He had cost the firm $15,000 for no reason at all. He was fifty-four and did not think he could ever find another job again if he lost this one. All his comfort and security was written in watercolors on silk sheets and he had come all over them, blurring and ruining his life for this pretty little dirty girl. He could not risk anyone finding out about tonight.

"Didn't you love me?" Lux asked angrily, as if he had broken his promise.

"Lux, you have to leave," Trevor said.

Lux was not prepared to face the reality that he was dumping her. All her life she struggled with the problem of men who wanted to steal her, trap her, own her, and control her. She didn't understand the concept that someone would actually send her away, and therefore, Lux could only focus on the physical problem of where to go. Her apartment was close but the tenants had already moved in. It was a long trip back to Queens, and she didn't want to ride the subway in her too-short skirt.

"I'll need money," Lux informed him, "for a cab."

She got out of Trevor's bed and walked naked into the shower. She steamed up the bathroom and washed herself clean. She used a pair of fresh towels and left them both on the floor in a heap. In the bedroom, Trevor watched as she dressed silently and at her leisure.

Lux snapped on the pink frilly bra that would show both bra and breasts through the white sleeveless tank top that went over it. She found the tiny scrap of fabric that masqueraded as underwear, but did not put it on. She purposely slid into the high-heeled shoes she'd borrowed from Jonella and then paraded around, underwear dangling from a fingertip, looking for her skirt. When she found it, she turned her backside to him and bent deeply at the waist to pick it up off the floor. She listened carefully for the grunts and hoots and "oh baby baby" that should have been spilling out of his mouth, but Trevor was sitting on his bed, looking a bit crumpled. The palms of his hands were pressed together, and he was considering the matching curve of the cuticles on his thumbs.

"Trevor," she said. She hadn't meant to say it so angrily. She wanted it to be soft and loving, but her voice was thick with Queens and the whine of a rejected mongrel dog, a fighting dog who knew the pound and all that waited there for it. She stood in her youth, high shoes, and nothing else, waiting for him to see her. It took a while, and when he finally looked up at her with everything except love and desire scribbled across his face, she finally understood that it was over. She threw her long legs into her tiny underwear and skirt. Then she grabbed her handbag and stood in front of Trevor with her palm outstretched.

He opened up his wallet and placed thirty dollars in her hand. It was almost enough to get a cab back to her mother's house, but she stood there and demanded more. He placed another twenty in her palm, but she did not close her fist around the money and leave. He added two more twenties.

"More," she said.

A fifty slapped down on top of the pile, but it did not appease the rage in Lux. Another pair of fifties and three one-hundred dollar bills. Still she stared at him.

"That's all that's in my wallet, Lux."

She imagined dragging him down to the ATM and making him pull out his daily limit of cash, but by then she might start to shake, and she didn't want him to see that. So she snapped her fist over the cash, clicked her heels to the front door and shot him the bird as she left his apartment. Fuck you Trevor, she wanted to shout at him, but, as she could barely breathe, she did not want to risk screaming.

Five hundred and forty of Trevor's dollars felt thick and hard in her pocket and Lux wondered if Auntie Who-ah had felt this much rage at all her johns. She got down to the street and tried to find a cab but on Trevor's quiet residential block there was little traffic at that hour. Lux walked to the corner, suddenly uncomfortable in her too-high heels and the colorful little outfit she'd thrown together hoping to ignite her old man lover. The world was quiet and deserted and Lux ran towards the lights of a main street.

She chose a busy diner with a waitress who was wearing too much makeup, the kind of girl who looked like she rode the bus back home at dawn.

"Pea soup any good?" Lux asked, her nose deep in the menu.

"If ya want it thick wit lotsa ham," the waitress confirmed.

Lux looked up, revealing to the waitress the darkness of telltale mascara streaks, the western world's understood symbol of bad date gone tragic.

"How 'bout a coffee?" Lux asked.

"At this hour?" the waitress warned. "It'll make ya crazy. I could do you an egg cream."

"My brother used to bring me down the street for egg creams when my mom was too sick to cook. He told me it was made a' eggs, and it was good for me."

"It is good f'you," the waitress confirmed. "You want one?"

"Nah. Just the soup. But thanks."

Lux handed back the menu. The waitress put a rush on the order and brought the soup with some extra warm bread, butter, and a box of industrial tissues. She wanted to tell her pretty customer with the raccoon eyes that whatever he was, he wasn't worth it. Oh the stories the waitress could tell of lost love and handsome men who were tragic assholes.

"You ah'right?" she asked as she set down the bread.

"I will be."

"Yeah."

Lux spread the first sheet of scratchy white paper across her eyes and pressed it there, letting the thin white tissue catch the next fall of tears as they washed more makeup off her eyes and onto her face. If life is going to be this hard, Lux thought, I'm going to have to get a waterproof eyeliner. And then she hiccuped a laugh that started the tears going. Snot and mascara flowed into the fragile tissues until Lux finally got up and went to the bathroom.

Sitting on the toilet, Lux tried to decide what to do and where to go. She easily wrote the whole scene with Jonella. What Jonella would say and how she would laugh at Lux being dumped for the first time; how she would crow about the fist full of money.

"Gimme some of it," Jonella would demand. "Let's go

shopping for clothes, buy some dope. Go out to a club. Come on prissy pants, this is the final payoff. Let's go play."

Lux scratched Jonella off her list. She didn't feel like playing; she'd lost her taste for drugs in grade school. And she intended to spend Trevor's money on a new sink for the next apartment.

If she told Carlos, he would be tender(ish) but only to get into her pants. If she went home, the ghosts that had been her family, the tired old stoners drinking beer and smoking pot in front of reality TV, would stare and say something that might border on comfort or philosophy, provided it could be enunciated clearly enough to be understood. All those people loved her, and Lux felt their love as poison. So sitting on the toilet in the diner, Lux flipped open her cell phone and called Brooke.

23. Cheese and Sympathy

"Brrrrrrrrrrring ba ba doo dah!" Brooke's cell phone sang from inside her tiny evening bag. Bill looked at her from across the sheets. They were lying naked in his bed, holding hands and talking about everything except the thing he really needed to tell her, when Brooke's cell phone rang. She leaned across his naked chest and collected her phone.

"Uuuuuuu, hello?" Brooke said, curious as to who would call her at such an hour. "Lux? No, yeah, sure it's ok to call me. I said anytime, right."

"You know someone named Lux?" Bill asked.

"Shh! What's up? Really? Shit. Wow. I'm sorry. Yeah, no, I'd love you to come over, but I'm not at home."

"Is her name really Lux?"

"Sh! No, I'm over at a friend's house. But I have a car, well it's my mother's car, and I could come get you."

"You could bring her here," Bill said. "I'll put out some cheese. I mean, if her name really is Lux. Who names a child Lux? Maybe her parents teach Latin. Is she French? What does she look like? Is she interesting? Where is she from?"

"Sh! Listen, I'm staying at my friend Bill's house. He's at 8 Fifth. Can you get here? The penthouse. Oh you'll have to tell the doorman you're visiting the Honorable Bill Simpson. He's really strict, especially after midnight, but I'll leave your name with him so he'll let you up. You sound terrible. No, of course it's ok. Nah, we're not doing anything. I said anytime, right. So come on over. Bill says he'll put out some cheese."

"Queens," Brooke said when she snapped her phone closed.

"You know people from Queens?"

"Only one person and she's coming here so get dressed."

When he said he'd put out some cheese, Bill Simpson really meant that he'd put out a variety of cheeses, with crackers, a bit of leftover pâté and smoked salmon on a silver tray with linen napkins. He was startled when Lux, in her too-short, too-loud skirt, walked across the grand parquet floor that he had inherited from his grandmother.

When Lux stepped off the elevator and stood in front of a set of huge mahogany doors stained blood red and varnished to a high sheen, she thought for sure she was in the wrong place. She rang the bell and heard Brooke's voice from inside call, "It's open."

Lux entered Bill Simpson's home and looked around. Her eyes popped wide in amazement. This was not an apartment but the main office of some large mid-city bank. A huge painting done by Brooke hung in the foyer. The painting depicted two men in three-piece suits sitting at opposite ends of a large, beautiful couch. A spaniel lying on the rug was looking lovingly at the gentleman sitting on the right. The gentleman on the left was stroking a sleeping kitten curled up on his lap. The two handsome men sat rigid and perfect, separated by an ocean of fine upholstery.

"Do you like my painting? It's my favorite," Bill happily volunteered when it seemed like Lux was never going to stop looking at the canvas.

"This is your house," Lux said as a statement, still staring at the painting.

"Yes, it is now."

"And that's the painting you picked. Or did you have Brooke paint it for you?"

"I bought it from one of her early shows. I just fell in love with it. How did you know it was one of Brooke's?"

"Duh," Lux said, still staring at the painting. The signature was far too small to be read from where Lux was standing but after several visits to Brooke's studio, her style became obvious to Lux.

"What do you think of it?" he asked.

"I don't know nothing about painting, except that more people like beige than purple, which is crazy, but I think you should live somewhere that you're really comfortable."

"What do you mean?" Bill asked as his eye flittered around his sumptuous home.

"No, I mean it's real nice," Lux said, "but all the gay guys from my high school dream about moving to like Greenwich Village, right, or that place in Rhode Island. Or is it at Cape Cod?"

"Cape Cod," Bill said as his mouth went dry.

"Oh," Lux said. She did not mean it as a test, but the fact that Bill immediately understood that she was referring to the gay enclave in Provincetown confirmed for Lux that Bill was either homosexual or clairvoyant.

As a judge, Bill Simpson was trained not to show his thoughts and so he just looked at Lux who just looked back at him. Standing on the grand staircase watching the scene unfold, Brooke began to laugh.

"Bill isn't," Brooke said but the tumblers in her brain had already started to spin, "gay, Lux."

Brooke's mind was reeling. Lux just called Bill a homosexual, Brooke thought. Next thing she'd be calling him a cocker spaniel.

"He's not? Geez, I'm sorry. I ah, geez, I ah guess I don't meet many guys who are so, ah, I dunno, clean-looking as you are. And ah, stand up as straight as you do," Lux stumbled, feeling like she'd come in with poop on her shoes. Real poop, not imaginary poop. As far as Lux could tell, Brooke's guy was gay.

"Not to worry," Bill assured Lux warmly.

"Uh, ok," she said to him. "I'm Lux."

"William Bradley Simpson IV, I'd like you to meet Lux Kerchew Fitzpatrick," said Brooke, wondering what other colorful sparks that might flare up if kooky Lux smashed into stiff, conservative Bill. Bill gay? How odd that Lux would say such a thing.

"Lux et Veritas? Your father was a Yale man?" Bill asked.

"No," Lux said.

"Your mum, then?" he asked.

"What about her?"

"Did she attend Yale?"

"No. She's from Jersey, but she graduated from Thomas Jefferson High in East New York because they moved there after my grandpa died, but she still thinks of herself as a Jersey girl. Weird, huh?"

"Um. Yes."

"Listen, do you know what the word 'lux' means?" Lux asked.

"Yes," Bill said brightly and then waited for her to say it.

"What does it mean?"

"Oh," Bill laughed, caught off guard. "It means 'light' in Latin. And the Latin phrase 'Lux et Veritas' means 'light and truth.' It's the motto of my alma mater. Yale. And that's why I thought maybe your father went to Yale also."

"Thomas Jefferson. Also."

"And Kerchew?" continued Bill in his grandmother's politeness. "Is that a family name?"

"It's the sound of a sneeze," Lux said absently, her eyes drifting across the other paintings and onto the books that lined the walls of the next room. Bill, smitten, followed her into the living room offering comfy slippers, a bathrobe, and some really good skin cream to stop the chafing of cheap tissues and tears.

They settled into the kitchen and the story poured out. Lux started in reverse chronological order, with getting dumped followed by bad sex and then legal papers. The timeline got messed up when Lux told Brooke and Bill about Carlos, Jonella, and Auntie Who-ah's real estate holdings. Bill gasped when Lux showed her still-mangled pinky finger. Brooke held her hand and agreed that Trevor had been an absolute pig to her and did not mention that she understood Trevor's side as well.

"You can find another crappy job," Bill said as he loaded a cracker with some softened Brie and handed it to Lux. "But you've got to think beyond that, too. You should look into getting a full bachelor's degree. Education is very important if you want to maintain your money. And you might want to diversify your portfolio. I mean real estate is good, but if that ship sinks, all your cargo is on it."

"Oh my God, you're so right," Lux said. "Ok, but like say you wanted to buy something like stock, right? How do you, you know, do it? I mean like, how do you pick one? And then like, ok, who takes your money and how do you get it to them?"

Every Cinderella needs a fairy godfather, Brooke thought as Bill zipped through the basics of creating a relationship with a brokerage firm. Well, not "fairy" she corrected herself. And then she worried about why she would feel the need to correct herself for that perfectly reasonable cultural allusion. Brooke listened as Bill began to tell Lux about the huge penthouse he had inherited from his grandmother, the origins of the woodwork and the imported tiles and the English furniture in the library. Brooke was surprised to hear him tell Lux how the rooms depressed him, how he longed to live somewhere without a doorman who noted all comings and goings. Brooke tried to concentrate on Bill and Lux in the present tense, but her brain was replaying and reexamining every erotic thing that Bill had ever said or done.

"Yeah, I've seen some of those lofts downtown. They're nice, but they're way out of my reach," Lux was telling Bill. "I'm focusing on like small condos in good neighborhoods that need work. Cuz I can make the work happen, but I'm afraid of getting caught with a huge mortgage if a tenant you know, totally flakes out on me. My lawyer says I should be bold cuz I can, you know, borrow from my own equity, but I dunno, that seems too risky. You know what I mean? Like some pyramid that could fall in ah, you know, a heartbeat."

"I think when you have three or four places under your belt, rented to good long-term tenants, you will feel more comfortable extending your capital to other…"

"What's my capital?" Lux interrupted him.

"Your cash," Brooke interjected as she offered the loaf of pâté to Lux.

"What is it?" Lux asked, eyeing the brownish gray lump.

"Pâté," said Bill.

"No shit?" Lux said shoving a knife into it and then directly into her mouth. She pushed it around with her tongue, flattening it against the roof of her mouth, then suddenly stopped mid push.

"You don't like it? Did it spoil? Not good?" Bill asked, sniffing the lump.

"The way everyone got excited about it, I just thought it would be sweet," Lux said as she tried to get the unruly liver paste under control in her mouth. "It tastes like liver."

"It is liver."

"Oh? Yuck!"

Bill handed her a linen napkin embroidered with his family's coat of arms. Lux spat the liver into the napkin and tossed it into the trash. Bill smiled. They ate and talked about Brooke's newest painting, about whom Lux should speak to about getting another job, about Bill's new drapes in the study, about where Lux should take classes, what Lux should do with her capital, do with her hair, what Lux should do with her beautiful life. The talking was good. And as they spoke, the long night of sex and rejection started taking its toll on Lux's neck muscles. When she found she could not hold her head up for another minute Bill urged her to pick a bedroom and go to sleep. Lux chose the lavender room. In the morning she would lie in the lavender sheets and consider the matching lavender walls, marveling that her beloved purple could be so whispery and tasteful.

Brooke said goodnight to Lux and closed the door. She walked back to the center of the apartment and found Bill in the foyer, standing in front of the painting he had purchased from her so many years ago. Brooke put her arms around Bill's smooth back and giggled in his ear.

"Can we keep her, Daddy? Can we keep her, huh, huh?"

"She is something," Bill agreed still staring at the painting.

"Can we adopt her?"

"Mmmmmmmm," Bill said, his mind elsewhere.

"What are you thinking about?" Brooke asked.

"What it's like to lead a life void of expectations," Bill said. "What would it be like if no one believed you had anything to offer? There would be no responsibility. And then, say you get even one or two places farther than zero. Say for instance, one day you manage to actually open a brokerage account. Would that be a huge celebration? What would it be like to have no one invested in you? No one watching you for signs of happiness?"

"Free, fun, sad, scary. What's the difference? It's not us."

"I think I would have made an excellent president," Bill said apropos of nothing.

"President of what?" Brooke asked as she slid her arms around and held him from behind.

"The United States of America."

Brooke, who laughed at everything, did not laugh.

"Did you paint this for me?" Bill asked indicating the image of two gentlemen on opposite ends of the sofa. "Did you intend to depict two gay men, lovers, sitting in public, not showing any affection for each other?"

"No," Brooke said suddenly feeling quite cold. "Is that what you see in it?"

"No, no, no. But that girl, she saw it in just a second. Does anyone else see it? Brooke? Do you see it?"

Panic had constricted his throat and the last questions came out in a higher pitch than Bill's normal baritone.

"What are you talking about?" Brooke asked. The sound of his voice frightened her.

Bill took Brooke's hand and held it to his lips for a long time before he kissed the palm. He didn't want to lose her. She had been his wife in all things except sex, fidelity, and cohabitation for more than twenty years. He had done something both foolish and special for her tonight when he tried to change himself to make her happy.

"What I did tonight, I did because I love you. I feel like we've sifted the water of sexual experimentation and found that thing that sometimes remains when passion and romance dies."

"I don't understand," Brooke asked again, although in her heart she knew.

"Nothing," he said, "I'm, I, I guess I'm trying to tell you that I love you."

"Is that all you wanted to tell me?" Brooke asked.

Following a large and expensive party, Bill's paternal grandfather had shot himself in the head on his fiftieth birthday. Bill's father, in spite of knowing some of the very best oncologists in the city, had not sought treatment for his simple cancer until it had become so complex and invasive that death soon followed diagnosis.

No one spoke to Bill of the sufferings of these beautiful, unhappy, homosexual men, tortured by sex, but his mother and grandmother had watched him grow up like a pair of lionesses protecting the last living cub. They watched him too closely, anxiously awaited the appearance of his impending sexuality. Their terror rubbed off on him.

The arrival of nubile, teenaged Brooke put everyone's mind at ease for many years. In the foreplay days of their sex life, the thrill of being naked and alone together overwhelmed any details of the desires they may have had inside them. It was all new and all good. In college they both experimented, sometimes together. As time went on, Brooke lost the taste for many of the things that had appealed to her in her youth such as threesomes, rum with coke, and girls. Bill's tastes changed in a very similar fashion.

When Bill was young and carefree and still drinking a lot, he would put his penis into just about anything, as is the nature of young, carefree boys who drink a lot. By twenty-five his love for Brooke was stronger but his passion for her body was beginning its slow fade. Other desires started to demand exercise. He pushed them away, clinging to Brooke and his denial. The lie festered and he could not stop the resulting ooze as it seeped into his most significant relationships like some unnamed poison. By thirty-seven, after visiting many urologists, Bill still refused to admit, even to himself, that he was a horny homosexual. He preferred to be an impotent heterosexual. That year Brooke designed her first tattoo.

The line of homosexuality running through his body was quite thin and simple. Bill wanted hard, rigid bodies, not soft, wet openings. He continued to have sex with Brooke as often as he could manage it because he was afraid of losing her. Sexually, he performed extremely well because it helped him believe the lie he told himself about his desires. He played the role of Brooke's lover with grand flare, almost as if his life depended on convincing her that his passion for her body was real.

But pretending took a great deal of energy and over the years it wore him down. By the time he was thirty-nine, Bill's mother, Eleanor, began to worry about him in a new way. When she saw the depression that had plagued her husband flare up in her son, Eleanor decided that she was ready to accept his gayness, but by then she could not reverse the fear and self-loathing she had silently instilled in her big, blond cub.

When his grandmother died and Bill inherited her vast amounts of money and real estate, Eleanor had taken him aside after the funeral. In the heat of a Palm Beach August she took him down to the beach, away from the house where no one could hear but the surf and told him that she thought it was ok to be a homosexual.

"Why would you say that, Mother?"

"Because your father and Miles Randolph never played a stroke of golf in their whole lives."

"Mr. Randolph?"

"Yes."

"Oh my God, at the funeral he was weeping so loudly!"

"Right."

"Wow."

"Miles Randolph loved your father. And so did I."

Bill's mother reached out and took her son's pale hand. She reached up and pushed the blond hair out of his green eyes and said to her boy, "Billy, I just want you to be happy."

And so he tried. He went to Mexico and tried. He went to Bangkok and tried really hard. He spent a lot of time in Paris, trying to be happy, and sometimes he was; but every time he got back to his home he found the weight of mahogany and family connections and the eyes of his colleagues would quickly squish happiness to bits. Even within the inviting world of his gay friends he felt he had to hide his desire for the beautiful men lounging poolside. Maybe it was all those years living under the watchful eyes of lionesses looking for a sign of danger that made him fear stepping out of his closet. Still, he was a passionate man who needed sex.

When he needed love, he called Brooke. She saw that his erection would soften when she removed her brassiere. She wondered why he was spending so much of his vacation time playing around in France. It had not occurred to her that he was pitching in a different league, until Lux gave it a name.

"I know you love me, Bill, but is there something else you want to tell me?" Brooke asked, not ready to believe that the man who had just made love to her three times in a night was not really attracted to women. She allowed herself to skip over the fact that he'd used a chemically enhanced penis to make it happen for her, and that he had not come at all.

"Brooke, I love you," Bill sputtered.

"Already established," she said.

"And I am…," Bill said and then stopped. He refused to commit to any specific adjective.

Brooke waited. The silence grew until Bill felt he had to fill it.

"It's just that upon occasion I find myself staring at beautiful men," Bill said as if it were nothing more than a very fine point of a specific rule of law. "Tom McKenna, for example, the pro at the golf club. He is a very handsome man and I ah, I don't think it's an unnatural attraction. And it ends there."

Brooke's bullshit meter flared up suddenly, registering

a high percentage of crap to truth in Bill's statement. She could have been angry with him except that he was obviously in such terrible pain.

"How long have you had this attraction?" Brooke asked and at the same time wondered how long she had known it was there. When Lux called it by name, an information virus had begun to work through Brooke's memories, highlighting a particular moment, a look, a gesture. How long had it been there?

"Since Jack Berenbott," Bill said.

Jack was an old school chum they'd run into while vacationing in St. Kit. He flirted with Brooke and Brooke flirted back. When Jack suggested a threesome, Bill agreed, thinking he wanted to see Brooke thoroughly pleasured. After it was over he tried to tell himself that he'd done it for her, but really he'd done it to see Jack.

"That long?" Brooke gasped, feeling like an idiot.

"I though I could outrun it," Bill said.

"Outrun it!" Brooke said. "It's not a pony, Bill."

"I am not totally gay, Brooke," Bill said. "Not really gay at all. I mean, if you were to graph it in a bell curve you'd see I have many, many more points in the straight portion of the curve than the gay."

"Except that you want to have sex with men," Brooke said.

"No. I've done some experimenting. That's all," Bill waffled, "my heart is with you."

"But your dick is with Jack Berenbott."

Bill was quiet for a very long time.

"I can cut it off," he said very seriously.

"Your dick?" Brooke asked.

"No! This gay thing. It's not a big part of me. Really. I love you. I have loved you since that very first hangover we shared at your grandmother's apartment. I can change for you."

Brooke didn't answer.

She turned to stare at her painting of lovers who would not touch. She wanted to pretend that Lux was very wrong. Lux had walked into Bill's apartment and said hello to the two thousand pound gorilla in a tutu that had been quietly living there for years. Now that the gorilla had been given a name, it was not going to shrink back into the shadows.

"There's only been a couple of men," Bill said sincerely. And, since he figured all the sex he'd had outside of the United States didn't really count, he honestly believed it was true. "And I haven't had sex with anyone but you for at least five years. I want to be with you more than anything else in the world. You are the best thing in my life."

Brooke tried to process the information. She thought about all the times she'd had sex with Bill. Lux had to be wrong. Crazy girl from Queens. What did she know?

Brooke stood in the foyer of Bill's apartment. Suddenly all she could see was that night in St. Kit that they had made love to Jack Berenbott. She picked over the evening, but couldn't find a single clue. They'd had a good time with Jack, then returned to their room and done it again just the two of them. There had been years of good sex between then and now. That had to count for something.

Then she weighed past great sex against his present

impotence. Maybe they just needed a break. Maybe he could control it. But did she want him to control it? Did she want to be involved with someone who was always holding his breath? Her head started to hurt. It was too big. She was standing at the end of the continental shelf. Everything in front of her was suddenly ocean.

"I'm going to go home now," Brooke said. "Would you please call up my car."

24. Winning

MARGOT LAY IN BED, thinking about masturbation. The Saturday sun was flitting through her blinds and nothing was on her agenda. She could, if she wanted to, dedicate the whole morning in bed to the most consistent and reliable lover she ever had. Thinking about herself, she slid out of her T-shirt and sweatpants and began to rotate her pelvis in a delightful figure eight, rubbing her naked thighs against the softness of her sheets.

She considered treating herself to a long, lovely bath. Margot started planning her morning. She would fill the deep bathtub with hot water only up to the point where it would lap at the bottom of her open vagina while her fingers massaged the top. Then, just before she came, she would lift her body up and throw it back into her bed where she would bring herself to a perfect orgasm, the kind that made her scratch at the pillows and shout to the ceiling. Then, Margot planned, she would take herself out to a fine breakfast.

As she was getting out of bed and heading towards

the bathtub, Margot's buzzer rang. Someone was at the front door. Margot guessed it was the newspaper delivery, unable to get into the lobby. She and her body would probably want the newspaper later, after, so Margot strode across her living room and hit the front door buzzer.

"Who is it?" Margot asked.

If he had called first, she would have told him to stay home. But Trevor was standing outside her building, ringing her buzzer unexpected and unannounced. He said he was out jogging and just happened to be passing her house. Could he come up for a quick coffee?

"Ahhhhh," Margot intoned into the intercom as she looked down at her waiting, naked body.

Through the squawk of Margot's intercom, her hesitant "ahhhhh" sounded like a groan and Trevor wished for a moment that he had not rung her bell. She was going to laugh at him or worse, lecture him about office policies again. But his family-sized apartment had seemed so empty that morning. He left the house with the intention of going for a good run, alone. He would stop on the way back for coffee and a bagel, alone. He would pick up the paper and return to his apartment, alone. When he found himself running down Margot's block, he suddenly could not bear the whole "alone" component of his day a moment longer and so he rang her buzzer. He was about to apologize for interrupting her Saturday and return home when she told him she was sending down the middle elevator. She gave him instructions to get on and turn the key in her private lock. That would send the elevator straight to her apartment.

This is the moment that compulsive shopping is all about, Margot thought as she dashed into her closet and pulled out a stunning silk nightgown with matching robe. It was a silky, peachy, shiny thing with well-placed inlays of ivory lace. She cut off the store tags and threw it on her body.

"Hey Trev, come on into the kitchen," Margot called as the elevator door opened. "I bought some special coffee from the farmers' market. It'll definitely perk you up."

"Do I look like I need perking?" Trevor asked as he entered Margot's spotless kitchen.

"Mmm, you're a little hangdog around the edges."

"Yes, well, I don't feel hangdog. I'm actually feeling very happy to find myself on dry land again."

It was then that Trevor looked at Margot. Her cheeks were flushed pink as if she had been exercising.

"You look beautiful. And that nightgown! Goodness, Margot, do you really sleep in that?"

Margot nodded calmly as she pulled a pot off the shelf and slid it onto the stove. She filled it with water, coffee, and sugar and set it to heat.

"You were saying something about dry land?" she asked and moved on to making toast.

"Yes, I'm just glad it's over with," Trevor said.

Margot did not respond as she stirred her pot of Turkish coffee and looked at Trevor. She liked his strong profile and the gray around his temples. In her stories, Lux had described him as an excellent lover, both gentle and exciting.

They drank in silence for a bit, each turning over their own thoughts.

"So," he said at last, "what are they saying about me?"

"Who?"

"At the office," Trevor said, wishing she would stop making him pull it out of her.

"Well, it falls into two categories. Intra-office and extra-office. Within the office we think you're an asshole. An expensive asshole that cost the firm $15,000 and a decent secretary. Warwick was beside himself on Monday when the temp faxed a confidential memo to opposing counsel. He complained about Lux all the time but now that she's gone he realizes what a great secretary she was."

"And outside the office?" Trevor groaned, expecting the worst.

"Unfortunately, outside the office they think you're a hot stud muffin who must have some big ride to have scored the hot chick that no one else could nail."

"Really?"

"Unfortunately, yes."

"How close am I to getting fired?"

Margot raised her hands and held the palms a good two feet apart from each other. The information raised Trevor's spirits a bit.

"Have you seen her again?" Margot asked.

"No, no, of course not," Trevor lied and she let him. Margot had already gotten the whole story from Brooke.

"Margot, do you think I made a mistake?"

Margot held the steaming warmth of her coffee cup to her face. She believed that Trevor had made so many mistakes that she didn't know where to start. He'd picked a volatile younger woman over a smart, beautiful peer and then he'd let himself be pulled penis-first into work where he disrupted their office and destroyed his own hard-won reputation as a cool-headed, reliable attorney. He would never make partner at Warwick and it was far too late to start again at a new firm.

"Yes. I think you made some serious mistakes," Margot said. She had more to say, but Trevor was already explaining.

"I was so small after my wife left me. Lux was so beautiful and so young. She got so…"

Trevor's voice trailed off into an embarrassed silence. Still, he was clearly pleased with whatever it was that he was embarrassed to say.

"She got so…what?" Margot had to know.

"So very wet," Trevor said, smiling. "Well, you know what I mean."

"Wet?"

"You know how exciting that is. You know, when you can get a woman all wet like that."

Margot sipped her Turkish coffee. The sweet steam curled up around her eye and then dispersed. She leaned onto the counter in her kitchen and tried to digest what Trevor just said. Trevor carried on with his confession.

"Lux made me feel really good and I'm sorry I had to hurt her."

"I see," Margot said.

"You think I should send her some money?"

"No."

"But she doesn't have a job. What will she do?"

"She's fine."

"Is there anything she needs?"

"I think she told Brooke she's saving up for a new

sink, but that's secondhand information. Listen, Trev, can we go back to the wet part?"

"What wet part?"

"The part where you said that I know what it's like to make a woman wet."

"Yes."

"And why would I know the thrill of rousing another woman?"

"Because you and that Brooke woman…"

"No."

"No?'

"No," Margot said definitively.

"Oh."

They both sat for a moment in Margot's kitchen, sipping their tiny pots of boiled coffee.

"It's just that when I made the move on you, you were clearly not interested in having sex," Trevor said.

"You made the move on me?"

"Chinese food? Mu shu chicken? Remember?"

"That was the move?"

"Well, yes Margot, that was the move," Trevor said, his voice growing a little hard. "And you were not interested in me."

"And so that made me a lesbian?"

"Well, that and I noticed that you and Brooke have lunch together at least once a week and sometimes after lunch you come back to your office all kind of, well, steamy. I guess I filled in the blanks to make myself feel better. So, the truth is you're not a lesbian and the Chinese food rejection was about me. You just didn't want me, then."

"You are so wrong!" Margot sputtered.

"Ah. Then you are gay."

"No! If I'd known that Chinese food night was my last chance to get into your pants, Trevor, I would have thrown down the mu shu, hiked up my skirt, and jumped on you."

"Really?" Trevor asked, smiling for the first time since he'd entered her apartment.

"Really," Margot said, feeling a great weight lift suddenly off her shoulders.

"So, you think I'm ok," Trevor said as he slid his hand across the counter and found hers. He ran his thick, rough index finger underneath her long, thin hand. He lifted up the individual fingers and then let them fall. She felt she should pull her hand away, but it was too pleasant, for a moment, to be the winner. She was noticing how big his hands were and how soft his eyes. For months she had fantasized about what she would do when this moment finally came, how she would unwrap and give herself to him. If she dropped the stunning nightgown on her kitchen floor and crossed to him now, Trevor would find that Margot was already quite wet herself. If she made love to him this morning, he would believe that she was passionate, easily roused, wild and full of fire.

"Can't do it, Trevor," Margot said suddenly.

"Of course you can," Trevor said as he moved further up her arm. He reached for her elbow and pulled her to him. Atlanta Jane stood on the sidelines in buckskins, cheering her creator on.

"I would have made love to you—in ways you could not possibly imagine—but you went and not only had sex with one of the secretaries, but you also got caught and made a big stink about it. You're branded at work. People are watching you. And you are completely and totally off limits to me as long as you are at Warwick. I'm not ruining my chances of making partner for sex."

He looked out her window, studying her view of the East River while Margot studied his face. Her body still wanted him. And her body feared that the years between fifty and sixty were her last chance to spend ten years getting really good sex. That after sixty she would lose the fevered interest that had defined her sex drive since thirty-five. If she could figure out how to throw away that ancient nagging worry that sleeping with Trevor would ruin her reputation, she could jump in and grab one long lovely swim with him before the sun went down.

"Well, I guess I should go then," Trevor said. He set his coffee on the counter with a clink and headed for the door.

"Ah, the sink," Margot instructed.

"Excuse me?"

"Put your cup in the sink and run some water in it so it doesn't stick. And then, if you want to go, you can. Although if you go now, I'll think you're an asshole."

Trevor paused at the sink. He looked at his hands. He looked at the view. He studied the water as it hit his cup, splashing Turkish coffee grounds all over Margot's white sink. Finally, he looked at Margot and saw she was smiling at him.

"And if I stay?" he asked.

"Well," she said, "I don't have any plans today that can't be changed."

"Do you cook?"

"Are you kidding me? You have just consumed the full extent of my cooking repertoire. In any case, I'm not cooking for you."

"No, no. What I meant was, I cook," Trevor said. "Really well. I could run down and get some eggs."

"You're gonna cook me breakfast?"

"If you want me to. Where's the best grocery from here?"

"You sit," Margot said. "I'll throw on some sweats and go down to the corner. Eggs and what else?"

"Juice, milk, whatever you want. I can cook anything, even a soufflé if you want one."

"Can you make the eggs over easy without breaking the yolks?"

"Uh, yeah, sure."

"Ok, don't move," she said. "I'm running to the corner and back."

Margot went to her closet and withdrew a lavender cotton skirt and the pretty little blouse that went with it. She brushed her hair, threw on lavender mules, a string of pearls that leaned towards pink and was ready to go. Trevor sat down on her couch to wait.

"You look lovely," he said.

"Thank you," Margot answered as she pressed the button for the elevator and wondered why his wife had dumped him. He looked contented for a moment, but then some bad thought walked across his forehead and he suddenly slumped into the soft pillows of the couch.

"You ok?" she asked.

"Yeah, sure," he said.

As she waited for the elevator to open, Trevor shouted to her from across the apartment.

"Margot, is it because I'm too old?"

Margot laughed at his deliciously absurd thought. Still giggling, she skipped into the elevator.

"I'm going to take that as a no," Trevor called to her as the doors to her elevator swung shut. Margot slipped the funny-shaped key into her personal slot and as the elevator descended she thought to herself, have I totally lost my mind?

When the elevator reached the lobby and the doors opened, Margot's downstairs neighbor was ready to get on.

"Sorry, Fritz, I forgot my purse," Margot sang as she twisted her key in the other direction and shot back up to her apartment. All the way up she scolded herself for being so pigheaded. Stupid, she thought. There is a man sitting in my apartment with whom I really want to have sex. This same man is willing to be my friend without sex and I'm going out to buy eggs! How stupid is that!

Passing the 4th floor Margot stepped out of her panties and slipped off her pretty little blouse. She tried to unhook the back of her bra at the same time she wiggled out of her skirt. It was impossible as the bra demanded greater attention and would not release. As the doors opened on her apartment, she hopped out, dragging her skirt off the tip of her toe.

Trevor, sitting despondent in the same spot on the couch, was wondering how many eggs he would have to cook before Margot agreed to make love to him. He was off by at least six months.

"Fuck work," Margot said as she raced nearly naked

into her apartment and tackled him on the couch. Her arms hit him square in the chest and pushed him back against the pillows. Atlanta Jane would have been proud.

Trevor had not seen such a delicate, lacy brassiere for a long time. His wife had worn dull cotton sports bras and Lux favored red and black sateen. He crushed the white lace of Margot's bra between his fingers and snapped the whole thing off in less than a second. His own baggy sweatpants were held to his hips by a simple drawstring that Margot was able to overcome in an instant. She pushed them down until they caught between the couch and his knees.

Margot sat astride his lap, a knee at each of his hips and one hand on each of his shoulders. He already had an erection, from when he first caught sight of Margot's breast pushing against her very glamorous, grown-up nightgown. All systems were locked and loaded, ready to go.

Then Trevor stopped. He took his hand off Margot's breasts and rested it on her face. She leaned her cheek into his hand. Trevor pulled her face close to him, until she could feel the heat of his mouth just above hers. He stopped there for a moment to let her tremble. She licked her lips.

Trevor looked in Margot's eyes and marveled that they were so soft this close up. Quite unexpected, he saw a little fear nestled in her longing. He wanted to tell her that he would never hurt her, but he saw there that he already had.

"This could get big," Trevor whispered instead of "I'm sorry."

For a moment, Margot worried that he was making a stupid joke about his penis, but instead of proceeding with sexual bravado, Trevor pulled her close and kissed her long. Then, with Margot in his arms, he stood up and, stepping out of the sweat pants that were now tangled at his ankles, Trevor carried her into her bedroom.

He started small, rubbing her breasts and stomach. He pushed her hand away when she tried to stimulate him in return. When her breath became short and slightly gasping, Trevor, fully confident of his sovereignty in the area of cunnilingus, began his campaign to secure Margot's undying love. When her gasps became a moan and her body trembled in his mouth, Trevor pulled Margot onto him.

For the first time in many years, Margot lost control. She wasn't orchestrating. She wasn't thinking. She wasn't planning her next move. As the waves rocked her again and again, Margot held onto Trevor like a shipwrecked swimmer clinging to a life vest. In the middle of making love to Trevor, she might have recalled how well they had danced together. She might have philosophized that this feeling of connection was why sex could make a women fall in love. Had she been capable of thought, Margot might have been brewing up any number of reflections. The closest she got to experiencing an intelligible thought that afternoon and for most of the next week, however, was a feeling like fireworks in her brain as she came again and again.

Margot called in sick for the week. And, in fact, she remained in bed for four days straight. On the fifth day, Margot and Trevor went to a movie. On the evening of the sixth day, Trevor asked if he could leave a toothbrush at her house. Margot, without a second thought, said yes.

25.
5 x 7

"*ATLANTA JANE GREW SOFTER,*" Margot read, "*as the orgasm spread up her belly and into her spine. Like fingers separating the vertebrae, pulling them straight, it crept up her back to her neck and released across my lips in a moan. She was done. She thought he was done too, but the wetness sliding down their legs was all hers.*"

Brooke wrote the word "my?" on her note pad to remind herself to mention the typo when Margot was done reading.

"*When he first started making love to her in the bright sunshine of her cabin, she had wanted to hide, to dim the lights or find a blanket to cover the flaws of her breasts, her thighs, her whole skin. He pulled off her buckskins and reveled in all of it. If he saw the damage of time, it didn't slow him down or cool his passion.*

"*For seventeen days, they lay under the thick wool blankets in her cabin doing little more than eating, talking, and having sex. They were so similar and so surprisingly well-matched that sometimes the talk was as good as the sex. Most of the time we were either laughing or making love. And the rumors were true. He was a big, thick wild ride. On Monday, Atlanta Jane had to go back to the business of keeping the town safe, but she would see him again and again and again."*

Margot put down her index cards with a sigh. Brooke had written several notes on how to improve the literary quality of the story. Margot looked so pleased with herself, however, that Brooke decided to hold her criticisms.

"That was great, Margot," Brooke said warmly.

"I liked it, too. But I think there were a couple of errors in pronouns," Aimee said.

"Really? I didn't notice any," Margot said.

"Yeah, you drop into the first person. But other than that it was really fun," Aimee responded.

"So Atlanta Jane finally got into the sack with Trevor the Texas Ranger," Brooke observed.

"Yes," Margot said, "he stopped by last Saturday looking very hang-dog and pathetic, needing coffee and offering to cook me eggs over easy."

"OH!" Aimee shouted from her bed as she made the connection between fact and fiction. "That's why you wanted to read your piece before Lux got here!"

"Are you planning to keep it from her?" Brooke asked.

"No, not the reality. But she was late and there seemed no reason to gloat in fiction while she listened," Margot said. "I'll just tell her the truth as simply as I can."

"Where is Lux?" Brooke asked.

"She promised to stop off at the printers and pick up those 5 x 7 prints of the baby shower lovers. The ones you ordered for me," Aimee said. "And you won't believe what she's letting me borrow!"

"What?" Brooke asked, pleased and surprised that Lux had something Aimee would want to borrow.

"Seems her dad is a huge science fiction fan," Aimee said.

"Makes sense," Margot said.

"He has in his collection a 1954 *Howdy Doody* episode in which William Shatner plays Ranger Bob."

"William Shatner in *Howdy Doody?*" Brooke said.

"Yeah. We're gonna watch that. Then a 1958 version of *Brothers Karamazov* with Yule Brenner," Aimee said, her voice full of excitement.

"*Brothers Karamazov* with William Shatner?" Brooke asked.

"And Yule Brenner," Aimee confirmed. "Then we're gonna finish up with Robert Burnett's indie flick *Free Enterprise.*"

"And the *Star Trek*," Brooke added.

"Well of course, all the *Star Trek*s," Aimee confirmed. "How could I do a William Shatner Festival without *Star Trek?*"

"Aimee, you are an entertainment nerd," Margot announced.

"Hey, trips to the bathroom are the highlight of the day," Aimee laughed. "That and I've listed some of my own prints on eBay."

"You're kidding!"

"It was one of the things I always meant to do if I ever had the time and now guess what I got—time."

"Anything sell?"

"Yep."

"Really?"

"Some of the old stuff does well and the baby shower prints are very popular. I made $5,600 and some change."

Brooke was quietly rolling it over in her mind. Trying to imagine the online auction house becoming the always-available gallery she'd longed for. The very thought of it made her temperature rise.

All three women looked up at the sound of the front door opening.

"Christ on a freaking crutch, Brooke!" Lux shouted from the front hall. "When you said 5 x 7 I thought you meant inches! This freakin' thing's huge!"

Brooke skipped out of the bedroom and called to Lux.

"Hey, Lux, we're in…"

Brooke stopped short at the sight of Lux.

"It's stupid right?"

"Ahhhhh…," Brooke stammered.

Lux stood before her, transformed. Blue penny loafers, khaki chinos, blue cotton shirt with a Peter Pan collar and a red cardigan sweater. Cable-knit. Pearls. From her toes to her chin she was a prep school girl on her way to English class. From her chin up she was the same red-haired, heavily made up, Lux of Queens.

"Oh my god," Brooke said finally. "Bill took you shopping."

"He's a monster. Try this on. Try this on. Wear this. Try that. He thinks I'm like 'Go to College Barbie' or something. He like, made me tell him the titles of all the books I've ever read all right, and, ok, and then he had his secretary type up a list of all the books he thinks I should have read already. Ok, that was one thing, right, and I thought that was a little weird but then this afternoon, ok, all those books start getting delivered to his house."

"He's a little intense," Brooke said.

"A little! He bought me six of these shirts! SIX! Six of these ugly boring shirts that make me look like a…oh fuck."

"What?"

"Nothin."

"What?" Brooke asked.

Lux realized that the shirts made her look like a boy. She didn't want to say anything else to hurt Brooke.

"These clothes make me look stupid," Lux said.

"Yes, they do," Brooke admitted. "Come show Aimee. She needs a laugh."

When Lux entered the room Aimee laughed. Margot laughed.

"You look like one of those children's books where you mix and match the head to the body," Margot noted.

Although Lux's transformation was very amusing, all Aimee could see was the enormous photograph she dragged behind her.

"My photograph!" Aimee gasped.

"It looks great!" Brooke said.

"But I asked you to order me some 5 x 7's!" Aimee said.

"That is 5 x 7," Brooke said with a glimmer of mischief in her eye. "Look, his vagina is gone. You've got a big empty wall there that needs something naked on it. Your photo looks amazing this size and anyway, it's my treat. I hope you like it."

"I love it," Aimee gushed. "Can you hang it in here? I want to look at it every day."

"Of course," Brooke said. Aimee stared at her photograph like it was some beloved child that has suddenly grown into adulthood. Aimee's lovers were so much better than the shock value of his finger-in-pussy "masterpiece." My work is good, Aimee thought. Why haven't I been this big all along?

As Brooke was hanging the photograph, her cell phone rang. If she'd seen the number that was flashing in her cell phone window, Brooke would not have answered her phone.

"This is Brooke. Oh. Hi…Yes. I have…I will…I said I will and I will. It's kind of a good idea but I'm just not sure…Yes. …Yes, I know I said I wanted it but I just have to think about it. Look, I'm in the middle of something and I gotta go….Yep. …YES, I will think about it some more. …Love you too….Hi to your mother."

Brooke adjusted the photograph on the wall where Aimee could see it. She looked at Aimee's swollen body, sighed, straightened her sweater and sat down.

"Bill wants to get married and have a baby."

Aimee and Margot looked at her, expecting more information than just that simple pronouncement.

"I don't know. I just don't know," Brooke answered. "I love Bill. But I think he's, well I think he's gay."

"Gay!" Aimee shouted. "Bill 'Best-Lay-of-Your-Life' Simpson cannot be gay!"

"I know," Brooke said, "I find it hard to believe also, and I was shocked when Lux called it…"

"Sorry, I shouldn'ta shot off my mouth"

"No, hey, it's ok," Brooke said. "I just keep thinking back over these moments and also, because our sex life, well, its current incarnation pales in comparison to its own former glory. If you know what I mean."

"I got no idea what you mean," Lux admitted.

"It's Viagra or bust," Brooke said.

"He's so young," Margot said.

"Exactly my point," Brooke said.

"Well, what does he say about it?" Aimee asked.

"He says he's not a homosexual. He promised me that when it's all said and done he's a pussy hound, not a butt pirate."

"Did the Honorable Bill Simpson really use the word 'butt pirate'?" Aimee asked.

"No," Brooke said, "I'm clearly paraphrasing for the entertainment value. If he's in love with a woman, if he's not having sex with other men, does that automatically make him heterosexual?"

"Ye—no," Margot said. "Is he having sex with said woman? Of course if he's attracted to men but insists on having sex with women that makes him a…"

"Psycho-sexual," Lux offered.

"Yeah," Brooke said. "Well, he said he's not gay. He's certainly not effeminate. He said he loves me and he wants me."

Brooke sat quietly and thought about it.

"How much does it matter? If he is gay, I'm not going to marry him, but I'll still love him. If he really wants a man, I'm not going to sleep with him anymore because that hurts my feelings. If this is who he is, ok, I'm still his friend. But I can't be the body he hides behind. It's not twisted to have desires, but when you hide them, they become twisted, and I don't want to be around that. It's the lying that's ugly."

"You're absolutely right. Honesty is everything," Margot said as she turned her whole body towards Lux. "Listen Lux, I've been spending a lot of time with Trevor and you were absolutely right, he is really well-hung. I intend to see him again. I hope you're not hurt and that you and I can still be friends."

Lux did not respond. As the surprise wore off, she sat quietly, thinking. In spite of her psychedelic upbringing, Lux was an intensely logical woman. She was, however, not very good at multitasking. Lux was unable to speak because she was busy concentrating on a complex problem, full of probability formulas. Lux silently weighed the probability of a friendship with Margot against the value of a relationship with Trevor. Margot won.

"Ok," Lux said quietly. Aimee stared at the ceiling and Brooke considered her nails.

"No, really, it's ok," Lux said. "He's a good guy. Geez you knew him before I ever met him. I hope you guys work out. Really. So listen, did you guys read yet? Cuz if Brooke is done talking about pirates and pussy, I wrote this piece about losing my virginity that I want to read to you."

"Sounds good," Aimee said, relieved that the life moment was over and they were moving back to art. "Who'd you lose your virginity to?"

"Carlos," Lux said. "Who'd you lose your to?"

"George Freeman, senior year, prom night. I was madly in love with him for several moments," Aimee said.

"I lost mine to Bill," Brooke sad sadly. "At sixteen at the Ritz-Carlton. He went down on me and I came. I mean, who comes when they lose their virginity?"

"Boys," said Aimee and Margot at the same time.

"But I dint write about Carlos," Lux said wistfully. "I wrote about how I would have liked to lose it, not about what really happened."

"Oooo!" said Margot, "I'd like to rewrite that moment."

"Ok, so here goes," Lux said as she unfurled her manuscript. The women got comfortable and Lux began to read.

"Ok, so first thing, I'm in love with an older guy. Not like twenty years older, but like five years older. And I'm not fourteen anymore either. I'm at least sixteen. And this guy, he's had sex before. And he loves me. So we agree to do it. And we talk about it. It doesn't just happen like that cuz he figures out how to get me alone. So one day…"

"During the day?" Aimee asked.

"Oh yeah. I would lose it during the day. So like, everyone is sober and there's light and I'm not tired," Lux said before she went back to reading.

"So one day, he takes me to a hotel. A nice place where the sheets come as part of the room, and we walk through the lobby and into the elevator and then up to the room he rented. He unlocks the door and we go inside. We start to kiss. And he takes my clothes off slowly. And I can see him and me in the mirror in front of the bed, which is kind of cool. But he doesn't look in the mirror. He's only watching the real me. So I'm naked but he's still dressed. And he starts to kiss me and touch my breasts and lick the nipples and then down to my belly button. And then he takes his shirt off. And then we lay down together on the bed. And he goes down on me, and keeps going

*down on me because he likes it, not just because he thinks he
has to so I'll suck his cock later. He keeps doing me until I'm
really, really wet. Soaking wet and I'm on the bed and my
body's almost bucking up and down because I want him inside
me.*

*"And this is important. I really want him to be inside me.
It's not like something I think I gotta do so everything else will
work out. I don't want him inside me because I think he'll like
me better if I do. Or that I don't have the energy to face the
begging and the abuse if I don't. I don't want to let him inside
of me cuz of what that might bring me. I just want him for
me, because I like the way it feels.*

*"But this is the first time and I know it's gonna hurt. He
tells me that he's gonna do it and then he puts the top of his
thingie just into the beginning of me, just at the soft fleshy
part. And he rubs it back and forth there. And he asks me if I
want a little more. And that just rocks me, I mean, that he
asks. And he says yes and more goes in and it starts to hurt but
I want it to happen. And he's getting psyched too, it's not just
me. And then he pushes in and it hurts a lot, but I was part of
the hurt too. And then we're off like a couple of racehorses. And
I'm part of it, not some girl watching on the sidelines hoping
that fucking him is gonna make everything ok. The end."*

The women sat quietly, thinking about all the things
in sex that have nothing to do with sex.

"So?" Lux asked. "Whaddy'think? I wrote it just like
I thought it. And then I crossed out all the 'rights' and
'you knows' and the other stuff and then I copied it over.
It makes a difference when you take out all that other
stuff, right?"

"It does," Brooke agreed.

"But you kept the honesty," Margot said. "That's good."

Lux smiled.

"So?" Lux asked, "how'd you rewrite your virginity?"

It was a big subject and they talked until the sun dropped low in the long windows. Then, Brooke started gathering up her bag and pulling out her cell phone.

"I'm going to just call Bill and I think I'll go over to his house and sit at the kitchen table and have a really long talk with him."

"I'm going running later tonight," Margot announced as they headed towards the door of Aimee's bedroom. "Lux, you want to come running with me?"

"Only if someone's chasing us."

Lux suddenly realized that once again she had no place to go. She'd left her stuff at Bill's house and if she returned there she'd interrupt Brooke's cozy evening of intense discussion. She could head home to Queens and try to avoid a contact high, but that was an impossible task. Lux decided she would buy a clean new notebook and a good sharp pencil and go park herself in the public library until they kicked her out. As Lux started to say good-bye, Aimee called out from her bed.

"Hey Lux, I mean, I thought you were gonna stick around and watch the *Howdy Doody* with me?"

Lux was momentarily startled. She was sure the voice had come from Aimee's bed, but that was just impossible. Maybe it was an auditory hallucination. Aimee hated her.

"Are you deaf, Lux?" Aimee asked when Lux didn't answer. "Do you want to stay and hang out?"

"Oh, yeah, sure. I'd love that," said Lux, who had seen

that particular episode of *Howdy Doody* at least a million times before.

In the elevator on the way down Margot and Brooke talked about Aimee and Lux. And as Lux settled back into the bedroom, she and Aimee began talking about Brooke and Margot.

"So you think Brooke should marry a guy who don't wanna have sex with her?"

"There are worse arrangements, such as filing for divorce while pregnant."

"Yeah, how's that going?"

"Well, I called Tokyo. And I called his agent. And they both agree that he has received the papers. The first papers don't say anything except that I have asked for a divorce. He's supposed to simply respond that he has received my filing."

"And?"

"No word. I got a message on my answering machine that had nothing to do with reality. He wants to know what my due date is. No mention of the fact that I think he's a useless bastard that I want out of my life. Although, how exactly does one respond to that sort of information?"

Lux and Aimee laughed. Lux was getting the hang of Aimee's use of sarcasm and irony. Her discovery of the word "sardonic" made her more comfortable talking to Aimee. Aimee told Lux about the wine and roses days of her early marriage, how happy she had been and how in love. Lux told Aimee that her brother in Utah had married a woman who had only one arm and they seemed very happy together. They talked and talked as the night grew cool and quiet.

"No shit!" was Lux's breathless response when Aimee admitted that she thought Lux might have real talent as a writer.

"Oh my God!" Aimee gasped when Lux recounted the full story of the night she accepted $50 to give a stranger a blowjob because she believed she desperately needed the money for a prom dress.

"Can you believe it? I was like, so totally afraid, terrified, of losing this loser that I did everything I had to do in order to look better than my girlfriend at a dance. A school dance. And in some ways it wasn't as bad as I thought it was gonna be. I mean the guy was youngish, and he was clean and he didn't hit me and he didn't hurt me but there was this meanness in the way he touched me that hurt my feelings."

Lux had never told anyone that story. Certainly not Jonella. Not even Auntie Who-ah. And here she was telling a woman who didn't even really like her. Maybe that's part of what made it ok, that Aimee already thought badly of Lux and so it wasn't going to get any worse. Let her call me a whore, Lux thought. We've already been down that road.

"And so, after that night I just had to get away, to you know, separate myself from my family because I think there was just too much pot and beer. And I know it was just pot and beer but it was like, all the time and it was clouding my thoughts and like I was losing, I wasn't, I mean, I wasn't able to reason things through in the right way. So I had to pull away from them. Luckily they never noticed because they love me and it woulda hurt them to think that I couldn't be with them no more."

Aimee was quiet for a while and then she said, "I'm really sorry."

"Fuck, it wasn't your fault."

"No, for…Um, what am I sorry for? I don't know. Sorry you got your feelings hurt, I guess."

"Well, no one made me do it. I used to feel bad, like some tragic thing had happened to me and then I felt bad, like embarrassed that I'd done something so nasty. On the upside, I started to brush my teeth a whole lot more."

"Really?"

"Oh yeah, for months after I was like, totally obsessed with oral hygiene."

"You got good stories, Lux."

"You think?

"Oh yeah."

"Cuz to me, my life seems like one stupid mistake after another."

"Well, yeah. So does mine. But not every day."

This thought, that someone as clean and successful as Aimee had mistakes and desires too, took root in Lux and started to grow as they talked. They talked real estate. They talked work. They talked clothes. They talked sex. They talked movies and they talked about their mothers. They talked until Aimee started to mumble and after she was asleep Lux kept talking on to herself.

As the sun came up, Lux grabbed a quick shower. She washed her face clean and tied back her wet hair in one of Aimee's barrettes. Then she let herself out the door and went in search of coffee and breakfast. Walking down the avenue, whistling, Lux caught sight of herself in a shop window. She looked tired from being up all night. Her flat hair and clean, pretty face was a bit of a shock to her and she was wearing really stupid clothes, but still on that morning, Lux felt better than she had in all the years of her life.

26. *Butt Pirate or Pussy Hound*

*B*ROOKE FELT HERSELF GROWING pale and suddenly she could not hold up her body. She let herself slump down onto the burgundy leather club chair in Bill's study.

"I'm sorry, Brooke, but it's true," Bill said, and then he reiterated the cold hard fact that had caused the blood to abandon Brooke's cheeks and the strength to leave her legs. "Ever since you left I have thought of nothing except how we can make this relationship work. I need to change myself. And I've finally realized. I'm not homosexual. I'm not heterosexual. I'm just non-sexual. Sex simply isn't that important to me anymore."

"Bill," Brooke said, "you're either dead or lying. You're still young and healthy and sexy. How can you say sex is not important to you?"

"It's not worth it to me," Bill said.

"Sometimes when I masturbate I use the thought of you naked to get myself going," Brooke admitted. "You can't look that good and be that dead. Maybe you should quit your job and move back to Paris."

"Will you come with me?"

Brooke thought about it for a moment.

"You want me to move to Paris for your sex life?" she asked.

"I can't live without you," he said and then turned away as tears suddenly dropped off his pale eyelashes and fell into his drink with a tiny "plink" that only Bill could hear. He abandoned his ruined scotch on the windowsill, confident the maid would discover it there within the hour and return it to the kitchen.

"Are you ill?" Brooke asked. "Maybe there's a better urologist."

"I'm fine," Bill said as he crossed to the cabinet, his right hand pulling out another crystal highball glass, while at the same time his left lifted the scotch and poured. "There's nothing wrong with me. I had a full physical yesterday. Everything works. I am in top health. No genetic diseases. If we have a baby now I will be about sixty when he or she graduates from high school, and I'll have plenty of time to be a father. I think I'll be a great father. And you'd be a great...oh!"

Scotch in hand, Bill turned back to Brooke and found her sitting naked on his burgundy leather club chair. Her legs were crossed at the ankle and she was still sipping the cabernet he had poured for her.

"Ah, you see," began Bill as he looked away, "I had rather imagined if we had a child, that we would do this part in a doctor's office."

"No, I'm sorry," Brooke said as she uncrossed her ankles and then recrossed them, demure in spite of her nudity, "I don't have any doctor's office fantasies."

Brooke began to absentmindedly play with her nipple as if it were a button on one of her cashmere cardigans. Bill remained unmoved. No interest. No erection. The closest he got to heavy breathing was a deep, sad sigh.

"I don't want to have sex, Brooke. Sex, at best, only serves to define my loneliness," Bill said, without allowing a trace of sadness to seep into his voice. "I'd rather just jettison it from my life."

Brooke took a lot of air into her lungs and then let it release slowly. She reached down and picked her underwear up off the rug where she had shoved it quickly under the sofa. Underwear was followed by bra, slacks, and then her shirt. As she slipped back into her jacket she told him that he had a serious problem, and that this particular problem could no longer be hers also.

"It's because your friend Lux said I was gay," he said without malice.

"No," said Brooke, "it's because I deserve better than this. I'm forty years old. I have a great life and I want a child. I was thinking about doing it myself but here you are. Handsome, smart, tender. You love me and I think you'd make a great dad except for the fact that you're really weird about sex. You have to be ok about sex to stay balanced. And I certainly don't want this kind of self-loathing around my child. And really, Bill, I don't think I want that around me, either."

In her haste to get all her clothes off before Bill turned around, Brooke had pushed one of her pumps a little too far under the sofa. She had to lie down on the floor and grope among the dust bunnies to find her shoe.

"You need help?" Bill asked.

"I got it," Brooke said.

"Ok then, we're all set," Bill said as if finding her shoe were the only problem they had. Brooke suddenly realized how often Bill used denial as a coping mechanism. Something deep and terrible had just happened. His best friend and longtime lover Brooke had just told him she could not love him anymore. But Bill chose to experience it on the shallowest level. Brooke felt a great pain for her old friend.

Bill watched her as she placed the exquisite shoe on her long, beautiful foot.

"Um, so next month I bought a table for the Sickle Cell Anemia party. We had a good time last year. Will you join me?"

Sickle Cell threw a cool party, good food, great band. It drew an interesting group of supporters including people from the arts. Last year they'd stayed till almost four in the morning, then continued the party at the home of some record producer.

"Can't," Brooke said. "I won't be part of how you torture yourself."

"Brooke, I love you so much," Bill said even as she slipped out of his grasp.

"You lied to me for twenty years."

"No, I thought it would go away."

They stood there among the deep, gleaming mahogany Bill inherited from his family. They stood there long enough for the light in the window to move across the carpet and catch on one of his dad's old sterling-silver golf trophies. It reflected a hard light into Brooke's eyes and reminded her that it was time to go.

"I'm so sorry," Bill said almost as a whisper, but she heard. Brooke found her purse on the sofa and headed towards the door.

"Friends?" Bill called after her as she left him.

"Can't change that," Brooke said. "But give me a month or two before you call me."

Brooke let herself out of his huge matched front doors. She decided to take the stairs instead of the elevator. They started out nearly industrial in design at the top but turned into heavy marbled grandeur by the time they reached the lobby. Still, at both ends they were stairs, and Brooke found that comforting. She waved to the doorman and stepped out onto the street. She stood for a moment outside of Bill's apartment building and then decided to walk south down Fifth Avenue towards the park.

27.
"O Fat Girl Needs a Job

*L*UX KERCHEW FITZPATRICK WALKED along lower Broadway looking for a bagel and a coffee. Maybe she would bring a bagel and coffee back to Aimee. Maybe Bill would call and say he'd found a great job for her, something with a solid salary that she could stash away until she had enough for a second all-cash real estate purchase. Maybe everything was going to be ok in spite of how it had all started out.

Lux ducked into a café near the university. It looked appropriately inexpensive so she walked up to the counter and ordered some food.

"You're in my psych class, right?" said the cashier as he rang up her order.

"Nah," said Lux.

"Really? Well then you've got a doppelganger hanging out at NYU."

Lux's hand immediately flapped to the opening of her shirt to see what, if anything, was hanging out. If her boob slipped from the mooring of her brassiere, it would certainly explain the way this boy was looking at her. As she was, without makeup or spray or glitter, dressed in boxy, colorless clothes, Lux could not imagine any other reason this boy would seem so friendly.

"Did you want milk in those coffees?" he asked.

"Uh, aren't they cappuccino? I mean, that has milk in it already, right?" Lux said, unsure of herself and the recipe for cappuccino.

"Oh yeah, right. Sorry. It's just, ah you look so much like this other girl. In my psych class. Her name is Monica, I think."

"Oh. My name is Lux."

"Wow. That must have been really hard in middle school."

"Why?"

"Well, because it rhymes with…well, ducks."

Lux laughed out loud. Not at the thought of how her name could be used in a dirty limerick, but because the boy had blushed so brightly red at the thought of how her name could be used in a dirty limerick. She looked into his eyes and saw that they weren't really hazel, but rather brown with big flecks of green.

"Nah," Lux said, "I had big brothers and a dangerous boyfriend. Nobody talked trash to me. I mean, other than the big brothers and the dangerous boyfriend."

"Is he still around? I mean, the dangerous boyfriend."

"His teeth fell out," Lux said.

The phrase dropped out of her mouth. Immediately she wished she hadn't said it. She assumed her comment about her ex-boyfriend's metaphorical dental work would be the death knell of this suitor's interest. In the past, guys who tried to hit on her were drawn in by her lips and turned off by what came out of her mouth.

"I think that happens a lot after high school," the coffee boy said, sounding truly sympathetic. "I mean, I never thought I'd end up pushing cappuccino, but school is way more expensive than I thought. So I'm doing half-time, which is a drag, but it's the best I can do. What about you?"

Lux was ready to lie. She was planning on telling him that she was out of school for a few semesters, but ready to go back in the fall. She liked who he thought she was, but before she could start reinventing herself for him a dark-haired woman in a white apron came out from the back of the café.

"Charlie!" his boss shouted, indicating the long line of customers queuing up behind Lux.

Charlie blushed again and Lux stepped away to allow him to take the order of the mousy woman standing patiently behind her. She stood to the side, finished her cappuccino and then started on the one she'd bought for Aimee. She hung out, hoping there would be a break in the line and she could talk to him again, but the café kept filling up. All the tables were taken and it wasn't long before Lux felt foolish standing there, ogling a counter-boy named Charlie. Her ringing cell phone bought her a little more time. She stood near the door with the phone to her ear, listening to Jonella explain their financial future.

"We could both get jobs together," Jonella was saying.

"I don't know, Jonella," Lux answered.

"Girl, if you ain't interested in easy money, I ain't gonna force it down you. Get your ass over here though. I'm getting this job, and I got stuff I need you to do."

Charlie was looking away, taking an order. A second later he was busing a table. Would he ever stop and look at her? She felt stupid and so, turning her back on the café, Lux hit the street, jumped on the subway and headed back to Queens to help Jonella solve her financial crisis.

"You crazy!" Jonella shouted when Lux again rejected her pitch for their bright new future. "We should be strippers! It's too freaking perfect for us! We could do it together. I mean, not on stage together cuz then we gotta share tips, but like work at the same club at the same time."

"I dunno," sighed Lux. "I'm hoping this gay guy comes through with an office job for me."

"No girl, we gotta do this," Jonella insisted.

"I don't think it's right for me. I don't think it's where I want to go with myself."

"Whatchoo talking about? Where you going? You taking yourself on vacation? With what money, girl? Strippin's big money. Girls like us need cash."

"Nah, I don't wanna."

Jonella thought Lux was an idiot who couldn't understand the big picture. She figured once Lux saw the benefits of stripping, she would jump right in.

"Well, jus come wit me then," Jonella said gently. "You come hole my hand cuz the first time gotta be a little scary. Jonella's gonna lay it down, rake in da green, and you come get with me when you ready, baby."

To her credit, Jonella had already done a lot of the research necessary to apply for the job she wanted. She found out from talking to one of the girls that worked at the Tip Top Club that the "strip" in stripping no longer included the tantalizing act of removing clothing. Rather, a girl simply appeared naked on stage and danced around. And, that very afternoon at the open audition, that is exactly what Jonella did. She did not make the first cut.

"Who do I gotta fuck to take my clothes off around here?" Jonella demanded. Lux came with Jonella, for moral support. She held Jonella's hand and her clothes. Lux thought her old friend had done an admiral job of gyrating naked across the stage, but the manager did not agree with that assessment.

"Listen," the manager said gently as he gave Jonella the bad news, "o fat girl like you, she need to do more than just shake her shit around the floor. Come back tonight you see my show, you see what my girls do."

It took Lux a minute to understand that the manager's heavily accented "o" in "o fat girl" meant "old." Jonella, like Lux, was all of twenty-three years old.

"You ain't old, girl," Lux whispered to Jonella as they stood in the dressing room of the strip club. Jonella waved it away as she threw on her clothes. She didn't care if some strip club manager thought she was old or fat. She just wanted money.

That night Jonella and Lux returned to the strip club to see what strippers actually did in lieu of removing clothes. The manager remembered the girls and waived the cover charge and two-drink minimum. The atmosphere in the bar was jovial and the audience coed. Jonella watched the stage with serious concentration as almost-naked women filled in the not-stripping part of stripping with some serious and athletic tricks that included flinging themselves towards the audience and then catching themselves on the pole in the center of the dance floor.

One woman hung upside down from the pole, her feet in the air. Then she shook her shoulders so her breasts wobbled. The second to last dancer was a very pretty girl with large young breasts who did very little other than dance around naked. The last girl on, the evening's finale, was a scarred, heavyset brunette who looked about forty years old. She stood on her head and breathed cigarette smoke out of her vagina. She got a huge round of applause and both the men and women in the audience inundated her with sweaty crinkled dollar bills.

As Lux watched the continuing parade of naked women shake the money tree, she tried to imagine what Charlie the Coffee Boy would say about a stripper whose name rhymed with "ducks." Would a guy who blushed like that understand how much she wanted to buy a second apartment? Should she care about what a guy like that was capable of understanding? In the end it was Auntie Who-ah gravely voice that growled the loudest. "Do what makes you happy," was always Auntie Who-ah's cryptic advice.

"I gotta work on my upper body strength," Jonella said as she pushed Lux out of the strip club and into the subway. "And I gotta get me some of them shoes. Them girls all had serious shoes. Wonder where you get shoes like that?"

"We'll look on the Net," Lux told her as the train took them home.

"What net?" Jonella asked.

"Internet. We'll Google 'shoes for strippers.'"

Jonella had no freaking idea what Lux was talking about, but that wasn't unusual. It sounded from Lux's tone of voice that she was planning to help Jonella find stripper shoes and even had an idea about where to start looking. That was enough for Jonella so she smiled and nodded in agreement.

Lux figured after this rejection Jonella would forget the whole stripping thing, but the next morning, Jonella showed up at Lux's mother's house earlier than usual. She insisted that Lux begin helping her search for stripper shoes.

"Take me to the net," Jonella said happily as she jumped into Lux's twin bed.

"Ok. We gotta get over to the public library," Lux said sleepily.

"They got stripper shoes at the lieberry?"

"Yeah."

Sitting at the library's computer, Lux quickly found Google, typed in "Stripper Shoes" and got more than ten pages of companies with websites that sold shoes for strippers.

"Hey, do that again and see what they got for cheap stripper shoes," Jonella suggested as she leaned over Lux's shoulder.

"Discount Stripper Shoes" brought up only three entries. Lux picked the first website and scrolled down to show Jonella what was available in her size. Jonella picked out two pairs that seemed good to her and then they proceeded to the checkout.

"You got a credit card?" Lux asked.

"Girl, I ain't even got a bank account."

Lux thought about it for a moment and then decided to go out on a limb.

"Uh, hi Brooke. This is Lux," she said into her cell phone. She explained the situation, that neither she nor Jonella had a credit card, and that Lux would promise to pay her back quickly. Brooke was delighted to help and, rolling out of her bed and over to her computer, she found the website and completed the ladies' transaction. She even bought a pair for herself.

"So?" Brooke asked lazily, "what do you need stripper shoes for?"

When Lux told Brooke that Jonella was trying to talk her into being a stripper, Brooke suddenly shouted into the phone, "No! Don't! Where are you? The public library? Which public library? Don't move."

"Why?" Lux asked.

"Because I am coming over there right now!"

Lux had never heard Brooke shout before. Her voice was surprisingly big with a bit of a growl. Jonella said the library gave her the willies, and she wasn't going to wait there all day to meet some bitch from the other side of the river. Jonella had scored her shoes and wanted to do other things with her day. In the end, Brooke agreed to meet Lux at Aimee's house.

"Margot!" Brooke shouted when Margot picked up the phone.

"Hello to you too," Margot said. She was just back from the gym.

"Drop everything," Brooke said, "we're doing an intervention."

"For whom?" Margot asked, wondering if Brooke was kidding.

"That Jonella person is trying to talk Lux into becoming a stripper."

Margot dropped her latte in the sink and ran out the door.

"But I could lose everything!" Lux shouted at her friends.

Aimee, Brooke, and Margot told her again and in no uncertain terms that she should not even consider becoming a stripper.

"It's a step backwards," Aimee said.

"Right! Number one, stripping is going to make you feel like meat," Margot began listing all the negative aspects of stripping. "You have just begun to own yourself; don't sell it back to a bunch of ogling strangers. Number two: that job will expose you to people and things that are not good for you. Number three: you have to spend a great deal of money on the costumes and so, number four: it will not provide you the income you think it will. Five: Jonella is a moron. Six: that kind of job will distract you from better work. Seven: it's night work. Night work sucks. Eight: it will…"

"It will make you feel bad!" Brooke interrupted. "And what are you so afraid of losing that you're willing to become a stripper just to keep it?"

"All my money," Lux said. "I got three grand a month coming in from one apartment. If that tenant flakes I got nothing, plus the thousand bucks each month I suddenly gotta pay for maintenance. Can you believe that? A thousand bucks a month!"

"What's the rent on the place?" Margot asked. She was confused as to how Lux was clearing three grand a month on a thousand square feet.

"Four," Lux said.

"And your maintenance is one thousand?" Brooke asked.

"Yeah," said Lux.

"So what's your mortgage?" Aimee asked.

"Well, nothing," Lux said. "I paid cash. I own it."

In the loft next door, Aimee's neighbor stopped and wondered for a moment what could be going on in Aimee's loft to make girls squeal and shriek so loudly.

"You own it outright and you're worried about money!" Margot exclaimed.

"I dunno what 'outright' means, but I'm saying I paid cash."

"Lux," said Aimee, "take the money out of the apartment. Buy two more apartments. Live in one, rent out the other."

"But I ain't got enough money to buy two apartments."

"You have more than enough money for a down payment on two apartments," Brooke said. "And the two rents will cover all three mortgages with enough left over for you."

"Lux," Aimee said, "it's time for you to live."

They devoted the rest of the afternoon to quelling Lux's uncertainties regarding debt and mortgages. Brooke sorted through the discarded newspapers around Aimee's bed until she found the real estate section. They reviewed specific apartments on sale in the area, and circled several to be visited. At their insistence, Lux enrolled in a course to acquire her real estate license.

"Ok! Ok! You're right. I mean, even if I don't use it I should know what the rules are, right?" Lux said.

"Right," her friends heartily agreed.

Some weeks later, just as Lux was bidding on a pair of apartments in the same building, Jonella called her on the telephone.

"Hey Lux," Jonella said over the phone, "can I borrow some money?"

"I thought you were raking it in at the club."

"Yeah, but I spend a lot of it."

"Christ, Jonella! What you spend it on?"

"Fuck you Lux, I spent $200 on that costume for the first set. And the rest on drinks and some other shit to get me through the night."

"Really?" Lux said.

"Fuck-yeah. Strippin fun but I dunno where the money goes. And girls like us need money, alright? And the thing is I'm momentarily outa cash, and I look like shit in the clothes I got. Let's go out, girl. Me and you like we used to."

"Nah, nah, nah," Lux said. "Can't. I got this class and a big test I'm studying for."

"That suck, girl. So can I get some money from you?"

"For what?"

"Well, I ain't got no big test I gotta study for. Just cuz you stupid why should I suffer?"

While Lux appreciated Jonella's logic, she said no.

Jonella believed that Lux was too proud to strip. She figured Lux was still taking cash from "old cock," and she believed Lux should share just a little of it with her. So Jonella asked again, this time not as nicely. Lux had rent coming in on her first apartment, but that money was earmarked for the future. She had a history with Jonella, but the future was somewhere else. Lux cut Jonella off.

"Girl, I just can't," Lux said. "I'm saving up for something big. Something for me."

Jonella was furious. She raged. She swore. She threatened, but Lux wouldn't give her another dime. Lux wasn't going out dancing and shopping and drinking; why should she foot the bill for Jonella's party?

"It's about the future," Lux told her.

"Fuck it," screamed Jonella, "and fuck you. I ain't helping you no more. And we ain't friends no more neither, Little Miss Lux Sucks and Fucks!"

The old nickname stung, especially coming out of Jonella who had once been her protector, slapping anyone smaller than her if she caught them chanting the ugly rhyme. Jonella had been her compatriot, coconspirator, compadre. Why she talking trash like this, Lux wondered. Don't she see how things are getting better for me?

"Girl, you driving on the D train?" Lux asked, inquiring if Jonella was doing any drugs.

"Hey," Jonella shouted, spewing some frothy spit onto the receiver of the pay phone she was using, "you ain't the boss of me! You owe me. An' Carlos owe me. He got him his house-painting business now, he owe me! You owe me, Sucks and Fucks!"

The icy fingers of an ugly adolescence squeezed tight

around Lux's soul. She rubbed her forehead, anxious to return to her studying. She wanted to call Brooke and talk about the apartments she had bid on. Aimee said she would rent one of them, if Lux got them both. Margot wanted to help pick out paint and sinks for the smaller, more broken of the two. As Jonella continued to explain in louder and more abusive language why and what Lux owed her, she sounded smaller and her words more garbled.

The world of Miss Sucks and Fucks seemed so far away from the tomorrow that was waiting for Lux of light and truth. This bright light that was coming at her off her books and investments was soothing over some of those old hurts. She wanted to share the light with Jonella. She wanted to tell her that there was a better way to make your way. Lux began to explain this new world, as best as she understood it, but Jonella had already hung up.

28. *Alexandra Grace*

"*Annie's nipples were growing hard* and pushing at the thin fabric of her bathing suit. She told herself it was the cool air racing across her wet suit that made them that way, and not a reflection of the previous seven months without sex. Annie looked down the bar at the young hotties all smiling back at her. The wind picked up over the water and for a moment Annie wished she'd brought a shawl or a T-shirt to cover herself, although that would ruin the effect of those last five weeks at the gym.*"

"Ok," Aimee said. "Now that I'm reading it out loud, it's a total fantasy. I haven't even seen my toes, never mind touched them, for four months. I feel silly. I can't read it. You go, Brooke. I'm done."

"No, no. Read it, Aimee," Brooke said.

"It's good," Lux said.

"I can't. I wrote myself beautiful," Aimee said. "How embarrassing."

Margot opened her mouth to speak, but Aimee, anticipating what Margot was going to say, stopped her.

"I know, I know," Aimee said, "but I want to be

beautiful in the way that makes a man want to touch me, not just in the joy-bubbled-up-from-within sense."

Brooke tried to interject a thought, but Aimee was on a roll.

"Yeah, yeah, you're right, both are good, I know. Ok, I'm just going to read what I wrote."

Aimee shifted on the couch and started to read.

"Her girlfriends were laughing at her. They'd all scored great guys the moment they stepped out of the van that brought them from the airport to the resort, but Annie was rusty. She couldn't remember where she'd left her bump and grind. Maybe at her desk. Maybe it was lost in the divorce papers. Everyone promised that the pool was hot. Annie had to just hold her breath and dive in."

Aimee tapped a button and the next screen on her lap top computer flicked up. She continued to read.

"The curly haired blond guy seemed sweet and easygoing. Annie took a step towards the bar when she felt a hand tug at her arm.

"'Annie Singleton?' he asked. The voice was warm, the eyes were blue and the face familiar. When she nodded he said, 'I think we went to high school together.'"

"See, I think what I'm looking for is something new, but familiar," Aimee said critiquing and psychoanalyzing herself as she went.

"Could you just read it?" Brooke said.

"The next twenty hours were a roller coaster of conversations, memories, and philosophical reflections on what ever became of the nastiest popular girls, and did they really deserve such bad luck. When they made their way to his cabana at dawn she was still wearing the same bathing suit

she had worn when she walked into the bar that afternoon. With his help, she slipped it off in the Jacuzzi. The water and his hands were hot and both were everywhere on her body. He jumped out of the hot tub without using the steps, lifting her out by the arm. Then they raced each other for the sheets."

Aimee suddenly folded down the cover of her laptop.

"And, of course, then they have sex," said Aimee in a way that indicated she was done reading her story.

"But we'd like to hear *how* they have sex," Margot asked politely.

"I don't know. I would have written that part except that I forgot how it happens," Aimee said. "It has something to do with a penis, right?"

"Yes, and if it's heading towards your ear, he's doing it wrong," Margot offered.

Aimee sat upright on the couch between Margot and Brooke. She felt a little woozy, but thrilled to finally be erect. When the baby weighed in at an estimated five and a half pounds the doctor ended her bed rest. Aimee was surprised to find it a difficult to maintain her balance and even stranger that a little piece of her missed the quiet of her captivity. So far, she had ventured out of her apartment only once, yesterday, for a short walk to the elevator, to pick up her Chinese takeout. Following that excursion, she returned to her living room and fell asleep on the couch.

In the middle of the night her nearly ex-husband called to say that he had received and signed the divorce papers. He would not contest the divorce. He would not drag her into court and pick over their lives in public. He promised to pay whatever sum of child support she and the court thought appropriate. After the papers were filed, their divorce would be final in about six weeks. Aimee said a very quiet thank you. In the silence that followed she heard a tinkle of dissonant Asian music and a background of daytime voices. His morning was her night.

"Aimee," he said, "are you ok?"

"Fine. The baby is due in a week and a half. She's your little girl too and if you want to be here for the birth you can."

"Week and a half? I'll see if I can get a flight."

There wasn't much to say after that. Where there was once such passion, now only silence.

"I'm going back to sleep now," Aimee said, "my writers' group is coming over tomorrow."

"All right then," he said and after polite good-byes, they hung up.

Aimee woke up the next morning with an inexplicable urge to clean her house. When her friends arrived around lunchtime they found her on her hands and knees, scrubbing the oven. When they suggested she stop, Aimee promised she was only going to finish the bathrooms and then she'd be done. Rather than scold her, Brooke, Lux, and Margot snapped on their own rubber gloves and gave the large apartment a quick once-over. The gleaming porcelain and stacks of folded laundry brought Aimee peace. When it was all in order, she was able to join her friends on the couch and listen to the other women's fantasies. She did not find it strange that she should feel so peaceful.

"So Brooke," Margot asked, "would you like to read your piece next?

"I didn't write anything," Brooke said. "I am momentarily flummoxed about sex. That's F-L-U-M-M-O-X-E-D, Lux."

"What's it mean?" Lux asked as she wrote the word in her book.

"Kind of what it sounds like," said Brooke as Aimee suddenly shifted uncomfortably on the couch.

"Sound like stomach flu," said Lux.

"Actually it means 'bewildered,'" said Margot.

Lux was not happy to hear that one could reach the ripe old age of Brooke and still be bewildered by sex. She wished she had some words of comfort for her friend.

"Um, I had lunch with your friend Bill a few days ago," Lux said.

"How is he?" Brooke asked with a little frost on her words.

"Good. He wishes you'd call him back."

"Has he started counseling yet?"

"If you're talking about a shrink, no. But he's hanging out a lot with this friend of his dads, Miles Rudolph or something."

"Miles Randolph!" Brooke exclaimed. "Miles is way too old for Bill!"

"Nah, nah, nah!" Lux said, waving her hands and laughing at Brooke's sudden, passionate, protective outburst. "The old guy's a friend of his dad's. He's just talking to him about you know, shit and stuff. Bill's boyfriend is younger, about thirty-five. Cute, but he like totally wins the title as 'most boring homosexual I ever met.'"

"Bill has a boyfriend!" Brooke gasped.

"Uhhhhhhhhhhh," Lux said, amazed that her attempt to cheer Brooke up had backfired so spectacularly. Since she'd come this far, though, she figured it was best to tell the whole story. "Yeah. He does. I stopped by to return some books and the guy was there, at Bill's place. And they were wearing bathrobes at four in the afternoon and it was pretty clear that they'd been naked not too long ago. Bill looked kind of happy, though. He introduced the guy as his friend. I think his name is Bannister. He was wearing this bathrobe and black socks. Dress socks. I'm pretty sure he'd had sex wearing those black socks cuz you don't just put black dress socks back on after afternoon sex, right. Anyway, this Bannister guy, he's almost as interesting as a fence post. He's got this English accent, and…"

"Alistair Warton-Smythe!" Brooke gasped.

"Yeah, that's him," Lux laughed. "Bannister Warthog-Smith. Tall, thin, blond. He kind of looks like you, Brooke. I mean, if you were the most boring homosexual man in New York City."

Brooke looked from Margot to Lux and back again. She wasn't sure if she wanted to laugh or cry. Margot tried to push the balance towards the former.

"Oh my gosh! Brooke! You are so lucky!" Margot said.

Brooke and Lux both turned to look at Margot. Neither could imagine how Bill's stuffy new boyfriend translated into Brooke's good luck.

"You just missed giving twenty painful years of your life to a man who prefers other men," Margot explained.

"Other boring men," Lux chortled.

"Yeah," Brooke said, smiling just a little. "Yeah, I guess you're right. I just gained twenty years of happiness."

Aimee sat quietly on the couch. She was listening, but felt very far away, as if other music was playing for her alone.

"So Margot," Brooke asked, "would you like to read your piece next?

"Ok, but I wrote about my vibrator."

"What's wrong with that?" Brooke said.

"Certain people have pointed out to me that my attachment for the mechanical will ruin me for the real man. But, hey, I'm fifty now. I don't drink or smoke. I think I should have a pleasurable vice just like everyone else in this city. And I'm teaching Trevor how to operate it."

Aimee suddenly got up and walked to the bathroom. She sat down on the toilet and checked her underwear. Then she sat for a moment in the quiet of her shining porcelain and wondered how she was going to do this all by herself.

Margot waited for Aimee to return from the bathroom. When she did, Aimee stood there, looking at her friends. She did not sit down.

"I just blew my mucus plug," Aimee announced.

"Oh my god!" Margot said. "What does that mean?"

"If she breaks the amniotic sac we're having the baby in the apartment," Lux said as she rose from her chair. "Jonella had most of her baby at home. Mucus plug went when we was out dancing, and we didn't know that meant we had to stop. So when we got home and the sack went, the baby starts flying out."

"We do not want to do that," Margot said firmly.

"I'm really excited," Aimee said quietly.

"So what do we do?" Brooke asked.

"Ok, ok, I've thought this out. I, ah, I know, ah," Aimee stumbled and faltered and couldn't remember what to do. Then she hit a giggle fit that would not stop. Margot took charge.

"Ok," said Margot, "we're going to the hospital. Lux gets the suitcase. Margot calls the car service, then the hospital and then Aimee's mom. Brooke helps Aimee down to the street."

Everyone stood for a moment, impressed with Margot's sense of order. Margot did not know why they were not executing her very clear instructions.

"Let's make it happen, girls!" Margot said cheerfully without a trace of the panic she was feeling.

Thanks to Margot's excellent planning, the car service was pulling up to the curb just as Brooke and Margot walked Aimee through the lobby of her apartment building. Lux took one last turn around the apartment to make sure everything that needed to be shut off was, that house keys were put in purses and cell phones slipped in pockets. She caught up with them as they stepped into the street.

"You ok?" Aimee asked Margot as they got into the cab.

"Fine, fine," Margot said.

"You're shaking," Aimee laughed. "I'm having the baby and you're shaking."

"I'm excited," Margot said. "And a little nervous. Oh my god! It's finally happening!"

Lux squeezed Margot's hand to try to calm her down. The thought that Aimee was fine but Margot needed to calm down made Lux giggle. It was contagious and suddenly the whole back seat was rocking with excited, nervous laughter. When the car arrived at the hospital emergency room, three of the four women rolled out of the sedan like drunken broads in front of a night club. Aimee rolled out like a beached whale on Coney Island. The florescent lights and quiet of the hospital quickly sobered them up. They gathered their wits and helped Aimee into the ER.

After a quick pelvic exam, Aimee was admitted to the hospital. When the attending physician announced that Aimee was dilated three centimeters and he was moving Aimee to Maternity, Margot switched from shaking to talking. As the women caught up with Aimee's wheelchair in the delivery room, Margot gave a detailed account of the room's décor and amenities to Brooke, Lux, and Aimee.

"Oh my gosh, my golly, look Aims, it's a Jacuzzi tub. Just like in your story. Isn't that useful although I don't know when you're gonna have time to get into it. And the wallpaper is surprisingly tasteful for a hospital. How interesting! It's like a lovely hotel room."

"Is there a mini bar?" Brooke asked.

As the nurse helped her into bed, Aimee started to feel some pulling deep inside her pelvis.

"It feels like I'm about to get my period. That's not so bad, right?" Aimee asked. "Right?"

Brooke and Margot looked at each other, then back at Aimee before declaring in one supportive voice, "Right!" Lux, who had been through this before with Jonella, offered more practical advice.

"You know," Lux said, "when you're at home if you wanna say 'shit' or 'cunt' or 'mother of freaking hellfire' or anything else you can scream it as loud as you want but once you get to the hospital they come and tell you you're disturbing the other mothers if you get too loud or crazy."

"Good to know," Aimee said and, even though she could not imagine she would ever want to scream or curse so loudly she added, "Thanks, Lux."

And then the first deep contraction came.

"Fuck me!" Aimee suddenly shouted in full-voiced terror. As the contraction subsided, a frowning nurse peeked her head into the room. She scowled at Aimee. The grumpy nurse closed the door to Aimee's delivery room in an attempt to shield the other women on the floor from Aimee's potty mouth.

"See what I mean," said Lux.

"I, I, I think I need that epidural," Aimee said in a slightly panicked voice. "And if I could get it as quickly as possible that would be really, really good."

Lux sprinted into the hallway to find the anesthesiologist. Aimee howled louder, but cursed less, through several large contractions. She squeezed Brooke's hand hard and practiced the breathing exercises they had learned in Lamaze class. The exercises didn't make the pain any less intense, but it did distract her, particularly when Margot, breathing along with Aimee and Brooke, hyperventilated and had to sit down. They were still laughing about it when the anesthesiologist arrived and the epidural took effect.

"Oh thank God!" Aimee said as her legs went numb.

"What do we do now?" Brooke asked.

"We wait," Lux said.

For six hours Margot, Brooke, and Lux sat with Aimee watching her contractions chart on the monitor.

"Woah! That was a monster one!" Brooke said as the contraction pushed almost to the top of the monitor.

"Did it hurt?" Lux asked.

"Didn't feel it at all," Aimee said. "Can't feel anything below my chest."

"So what are we naming this baby?" Brooke asked.

"I like the name 'Grace,'" Lux said. "That's the name I always called myself when I played that I was someone else."

"What about 'Tuesday?'" Brooke suggested.

"Nah, nah, nah," Lux warned. "A name is not a joke."

"For a while I really liked 'Lily,'" Aimee said, "or maybe 'Dahlia.'"

"Flower names are nice," Margot said as she zipped off a quick list of flower names. "How about Lilia. There's also Rose, or Petunia. Oh no, not Petunia. There's Violet, Poppy, Viola, Willow, Posy, Lilac, Primrose, Pansy, Veronica, Angelica, Iris, Holly, Heather, Hyacinth, Tiger Lily, well, that's from *Peter Pan*. There's Lavender, Fern, Flora, Rosemary, Saffron."

"Stop!" Aimee called out. "I'm naming the baby 'Alexandra.' I decided last night."

"Alexandra is very nice," Brooke said warmly.

"What do you guys think of the name 'Alexandra

Grace'?" Aimee asked the people who really mattered to her.

"I like it," Lux said, and everyone agreed.

"How are we doing here?" the nurse asked crisply as she entered the room. She walked to the bed and checked Aimee's progress.

"I feel good," Aimee said. "Actually, I don't feel anything at all. Totally numb from my chest to my toes."

"Oh my!" said the nurse. "You're at six. You're ready to push. Now, I'm going to get the doctor and then we're going to push, push, push like we're having a bowel movement."

"Great, except I have no idea where my anus is currently located," said Aimee, pointing to the epidural drip.

"Oh!" said the nurse and she scurried off to find the anesthesiologist.

When Aimee's doctor strode into the room, she still had the pillow marks on her face.

"What time is it?" Brooke asked.

"Three in the morning," the doctor said, followed by, "Who are you?"

"These are my best friends," Aimee said, gesturing to Margot, Brooke, and Lux.

"Ah," said the doctor, "a tribe of women. That's good. You'll need the support. So the epidural has been turned off. Tell me, can you feel your butt yet?"

Aimee nodded. She could feel her butt and a whole lot more. The pain was washing back into her body in big ocean waves.

"You," the doctor said as she pointed to Margot. "I need you to rub her legs. They're a little cold and stiff from the epidural."

"Yes, ma'am," said Margot as she sprung into action.

"Who's the Lamaze coach here?" the nurse demanded.

"I am," said Brooke.

"Good, you're at momma's right. And you," the nurse said pointing at Lux, "you're at her left. We're gonna move the bed so she's sitting up. Then we're gonna push."

"How are you feeling, Aimee?" called Aimee's doctor above the whirr of the moving bed. A mirror on the ceiling came down so Aimee could see her baby as it was born. The doctor snapped a glove over her manicured hands and took her position between Aimee's legs.

"If you're ready," the doctor said, "we're going to push for a count of ten. If you can do fifteen that's better but I want you to push at least till ten."

"Come on Aimee, give us a good fifteen," Margot cheered from her position at the foot.

When they reached eleven, Lux, Brooke and Margot joined in a chorus of counting. Buoyed, Aimee bore down hard.

"Eighteen, nineteen, twenty, twenty-one," her friends sang out and with her cheerleaders whooping, Aimee found the strength to push for a count of thirty. The baby was small and Aimee's body had been rehearsing her exit for several months. Still, with what seemed to Aimee an unimaginable amount of pain and time, Alexandra Grace came into the world.

She was pink and wet with heavy lips and a full head

of Aimee's curls. When Aimee cut the cord that physically bound her to her baby, she felt a deep surge of love and passion for this creature who was finally a separate person. Margot held Alexandra while they stitched up the damage to Aimee's body. Although, per her own well-thought-out lists, it was Margot's job to make the phone calls, Margot did not want to put the baby down. Brooke called Aimee's family to give them the good news. She called Tokyo and left a polite, if breathless, message on his answering machine.

Finally, the doctor took Alexandra Grace from Margot and handed her to Aimee. Aimee held her breath as six pounds of baby and blanket settled into her arms. As if she knew she had come home, Alexandra turned to Aimee, opened her dark eyes and regarded her mother with a deep, thoughtful stare. Love gripped Aimee in the chest like an asthma attack and swelled through her, changing so many things about her that Aimee was almost a new person herself. Aimee started to breathe again, and with the first breath, made a silent promise to lay down her life to protect this little girl.

Hours later, resting quietly in her room with a soft pink mound of baby sleeping on her chest, Aimee was surprised at the amount of damage and bruising to her pelvis and vagina, inside and out. The birth by all standards had been easy, and yet when Aimee got up to go to the bathroom, she needed Lux to help her across the floor.

"I'm a battlefield," Aimee sighed when Brooke sat down next to the bed and asked how she was feeling.

"Yes, baby, but the war is over now," Brooke told her.

"You think?" Aimee asked.

"Of course," Brooke said, "now you just have to be a parent."

"I think I should marry your friend Bill," Aimee said.

"Why?" Brooke asked.

"I never want to have sex again either," Aimee laughed. While they were laughing a harried nurse rushed in with her nose in a chart.

"Do you need a consultation on the circumcision?" the nurse asked.

"I have a girl," Aimee said.

"Oh, sorry. Not a decision you have to make today," the nurse said as she scurried off to find the boys.

Aimee suddenly reflected on all the decisions she would have to make for her fatherless little girl. In their urban life, that first visceral promise would probably never be pushed to its extreme. She would never be asked to lay down her life, but how many times would she have to put aside her own life and desires to fulfill the baby's needs. The constancy of those needs could prove as hard to fill as any one-time heroic sacrifice. I'm so selfish, Aimee thought. I'm too critical and I'm so alone. How am I going to balance this? How am I going to pay for this?

Alexandra's little hands, with their ghostly white fingernails formed in the exact shape of Aimee's grandmother's, were curled around Aimee's pinky. Compared to Aimee, Alexandra's new hand looked very olive, even a bit yellow. Was yellow the right color? What happened to the perfect pink of a few hours ago? Would she hate her curly hair? Would she want to pierce her ears? Would she fall in love with a bad boy and get her heart stomped? Aimee's eyes filled up with tears as she reflected that Lux's mangled little pinky was once as perfect and new as Alexandra's.

"Here comes the doctor," Brooke said. "I guess it's discharge time."

"So soon," Aimee murmured, worried about how she was going to manage it all alone. What if something happened? What if she wanted to take a shower? In a snap, the doctors were upon her.

Her doctor strode up to the bed, flanked by the Alexandra's assigned pediatrician.

"We have to take the baby. Right now," Aimee's doctor said.

"W-w-w-where?" Aimee asked, shocked at their quiet seriousness.

"ICU," said the pediatrician as he reached into Aimee's arms and lifted a sleeping Alexandra Grace. Holding Alexandra close to his body, the pediatrician sprinted for the door. Aimee's doctor was close behind him.

"Halfway down the hall take a right then a left. Get dressed and meet us there," Aimee's doctor said as she quickly grabbed the baby's chart and followed the pediatrician to the Neonatal Intensive Care Unit.

Aimee gasped like a fish out of water. A second ago she was worrying about how she was going to get into the shower.

"Lux," ordered Margot, "run down the hall and follow those doctors. It's a big hospital. Make sure we know exactly where they've taken our baby. Brooke, get Aimee's clothes out. If you can't find them there's a bathrobe in the washroom. Aimee, I'm going to pull your IV unit around to the side of the bed and help you stand up."

The women leapt into action and within three minutes Aimee was wobbling into ICU. At the end of the ward, Alexandra Grace was lying in a glass bassinette under what looked like a cross between a tanning lamp and a french fry warmer. She was stripped to the waist and even had tiny sunglasses taped across her eyes.

"Jaundice," the pediatrician said. "We caught it on the second blood test. We can treat it. I'm sorry if we frightened you, but it moves fast, so we had to move fast."

The explanation continued, but Aimee couldn't understand a word of it. Eighteen hours old and already there was trouble. Brooke listened closely as the doctors explained that the lamps would draw out the blood toxins that Alexandra's little liver could not yet process. They'd caught it early and there was little to no chance of permanent damage. In thirty-six hours Alexandra Grace would be pink and perfect and ready to go home.

"And what should we do until then?" Brooke asked.

For a moment the pediatrician looked at her blankly, not understanding which "we" Brooke meant. Then he got it; these four women were the family.

"You should make sure the momma gets as much rest and nutrition as possible," the pediatrician said.

"Yeah, we could do that," Lux said.

Aimee was silent as they settled her back into bed. As if roused from a trance, she turned to her friends and said, "She's gonna be ok."

"Of course she is," Brooke said warmly, and then Aimee started to cry.

The first tears were a sudden cloud burst, accompanied by an exhalation of Aimee's pent-up fear. Those light showers were followed by the heavy artillery of Aimee's great thanksgiving that she had such good friends. When Aimee blew her nose straight through the chintzy hospital tissue she really meant it as an offer of gratitude that these exciting women, who each had their own desires and needs, had called her little daughter "our baby."

And when her friends responded by grabbing handfuls of toilet paper to wipe the snot off her face, they were really saying we'll be there for you and for her, even when she spits up on our good wool suits, even when she turns thirteen and runs up our cell phone bills with inane blather about some boy she has a crush on. We'll be there to help change diapers, to talk her out of piercing her nose. We'll be there to explain to her that mommy really loves her and that's why she has to be home by nine, even though the other girls can stay out until eleven. And when they gathered up the ruined tissues and toilet paper and tossed them in the trash without being grossed out by the mess, they were really making the most serious promise of all: we'll babysit for free.

"It's gonna be alright, Aimee," Lux said and by that she meant we'll be there when she's an infant, when she's a little girl. We'll be there to help her become a woman.

"Yeah, it's gonna be fine," Aimee agreed and she believed it to the bottom of her heart.

Hospital food was out of the question. Margot took a poll of everyone's favorite restaurants and then phoned up the one she liked best and added a bottle of champagne to the order. Within the hour the members of The Tuesday Erotica Club raised their plastic glass in the air.

"I wanna make a toast," Brooke said. "To Aimee's woo-woo. May it heal quickly and well."

"Here, here," agreed Margot sounding like a grand English barrister. "To Alexandra Grace," Aimee said, "and to us."

YEARS LATER

"He traced his hands up the side of my body. One hand shifted and went into the small of my back and the other settled on my breast. I sighed and found the buttons on his pants, pushing them off as we kissed."

Lux suddenly stopped reading as the door swung open.

"Mom!" said Alexandra Grace. "When Rosie cleans she hides all my stuff. I can't find any of my fun socks."

"What are fun socks?" Brooke asked.

"Socks with fun stuff on them," Margot informed her. "She likes the ones that have lipstick and fancy handbags detailed into them.

"And Rosie hides them when she cleans!" Alexandra complained to her Aunties through the closed door.

"When we're done," Lux promised, "we'll all help you find your fun socks, ok?"

"Mmm," Alexandra thought about it, "ok."

Alexandra hunkered down to wait for her favorite women to finish whatever it was they were doing.

"Go play," her mother ordered her.

"But I want to see what you guys do in here," Alexandra said.

"We'll tell you all about it," Auntie Margot said.

"When you're older," Auntie Brooke said.

"When you're ready," Auntie Lux promised, "you can join our club."